The Weight
of the Sun

ANDREW HUMPHREYS was born in 1970 in Sydney, Australia, where he currently resides. He was educated at Sydney University, where he studied Arts and Law, and has worked as a magazine writer, editor and publisher for the last seven years. He refuses to sing in public, not that anybody ever asks, which would be nice once in a while. *The Weight of the Sun* is his first novel.

The Weight of the Sun

Andrew Humphreys

ALLEN&UNWIN

The author and publishers would like to thank the following for the use of copyright material: lyrics from 'That's Amore' by Jack Brooks and Harry Warren (p. 35) © Copyright 1954 Paramount Music Corporation and Famous Music Corporation (50%). Used by permission of Music Sales Pty Ltd. All rights reserved. International copyright secured. © Four Jays Music Publishing. Frankdon Music Pty Ltd for Australia and New Zealand. Used by permission. All rights reserved.

First published in 2001

Allen & Unwin
83 Alexander Street
Crows Nest NSW 2065
Australia
Phone: (61 2) 8425 0100
Fax: (61 2) 9906 2218
Email: frontdesk@allenandunwin.com
Web: http://www.allenandunwin.com

National Library of Australia
Cataloguing-in-Publication entry:

Humphreys, Andrew, 1970– .
    The weight of the sun.

    ISBN 1 86508 536 7.

    I. Title.

A823.4

Set in 11/15 pt Baskerville Berthold by DOCUPRO, Canberra
Printed by Australian Print Group, Maryborough, Victoria

10 9 8 7 6 5 4 3 2 1

The letters in this book and the words
they form are for Jenny

Metal chair legs, the protective rubber feet long since gone, scrape across the polished wooden floor. Somehow, thirty-four children manage to perform this motion in unison, without a plan, without so much as a signal, filling the room with a single, shapeless noise. There is no talking, the morning chatter having given way to a tired acceptance: lessons are about to begin, books and pens are being placed on desks and the children, two to a desk, face front and exhale.

At the front of the class the teacher turns her back to the children and begins to clean the blackboard with broad sweeps of her felt duster. Older children, boys particularly, may have noticed some small grace in her movements, her hips held steady, the long black skirt barely revealing a trace of her body underneath, her arms occasionally rising to such a height as to show the curve of her breast under a pale blue sweater. She can be no more than twenty-eight years old, her light-brown hair swept back from her sharp-featured face and held at the back with a black plastic comb. Outside of the school grounds, her hair released and her cheeks dusted in a fine powder, men have often told her that she is beautiful. She knows that she is not but sometimes she gives herself to their soft-spoken lies.

None of the children think of her as beautiful. She is simply their teacher. Some of them think she is nice, some do not; most barely think of her at all.

Still there is no talking, only the sweep of the duster and the sounds of schoolbags unzipping, the arrangement of arms, legs and the day's equipment.

Three rows from the front, the second desk from the right, a boy reaches into his Samsonite case and pulls out a small circle of gold, which he places, very deliberately, in the centre of his desk, in line with his pencils, eraser and sharpener. The arrangement is neat and uncomplicated but the gold circle is clearly its centrepiece. It appears to be a chocolate, at the very least a sweet of some sort, encased in a stamped foil wrapper.

The day outside is warm and bright and the sun is streaming through the windows, spilling across desks and onto the classroom floor. The teacher, her back still turned to the class, catches a glint of gold at the very edge of her field of vision. A chocolate? If it is a chocolate, she thinks, it will soon melt. This gives her some small satisfaction. She turns towards the boy with the gold. He is smaller than some of the other boys but not the smallest boy in the class. His hair is dark and prone to curling. His face, like his body, is slightly puffy. He is, she thinks, a pretty child, at least for now. That fullness will turn to fat in time, his features will be lost and no one will think of him as a cherub in his teenage years. He may yet become a good-looking man. But now, at eight years of age, who can tell?

She stares for a moment at the chocolate then fixes her stare upon the boy, willing herself to convey through her eyes a simple truth: if you eat that chocolate, I will punish you, I will embarrass you and perhaps make you cry. Do not eat that chocolate. The boy does not blink, holding her stare and moving his hands slowly towards the glittering prize. The teacher is so intent upon maintaining her stare that the boy has unwrapped the chocolate before she even notices that his hands have moved. She strengthens her stare.

The boy takes the unwrapped chocolate and places it in his mouth. His eyes remain fixed on hers. He doesn't chew the chocolate but rolls it slowly around his mouth, from side to side, up and down, occasionally straying into a clockwise rhythm. The effect on the teacher is, it seems to the rest of the class, somewhat hypnotic, and it is only after the boy has finished moving his tongue over his little teeth, completing his cleaning ritual, that she opens her mouth to speak.

'I hope,' she says, feeling the hollowness of her words before she speaks them, 'I hope that you have brought enough for the rest of the class to enjoy.' She is satisfied that she has delivered her line correctly, with just the right mix of sarcasm and threat.

The boy is unmoved, his lips settling into a straight line.

'Yes,' he says flatly, 'as it happens, I have.' He reaches down into the Samsonite case and produces a red and gold box. There are, he knows, thirty-three chocolates left inside. Fine Belgian chocolates, all with ornate gold wrappers, which he has taken from the second drawer of his mother's bedside table. There were five other boxes in the drawer, each exactly the same. Only one was open.

'If the children would like to form an orderly line to the right of my desk,' he says, 'I'll distribute the chocolates as I see fit.'

The teacher turns her back to him, gripping the duster in her right hand. Her hand begins to shake so that the chalk dust is falling to the floor, white powder caught in brilliant sunlight.

'Very well,' she says and continues her sweeping movements over the blackboard. After some hesitation the children do form a line, more or less orderly, to the right of the boy's desk. The line moves steadily and without a sound, save for the steady shuffle of the children's feet. Each child takes a chocolate and returns to their desk. No one, the boy notices, says, 'Thank you.'

He gets off the school bus at his usual stop, three houses down from his mother's house. He notices that a lot of children who normally do not alight here (it is not a popular stop) are also getting off the bus. He stops walking and watches as a circle begins to form around him, a circle of children from his own class, children who had earlier eaten his mother's chocolates. There are other children too, boys and girls who had not been offered chocolate, children older than himself. He does not recognise all of their faces, there are so many.

The first hit is high. The fist, as he remembers it, is remarkably small. But then, so is he. As his head rocks back he can see an arc of blood, probably from his left nostril, framed against the deep blue of the sky. The sun is still very bright and he can feel its warmth as the circle closes in.

A week later his mother notices that her chocolates are missing.

Chapter 1

The concrete sidewalk beneath him is cool to the touch. Concrete and steel towers reach for the sky, a haze of brown and blue, casting long shadows over the asphalt roads that cut between their foundations. Pedestrians move freely between the traffic, crossing the roads and mounting the curbs, moving in two directions through the broad lane, one leading to the railway station where the waiting electric trains will carry them away in packs, the other leading to the city within.

They walk at different paces at this time of the day. Later, as they move towards the railway station's entrance, they will all maintain the same speed, the weak caught up in the long strides of the strong in the rush for home. But for now they choose their own pace. Some walk briskly, as if to prove to others as well as to themselves that their sense of purpose will carry them through the day. Others, affected by the morning heat, limp towards an uncertain goal, staring into shopfronts, fumbling with pocket-change and stalling for time at traffic lights. Some will talk to others; most will not.

He sits with his back propped against a cream-coloured building, deep in shadow. Beneath him is a flat strip of cardboard that was once a box. It was almost certain that groceries had once been carried in this box, from a supermarket to a car and finally to a home somewhere at the end of one of these roads. The box would be packed with smaller boxes containing cereal, perhaps; toothpaste, biscuits and packets of pantihose, flat and tall.

He is wearing too many clothes for the summer heat – jeans, an undershirt, shirt and woollen jumper – but they are not tattered. They appear to be the right sizes. Because he stays so still, because the concrete he chooses for a sitting area is always damp and the small passages between the buildings manage to channel the wind into a powerful force, he never feels the need to take off his jumper. In fact, sometimes he feels a chill and wishes he was wearing an overcoat.

He does not, like many of the other men he has seen passing their days on cardboard boxes, have a sign – no 'Homeless, Please Help' in sight – and he remains perfectly quiet, looking at the dirt-covered concrete below him. Still, people throw their loose change in his direction. Silver and gold coins are scattered around him.

It is almost time. He can tell by the cast of the shadow of the building he sits below. Time for his daily visit.

He hears her steps first, precise, measured and rhythmic. The paces are not brisk (others walk by him far more quickly) but they are certain in their approach. Soon he will see her feet. The shoes are always the same, though never, he thinks, the same pair: black leather, low heeled, double stitched, with an almost square toe. Her strong, thin calves are always covered in a tan stocking; her knees and the tops of her legs, her thighs, disappear into a navy skirt. She wears a white blouse, never any other colour. Usually the blouse is plain; sometimes he notices the occasional embroidered flourish around the buttons or collar.

Today she is wearing a navy jacket and a single fine gold bracelet around her right wrist. Her brown hair, cut short, almost boyish, is flecked with grey. Her eyes are also brown. The bridge of her nose to her chin, as always, is covered by a white, disposable air-filtration mask, the kind he remembers seeing spray painters and mechanics sometimes wear.

His eyes return to the ground and he begins to count, spacing out the numbers with what he believes to be the correct interval: one thousand. She will stare at him for forty-two seconds – never any shorter, never any longer – and then she will turn on her left heel and walk away, back into the city she came from.

Chapter 2

'Let me see that. What the hell are you reading?'

'One of the morning's submissions, sir. It's an essay on *Moby-Dick*.'

'Show me that. "Hello, Sailor! Homoerotic Imagery in Herman Melville's *Moby-Dick*" by Joost P. Sandal. We can't run that. Too fruity by half.'

'Fruity but scholarly, sir.'

'What the fuck are you talking about?'

'Well sir, if I recall the novel correctly, it was, as you say, very fruity. I vividly remember images of the seamen slipping and sliding about on decks covered with sperm – yes, it was sperm oil, but the image is still very strong. All those men alone at sea . . . and let's face it, Queequeg is more than just an ordinary harpooner, so to speak, to Ishmael. Mr Sandal states his hypothesis very early: that *Moby-Dick* is not a story about Ahab's obsession for the white whale but rather a love story, the love story of Ishmael and Queequeg. Look here . . . "Upon waking next morning about daylight, I found Queequeg's arm thrown over me in the most loving and affectionate manner. You had almost thought I had been his wife." The text is certainly open to Mr Sandal's interpretation.'

'Jesus, Bloomington, you sound a bit fruity yourself.'

'Yes, sir. I've often been told that. Once as the prelude to a particularly unsanitary invitation.'

'Yes, I imagine it was. Well, throw it away. That one's a waste of time.'

'But I've always wondered why the whale had a "Dick" in it . . .'

'Bloomington, what the fuck are you talking about? There was no dick in that whale. It was a fucking harpoon.'

'I was talking about the name, sir. "Dick". "Moby-Dick". But you've just made a very interesting connection, sir. Are you familiar with Mr Sandal's work?'

'Shut the fuck up and throw that shit in the shredder. We can't run it.'

'But surely I owe the author the courtesy of finishing the manuscript?'

'Bloomington, we are not going to run "Hello, Sailor! Homoerotic Imagery in Herman Melville's *Moby-Dick*" by Joost P. Sandal or by anyone else for that matter. Not today, not tomorrow. Not in a million fucking years. What do we do here, Bloomington?'

'Publish a monthly journal, sir. And a very well-respected one at that.'

'What kind of journal, Bloomington?'

'It's a legal journal, sir.'

'That's right. *Uncommon Cases and Commentary on the Common Law* is a legal journal. And what the fuck does "Hello, Sailor! Homoerotic Imagery in Herman Melville's *Moby-Dick*" have to do with the Common Law?'

'I was hoping Mr Sandal would get to that, sir.'

'For fuck's sake, Bloomington. He's not going to get to that, is he? "Hello, Sailor! Homoerotic Imagery in Herman Melville's *Moby-Dick*" has nothing to do with the Common Law. It's just another weak-as-piss, piece-of-shit, bullshit submission that belongs straight in the fucking shredder, which is where you're going to put it.'

'Yes, sir.'

'Jesus fucking Christ, Bloomington. Just get on to the next one. Here, what's this one? "Family Court Practice in Australia since *Kramer v. Kramer*" by Arthur Chesterfield-Price. That seems far more likely, wouldn't you agree?'

'Yes, sir. It does seem more likely.'

'Then read it and give Whitely-Smalls a summary by this afternoon. Then get on to the next one. And if you get more bullshit submissions, throw 'em straight into the fucking shredder, you understand?'

'Bullshit. Shredder. Yes, sir.'

. . .

James Bloomington had been working as a junior editor at Sandler and Harris, publishers of the monthly *Uncommon Cases and Commentary on the Common Law* and other small-circulation specialist titles, the most successful of these being *Saddlery and Stirrups Monthly*, since he graduated from the University of Sydney Law School five months before. He was, said his employer Geoffrey Sandler, son of the company founder, the long-deceased Jeremiah Sandler (there never was, as far as James could tell, any Harris of any sort involved with the company), 'the next best thing to totally fucking useless', but he enjoyed the solitude his employment provided and occasionally, as with 'Hello, Sailor! Homoerotic Imagery in Herman Melville's *Moby-Dick*', the intellectual stimulation that accompanied it.

Geoffrey Sandler, on the other hand, seemed committed to ensuring that James's moments of bliss were few and far between. He was not a large man (judging by the official Sandler and Harris portrait of Jeremiah Sandler, who appeared almost dwarfish seated behind a large mahogany desk and the leather-bound volumes that sat atop it, height was not a Sandler family trait), but Geoffrey Sandler was any man's match for anger and nervous energy. His red and blue eyes never seemed to rest, darting from room to room and person to person, rarely settling upon anything – be it a face, a pair of shoes or a bookshelf – for more than a few seconds. Detail was simply not important to him. If he could name it – a chair, a doorway, a dickhead in a bad suit – that was enough. He had no time for more.

Part of, in fact all of Geoffrey Sandler's job as publisher and editor-in-chief seemed to depend upon constant motion. He would circle the Sandler and Harris offices, which took up the bottom floor of Yeats' Towers, an anonymous fourteen-storey office block on the fringes of Sydney's legal district, for the duration of every working day, stopping only when an exchange with a wayward employee (usually Bloomington) was necessary.

The employees of Sandler and Harris were not large in number and James was not on familiar terms with any of them. Each journal (Sandler and Harris currently published five journals: *Uncommon Cases and Commentary on the Common Law, Australian Jurisprudence Quarterly, Handicrafts Australia, Modern Horsewoman* and *Saddlery and Stirrups Monthly*) was staffed with an editor, a junior editor and a team of freelance subeditors and contributors (the exception being *Saddlery and Stirrups Monthly*, which employed two junior editors and a full-time subeditor). There was also a production manager, a deeply unpleasant man by the name of Ray Beetle, a part-time accountant (whom James had often seen but had never been formally introduced to) and the office receptionist, Betty Palmer.

Social activities, even the most basic ones, were not part of the daily routine of Sandler and Harris employees. Perhaps as a result of Mr Sandler's regular

13

excursions throughout the office and his predatory manner, employees tended to keep to themselves, remaining largely silent throughout the day. It was an environment that James found entirely to his liking.

As a junior editor, James was responsible for various tasks, each of which he approached with an uncommon zeal. At the beginning of each production month he would read, assess and edit submissions before passing them on to his editor, a Mr Michael Whitely-Smalls.

In his five months at Sandler and Harris, James had never once seen Mr Whitely-Smalls, although he was by now very familiar with his handwriting: tightly looped, not quite neat words produced from a cheap (judging by the uneven ink flow) red ballpoint pen. It was all over the edited pages of text James would find in his pigeon-hole on Tuesday and Thursday mornings. Sometimes the only mark would be a large red cross through every page, informing James that the submission he had championed was not up to the high standards of *Uncommon Cases and Commentary on the Common Law*.

That Mr Whitely-Smalls never once left his office, if indeed he ever entered it, did not seem to bother other Sandler and Harris employees (including Mr Sandler himself) and consequently it did not bother James. Occasionally he could hear a low, rasping cough coming from behind the door to Mr Whitely-Smalls' central office. Whether this cough emanated from

Mr Whitely-Smalls himself, James was in no position to judge. Only Betty Palmer, who actually claimed to have seen Mr Whitely-Smalls some time in the late 1980s, almost twelve years ago, had any authority to pass judgment as to the origins of the cough, which could be heard throughout the entire floor on a good or bad day, depending on your point of view.

Betty, who, with her long, dark curly hair and penchant for head-scarves, bore some resemblance to the once-famous tennis player John McEnroe, did not like to betray a confidence, however small that confidence may have been, and was unwilling to entertain public speculation as to the owner of the Sandler and Harris cough. She was almost impossibly soft-spoken for a receptionist and must have been, James guessed, in her early fifties. That James had been careful to wish her a good morning for every day of the past five months, and always addressed her as 'Miss Palmer', earned him a special place in her heart; and once, as he was walking after work through the city streets towards the underground train station, Betty Palmer had glided up beside him and confessed that she did indeed suspect that the cough was coming from Mr Whitely-Smalls. At least she believed the cough to be consistent with the appearance of the man she had seen all those years ago. Mr Whitely-Smalls, as she recalled, was a rather large, one might say obese, man with an unusually red complexion – it was not difficult to imagine him as a consumptive – and she was sure his throat would be capable of delivering such a power-ful and distinctive sound on a regular basis.

James was busy with 'Family Court Practice in Aus-tralia since *Kramer v. Kramer*' – he was not sure that the legal scholarship was going to be up to the correct standard but he could tell immediately that the vigour of 'Hello, Sailor! Homoerotic Imagery in Herman Melville's *Moby-Dick*' was nowhere to be found here – when he looked up from his corner desk to see a woman enter the Sandler and Harris offices through a door immediately adjacent to Betty Palmer. The woman did not stop to address Miss Palmer but brushed straight past the reception desk and into the office proper. James could see Betty's still open mouth. He imagined her feeble voice had begun to ask, 'Can I help you, ma'am?' but was cut short by a total lack of interest in a response on the other woman's part. The woman made her way quickly through the office, her body upright, back supremely straight, passing close by the Sandler and Harris staff but not touching any of them, not even with a brush of fabric from her navy skirt or jacket.

Some of the staff continued with their work, others stopped and stared for an instant as the woman passed them on her way, the most direct route, to James's desk. When she arrived, James, who remained seated, looked up at her. She was wearing a white, disposable air-filtration mask.

'Hello, Mother.'

'Hmph npht ungh ha ha.'

'Take off the mask please, Mother.'

'Hmph neehoffer nit not.'

'Please, Mother, the mask.'

'Hmpht npht. Nit Not!'

'Really, Mother. I can't understand a thing you're saying. Take off the mask.'

'Hmpht.'

She reached across James's desk, across a computer terminal and James himself, to find a ballpoint pen, one of four lined neatly along the right corner of the desktop, parallel to the side edge. She took a sheet of paper from James's hand. It was a page from 'Family Court Practice in Australia since *Kramer v. Kramer*', which she turned over, placed on the desk and began to write upon.

'Do you mind, Mother? That happens to be a particularly important document you are in the process of defacing.'

'Hmpht nit neehoff hoo ha ha.'

'Yes, I know you're only writing on the back of the page, Mother, but that's really beside the point. I still need to pass that document on to my editor. If only you'd have asked I would have fetched you a clean sheet.'

She continued to write in a clear, plain hand – no unnecessary flourishes, a graceful economy of movement. She turned the paper towards James. It read: 'I will not take off my mask until we are in a secure environment. You know better than that. And I did ask you for a clean sheet of paper. What did you think I was doing here huffing and puffing?'

James should have known better. One day, shortly after his seventeenth birthday, his mother, looking up from the colour supplement of her regular Saturday newspaper, announced, 'The air is impure.' And who could argue? James certainly did not attempt to do so. The air was impure. Three hours later she returned from a hardware store with a box of fifty disposable air-filtration masks (the literature inside the box preferred the term 'particulate respirators') from the Safe-T Services Corporation of Boise, Idaho. The respirators themselves were made in the People's Republic of China, where they were individually sealed in hygienic plastic bags, packed in lots of fifty and sent to Boise, Idaho, for distribution around the world as model number STSC-720 N95. The first box was empty within two months, but not before another box had been purchased and stored in his mother's bedroom closet. James had no idea how many boxes had been purchased since, nor did he know how much the retail price of a box of fifty STSC-720 N95 disposable particulate respirators had risen in seven years. (The amount was, if he cared to consult his mother, $12.45. He did not care to consult his mother.)

His mother's requirements of a secure environment, James knew, were not as strict as they perhaps should have been. She preferred to be in a continuously air-conditioned space, without open windows or other obvious opportunities for the impure air of the outside world to intrude. Thus, large city department stores were her natural home. (She minimised the threat of legionella bacteria and other airborne particles by frequenting only stores and complexes of the highest quality.) Perversely, the ground floor offices of Sandler and Harris were not air-conditioned. James himself sat next to an open window, hoping for a breeze to deliver him some respite from the punishing summer heat.

But his mother's demands were, when faced with obvious practical limitations, usually flexible. She would settle for a single air-conditioned room and the offices of Sandler and Harris contained just such a room: the Jeremiah Sandler Memorial Boardroom, located directly opposite James's desk, in the far left corner of the floor. Hopefully his mother would not notice that the two window-mounted air-conditioners that kept the Jeremiah Sandler Memorial Boardroom cool were well over eight years old and not, as was plain to see, operating at full capacity.

'Follow me, Mother,' said James, rising from his chair and making his way towards the boardroom. His mother followed, a steady two steps off his heels.

The Jeremiah Sandler Memorial Boardroom contained a round oak table around which eight high-backed leatherette chairs were arranged. It was rarely used and, if not for the air-conditioners (which, for reasons best known to Geoffrey Sandler, were always running), would surely have been musty. James seated himself on the chair closest to the room's entrance. His mother closed the door behind her and remained standing. She slipped the disposable respirator over her head and faced her son.

'Those air-conditioners must be well over eight years old, James. And it's plain to see that they are not operating at full capacity. No matter, every small exchange between us hurries me towards my death.'

'It's lovely to see you too, Mother. You're looking well.' It was true, she was looking well. Her eyes were clear and her thin, set lips lent, as always, an air of dignity to her appearance.

'I've seen him again.'

'Who have you seen, Mother?'

'You.'

James paused for a second.

'Who did you say, Mother?'

'You.'

'Who?'

'You.'

'What?'

'You.'

'Me?'

'You.'

'Me?'

'You. It's you.'

James paused again.

'What are you talking about, Mother? Are you entirely sure that those masks you insist on wearing are not restricting the necessary flow of air to your brain? I've always suspected that to be the case. In fact I suspected something of the kind before you even began to wear the masks.'

'I've seen you. Your future.'

'Have you been having visions, Mother? Finding religion at this late stage of your life is a little crass, I would think. You're not drinking again, are you?'

'Please, James. Your attempted sarcasm — that is what you think you're doing, isn't it? — only serves to paint you as the attention seeker that you are. It gives you a certain air of desperation, which I for one find repulsive.'

'Thank you, Mother. Please forget that I said you were looking well.'

'You think I'm looking well?'

'Yes, Mother.'

'Thank you, darling.'

'Don't mention it. Now, what on earth are you talking about?'

'There is a man I've found. He looks like you.'

'Please, Mother. Stop this conversation right now if it's heading where I fear it may be heading. I don't think I can afford the therapist's bills.'

'I said stop that, James. There is a man. He sits on a flattened cardboard box. I suspect that he is one of those homeless men. He looks like you. Not like you now, but you in ten or twelve years' time.'

'How do you know what I will look like in ten years' time?'

'I am your mother, James. You were pulled from my stomach. You caused me to lose my figure, albeit temporarily. I know.'

'That's a lovely story, Mother. Thank you for sharing it with me. My destiny is to be homeless. Something to look forward to, then. Now, if you don't mind, I really must get back to work.'

'Come look at him with me.'

'Pardon?'

'Come look at him with me. I want you to look at him. With me. Come with me now.'

Chapter 3

They walked through the city streets, James Bloomington and his mother, Veronica. As a child he had admired her self-possession. People would see her, notice her, even if it was unconsciously, and give her the room she required. It was clear to everyone, no matter their purpose, that Veronica Bloomington's purpose was greater, and people deferred to the rightness of her movement. James would follow behind, moving his legs as quickly as he could to keep pace with her. She would never, like other mothers he saw, reach back for his hand; she would never drag him along. They both understood that it was up to him to keep up. Usually he did.

Now they walked side by side, James easily matching his mother's pace. It was early afternoon and the streets were busy with people making their way back from their daily lunch breaks. James could feel people – their bodies – all around him, brushing his own body as they passed. Arms, shoulders, hips, faces. To his left, his mother remained untouched. Always, often at the last moment, people would contort their bodies to avoid disturbing her. Perhaps, James thought, it was the sight of the respirator, although he knew better. In transit, people, children especially, would often turn their eyes towards the mask before they continued on their way. Rarely, however, did anyone take a second look. Once they had taken in her full appearance, the white mask – neat, tidy, not strange of itself – seemed perfectly in its place and it was obvious that Veronica Bloomington was not a woman to be either feared or shunned. She was a woman to make way for.

They did not speak; his mother's mask made conversation impossible and, besides, James had nothing to say. Here he was, roaming the streets with his mother – in search of what? Himself? His future? – when he should have been back at the Sandler and Harris offices doing the work that he was paid, not handsomely but paid nonetheless, to do. They walked five blocks to Wynyard Station then took a train south two stops, to Central.

They rode in the compartment closest to the carriage doors, two rows of brown vinyl seats facing each other across a small section of floor space for standing passengers. James noted the usual harassed faces of workers, shoppers, students. Directly across from him was a man in heavily stained blue jeans and a pale green t-shirt with a long, straw-coloured beard. His hair was not brushed and his eyes darted constantly about the carriage. He was carrying a yellow plastic bucket full of mud. There was a small section of a tree branch standing straight up in the mud. The man appeared to have soiled himself. He was half-mumbling, half-singing God knows what to God knows who. Nobody paid him any attention.

James followed his mother through the station's exit. Already he could see a collection of men sitting on collapsed cardboard boxes in various locations. Which, he wondered, was his mother's particular favourite? Two blocks later they came to a halt in a rarely used one-way street. Cars avoided it, so people walked all over the road in both directions. Some stuck to the concrete footpaths on either side out of habit, but most simply meandered across the road. The sun was shining high above them but the entire street was cast in shadow.

His mother's eyes were directed to a section of the base of a concrete building that met the left footpath. She kept her gaze perfectly still for ten seconds or so then looked up at James, who was waiting for her signal. She shrugged her shoulders: there was, obviously, no one there. James shrugged back at her, turned, and began to walk towards the station. She did not follow him.

· · ·

As he approached the entrance to Yeats' Towers, James could see the shiny head of Oliver McDonald-Stuart. He and Oliver had first met at university. Oliver's great aim in life, James suspected, was simply to be liked by as many people as possible, preferably at the same time. He liked people and thought it was only natural that they, in return, should like him. To be liked by as many people as possible, one had to be known by as many people as possible and thus Oliver had introduced himself to James, during a particularly dry lecture introducing the concept of bailment, by sliding up to him along the long wooden bench and imploring him to 'get a load of the tits on that'. The instruction was backed up with Oliver's slyest grin. James was, of course, appalled but, by following the direction of Oliver's eyes, and failing to show his disapproval in an unambiguous manner, found himself in constant contact − never initiated by himself − with Oliver throughout his university life and now beyond. James's elaborately stiff civility only seemed to encourage his attentions.

Oliver was working as a solicitor with Handley, Hanson and Short, a small firm specialising in personal injury liability that took up the eleventh and twelfth floors of Yeats' Towers. For an arm and leg man, Oliver was handsomely dressed in a double-breasted grey pin-striped woollen suit, neatly polished brogues, a fine pale-blue cotton shirt (Italian, James guessed) and lightly patterned red silk tie. Despite the premature loss of much of his hair (a few unconvincing blond strands remained around his ears), he was not an unattractive man. His clear blue eyes were set back in a face made up of very straight lines and softened by a pair of almost oversized lips. To everyone's great surprise, not least his own, Oliver had shown a prodigious talent as a personal injury claims lawyer and had quickly become a valued member of the Handley, Hanson and Short team. A partnership offer, it was rumoured, was only a matter of a year or so away.

James slowed his pace, hoping that Oliver would turn his back and allow him to slip through the entrance way to Yeats' Towers and on to Sandler and Harris unmolested. Oliver had his arm around a smaller man dressed in an ill-fitting green – was that what was called gabardine? – suit. The man was walking with some difficulty, but thankfully he was moving away from James and the Yeats' Towers entrance. James looked down and noticed that the man's left leg was a prosthetic. Where the flesh ended and the plastic began he couldn't tell – the man's trouser leg covered the view down to his ankle – but the exposed foot was clearly artificial. For some reason (James later learned that the man was under direction from Oliver) he was not wearing any shoes.

Oliver's voice could be heard by anyone within a five-metre radius.

'Yeah, I'll admit it's a good offer. Have to admit that, at least. Fair and equitable, some might say. Nothing to be sneezed at, oh no.'

James could not hear the man's reply but his manner suggested he was posing a question.

'Because if we just hang in there for a month or two, we'll be looking at a lot more. Maybe even double. We all want the best deal we can possibly get, right? It's good for you and I make no secret of the fact that it's good for me too. Maybe double! That'll get you back on your feet in no time.'

After a pause for burlesque effect, Oliver laughed loudly. The man laughed with him, shaking his fragile head back and forth before slipping from underneath Oliver's arm and continuing on his way with a surprisingly steady gait.

Oliver yelled down the street after him: 'Keep your pecker up, matey!'

He was still smiling, his face red from the strain, when he turned back towards Yeats' Towers and straight into James Bloomington.

'Jimmy!'

'Hello, Oliver.'

'Jimmy Bloomers!'

'Hello, Oliver.'

'Would you believe, you're just the man I'm looking for?'

'Be still my beating heart.'

'Be still your beating off, more like it!'

'Thank you, Oliver. I'm not sure that old woman with the hearing aid over there heard you, but thank you.'

'Don't mention it. No, seriously, I've been looking

for you. Popped in to the office but you were out. No one seemed to know where the hell you were. Away with the fairies, I said, and the little guy, what's his name? Sandler? Sandler said yes, he does have a way with the fairies. Funny little fucker sometimes.'

'His hilarity often knows no bounds.'

'Much like your own.'

'Yes, very much like my own.'

'So anyway, I've got a date for us – now don't give me that look, Jimmy. I know the last one I set you up with wasn't exactly a winner, but how the hell was I supposed to know she'd salivate like that at the sound of a dinner bell? Yes, I was aware she was known by the name of Pavlov's Dog in certain quarters, I'll admit to it, but I didn't expect that, did I? I thought she'd be a real goer, you know? And I did cover the dry-cleaning bills, didn't I?'

'Yes, that was very decent of you.'

'Yes, it was. Anyway, this time it'll be fun. Fun for me, fun for you, fun for anybody within a ten-mile radius. Fun, fun, fun. And you're a fun guy, Jimmy, you just don't know it yet. Her name's Alison, she's a sales girl at Ralph Lauren Polo, in the Pitt Street Mall – you know the one, flashy entrance, lots of pictures of guys on horseback. I've never met her – now don't look at me like that – but Trudi, that's Trudi with an "i", the one I've been trying to get interested for the last couple of weeks, assures me she's a lovely girl. She's just a bit nervous, Trudi that is, of going out with me all by herself. Thinks I've got a touch of the serial-killer about me. Fuck that Ted Bundy. So I need you to help me out here, although if I really want to convince anyone of my sanity, I'm not going to do it by hanging around with you, am I? That was a joke, Jim.'

'Was it?'

'So I've told her all about you, built you up as the strong, silent type. Said you'd been hurt before, wary of commitment, all that shit. Made you interesting, Jimmy – far more interesting than you really are, truth be told. All you've got to do is sit there through dinner. No dinner bells this time, we'll go somewhere else. Be as moody as you like, I don't give a fuck, just be there and be . . . interesting. We'll have a nice dinner and then go our separate ways. What do you reckon?'

'I really need to get back to work, Oliver.'

'Yeah, me too. But what do you reckon? Are you up for it? Come on, Jim . . . one night and you might get lucky. Lord knows you could use the release, right?'

'I'll think about it, Oliver. I could do with some companionship at the moment but I'm not sure that a sales girl is exactly what I'm after. And besides, I'm perfectly capable of finding companionship by myself.'

'Yes, I know you are. You're a good-looking man, Jimmy. That's why I need you. Look, it'll be fun. If it turns into a nightmare, at least you know I'm good for a couple of trips to the dry-cleaners.'

'I'll think about it, Oliver. Now, if you don't mind, I really must be back at my desk.'

'It's tomorrow night, Jimmy. I'll come down and grab you after work, OK?'

'Yes, fine.'

With that, spoken over his shoulder, James ascended the front steps of Yeats' Towers and made his way towards the desk waiting for him within.

Chapter 4

The sound of music drifting on the wind towards him told James that he was home. The song was 'That's Amore', the singer was not, unfortunately, Dean Martin, but an anonymous session vocalist doing his best to disguise the fact that he was not, unfortunately, Dean Martin.

The trip home took him under a half-hour in the evenings: three stops on the North Shore train line followed by a short, usually pleasant walk to his current domicile in Watterson Avenue, Waverton. James rented two rooms at the rear of well-kept brown-brick house that lay in a row of similarly well-kept and coloured houses. The real estate notice had, to the best of his recollection, described the two rooms as a 'self-contained unit' – words which had very much appealed to him at the time – but he shared a common entrance, a bath-room, laundry and occasionally some living area with his landlady, Mrs Salvestrin.

It was Mrs Salvestrin who was playing 'That's Amore', the favourite track on her favourite album (or so she had repeatedly assured James), *Great Italian Love Songs*. James did not know what other songs appeared on the album (he would not pick up the album's sleeve for fear of being suspected of displaying an interest in other, perhaps greater Italian love songs); all he ever heard, every evening on his scheduled return home at 6.25 pm, was 'That's Amore'. It had begun shortly after he had moved in, almost five months ago. And every evening, as he approached the steps, Mrs Salvestrin would be waiting for him, her shoulders back against the brick, feet planted further forward, as he walked up the steps and onto the small concrete patio.

She exhaled the smoke from her cigarette.

'Bongiorno, James darling.'

'Hello, Mrs Salvestrin.'

'Please, James, call me Sophia. Don't I tell you this every day?'

'Yes, you do,' said James as he walked past her and into the hallway.

The widow Salvestrin was, James guessed, in her early fifties. Mr Salvestrin had been a successful if (according to his wife) unambitious accountant. He had died of a heart attack seven years ago, four days short of his forty-eighth birthday. Mercifully, he had left Sophia well provided for. She did not, for instance, need to take in a tenant. She did, however, enjoy the company.

She was probably considered a handsome woman in her youth. Even now people often told her that she resembled the post-war Italian movie siren Sophia Loren. At least she told James that people often remarked upon the similarity. So much so that she was getting sick of hearing it. And besides, it was obvious to her that Miss Loren was of late resorting to plastic surgery to maintain her looks, particularly her generous cleavage. Probably had it done in Beverly Hills. Or somewhere in Italy. Genoa, perhaps. Sophia Salvestrin did not need to do this.

James had a vague recollection of Sophia Loren on late-night television wearing a nun's habit, white and pure. He could not remember if the movie had been in colour or in black and white. But he did remember that the camera was often framed tightly on Miss Loren's face, which was frequently required to display a diverse range of emotions. The movement on her forehead during moments of indecision had been remarkable. Perhaps it was the habit and head-dress, but as far as James could tell, Mrs Salvestrin bore only a superficial resemblance to the woman he recalled. Her lips were far too thin, her chin lacked the required sharpness and her forehead was totally unremarkable. He also suspected that Mrs Salvestrin was not Italian: some of the correspondence she received in the mail (which James collected from the green tin letterbox at the property's boundary as he came in of an evening) was addressed to a 'Miss Sophie Watkins'.

Still, she may well have been a handsome woman in her day. Her posture was good and even now she retained much of her figure. If only her arms didn't appear so unusually large, the flesh, particularly on the upper areas, so loose . . . But her face was, for the most part, pleasant, although James often found the longing in her dark eyes unseemly.

The song continued, shifting to a higher key.

'When . . . the . . . moon hits your eye like a big pizza pie . . .'

James walked down the hallway towards the rear of the house and the smoked-glass doors to his rooms. The first room contained a small kitchen, for which James had little use. The only appliances were a mid-sized refrigerator and a small microwave oven, which sat against the left wall on a wooden benchtop next to the sink. There were drawers and cupboards underneath. A small round table, the top finished with white formica, was pushed against the right wall. Two chairs, steel framed and covered in orange vinyl, sat on opposite sides of the table. James took a glass, turned upside down, from beside the sink and opened the refrigerator door, taking a plastic bottle of orange juice, 'No Added Sugar! 100% Juice!', from within. He filled the glass, half emptied it and sat it on the table, moving into the second room.

The second room served as both his bedroom and main living area. His bed, a single, inner-spring mattress on an unfinished pine-slat base, was pushed into the near left corner. A pair of sneakers, white socks sticking out from their insides, lay underneath the bed. A wooden bookcase stood against the wall at the foot of the bed, filled with a mix of legal texts and novels from his early classes in English literature. His clothes were arranged on two large steel-framed hangers that sat against the right wall; socks, underwear and t-shirts were folded and placed in a set of white steel-mesh drawers. A television set, a 51-centimetre Sony, sat on the floor opposite the bed. There was a single, aluminium-framed window on the far wall, which looked out onto a small backyard overgrown with grass and weeds. The sun was still high in the sky, filling the room with light. James pulled the curtains across and began to loosen his tie.

He turned on the light, a bare bulb in the centre of the ceiling, and the television – a teenage soap opera of some sort – and sat down on the bed, which had been neatly made, he assumed, by Mrs Salvestrin. The bed was always made when he came home but neither of them had ever mentioned it. A girl on the television, small but very pretty, her belly button on prominent display in the space between her tight t-shirt and jeans, was talking to a blond boy with a bad complexion.

'But Travis, you've got to come to the dance with me. Or else all the girls will think I've been lying about me and you!'

'*Yeah, but there's an awards night on at the footy club –*'

'*Travis! But you said you loved me! Otherwise I wouldn't have let you do that thing we did with the you-know-what under the pier! It's still itchy down there, Travis!*'

[hysterical sobbing]

'*Settle down, Jamie. All right, I'll go to the dance . . .*'

His attention drifted away from the television and he kicked off his shoes and socks. He emptied his pockets and threw his watch onto the floor. He was more careful with his jacket, a single-breasted plain grey woollen, which he placed on a hanger at the front of the rack. The suit was two years old and not from a recognised tailor, but James thought it notable for its classic cut. He could, depending on the state of the pants, wear it for another couple of days this week before he needed to switch to the double-breasted navy. He took off the pants and brought the seat up to his nose. Fine. He folded each leg along its crease, hung the pants next to the jacket and returned to the bed in his boxer shorts and shirt. His briefcase, Samsonite, not leather, was on the bed. 'Hello, Sailor! Homoerotic Imagery in Herman Melville's *Moby-Dick*' was inside it. It certainly was not suitable for a legal periodical but it was a fascinating subject nonetheless. Perhaps he would return it to the author with a few well-chosen words of encouragement.

He was just finding his place in the manuscript when Mrs Salvestrin walked in.

'Oh, pardon me, darling. I didn't know you didn't have any pants on.'

'No. That was very careless of me. Please accept my apologies.'

James raised himself from the bed and headed towards his pants on the rack.

'No, don't get up. It's perfectly OK. What are you reading, dear?'

'Oh, I've just brought some work home with me.'

'My, you're such a hard worker. If only my Guido had had your initiative, your . . . drive, he might be alive today.'

Silence.

'I was wondering if you've had any dinner, James?'

'No, I haven't as yet.'

'I've just made some pasta, a little fettucine carbonara. There's more than enough for two. If you'd like.'

'Thank you, Mrs Salvestrin. I'll be in shortly.'

'And there's a movie on television tonight, one of my favourites, you know. Perhaps we could watch it together.'

A pause.

'It's *The Graduate*, with Dustin Hoffman and Anne Bancroft. You know, people used to tell me that she and I looked very much alike. Similar sense of style – I could see that – but really, they flattered me.'

'Yes, I expect they did.'

'Have you seen it?'

'I don't believe that I have, but I shall be quite busy with my work tonight, I'm afraid.'

'There's that drive again. Well, I'll see you for dinner soon.'

'I'm very much looking forward to it.'

As James got up to put his pants on he could hear the ring of the telephone in Mrs Salvestrin's kitchen. He did not have a phone of his own, and was permitted to receive calls on Mrs Salvestrin's line. He did not make out-going calls. Just as he had finished with his fly, Mrs Salvestrin came back into the room.

'James darling, it's for you. It's your mother. I got quite a surprise.'

'Thank you, Mrs Salvestrin. I'll be right in.'

He moved through his own small kitchen and up the hallway into Mrs Salvestrin's kitchen. A shallow pan of carbonara sauce was simmering on a hotplate above the stove. A pot of water was about to boil beside it. The phone was mounted on the wall. James pulled up the cord until he reached the handset.

'Hello, Mother.' He could hear the hum of the air-conditioner in the background.

'Who is that woman, James?'

'You know perfectly well who she is, Mother. Mrs Salvestrin. This is her house.'

'Are you sleeping with her, James? Are you fucking an old woman? My God, James, how old is she, anyway?'

'Stop that, Mother. I'm not sleeping with anybody.'

'That's what I'd always suspected, but James — with an old woman? How can you stand that voice? "*Oooooh,*

Mrs Bloomington! It's lovely to hear from you. You know, James is just a *per*fect darling. He's such a well-mannered young man, and so handsome. You must be very proud of him." My God, James, she must be at least ten years older than me. It's almost perverse.'

'Stop it right now, Mother.'

'She said you were just about to sit down to dinner. Are you just about to sit down to dinner?'

'Yes, Mother.'

'Are you wearing your pants?'

'Yes, Mother. As it happens, I am.'

'What are you having for dinner?'

'Fettucine carbonara.'

'Are you fucking that old woman, James?'

'No, Mother, I am not.'

'Very well. I want you to come with me again tomorrow morning. To see him. But it has to be in the morning. I know he'll be there, he always is.'

'Mother, you know I have to be in the office in the morning.'

'James, I'm sure the legal periodical industry — that is what you do, isn't it? — will not come crashing down to earth from its dizzy height in the heavens simply because you are absent from your chair for half an hour. I will be there, at the spot we visited this morning, at fourteen minutes past ten. I expect you to be there as well.'

'Yes, Mother.'

'What time do you have now?'

'I'm not wearing my watch, Mother.'

'No, of course you're not. What need does a young man in love have for time?'

Before he could answer, the phone went dead. James hung up the receiver and went to the bathroom to wash his hands for dinner.

Chapter 5

It was hotter today, the sun, high as it was, burning everything that it touched. Even in the shadows the concrete had lost its chill and he was aware of its warmth as it seeped through the cardboard below him and into his body, or, more specifically, his arse. He was already beginning to feel uncomfortable and it was still only morning, probably around ten or so. Not much traffic about and the passers-by were, not surprisingly, largely lethargic and uninterested.

He wondered if she would come today. Perhaps it would be too hot for her. Maybe the mask wouldn't function right in really hot weather and she'd need to stay at home, wherever that was, hooked up to some sort of machine. Like an iron lung, maybe. Only smaller. Sleeker. Modern times, after all: what'll they think of next? He fixed his eyes on the concrete expanse in front of him, picking out an expelled piece of chewing gum slightly to his right, bright pink, still glistening with moisture. The teeth marks wouldn't last long. Sooner, rather than later, somebody's shoe would squash the gum flat against the concrete. The gum would stretch with the upward movement of the foot, snapping at some point to leave two smaller pieces, one leaving with the foot, one remaining. Who knows how far it would travel?

And then he heard the sound of her footsteps approaching. The steps. The shoes. The ankles. The stockings. The skirt. A white, light cotton blouse. The mask. Today, a wide-brimmed straw hat with a navy ribbon and black-rimmed sunglasses. He began to count . . .

Thirty-eight, thirty-nine, forty, forty-one, forty-two, forty-three, forty-four, forty-five. Unusual. Maybe she was tired, exhausted from the heat, needed to rest a while. He raised his head from the ground, past her waist and up, briefly, to her face. The sunglasses had oversized round lenses, impenetrably black. Still she stood her ground, looking down at him.

After a few minutes a man in black leather shoes and grey pants walked up and joined her. A grey suit, actually. White shirt. Some sort of blue tie. He was sweating and looked uncomfortable but vaguely familiar. Quite good-looking, really. Young and almost pretty, dark hair cropped close to his rather round head. Drops of sweat ran from his forehead and down his protruding chin; some hit the concrete surface below, where they were quickly absorbed by the covering of dirt.

'Hmpht nay.'

'Yes, Mother, I know I'm late. I apologise. The trains this morning were very disagreeable. Far too many people, far too much heat.'

'Npht it he mo ng hit foo hook nee.'

'Mother, if you're going to continue talking to me through that mask, I'm going to go straight back to work. It's really quite unbearable. So either take the mask off or start writing.'

'Me nit ot ne humho nerry.'

'I know it's not a secure environment, Mother. I would never suggest that any street in this city is a secure environment. But the sun is unreasonably volatile today, as you can see. It's probably burning the impurities from the air even as we speak. Besides, I don't intend to be here talking to you for very long. Whatever damage is occasioned to you will surely be reversible.'

'You'd like that, wouldn't you? If I was damaged?' She had taken off the mask, which now hung loosely by its elastic straps around her slender neck. At the sound of her voice he looked up from the ground to see her face. She was looking at her son and did not notice his gaze. Despite her thin lips, which seemed to set her mouth into a straight line, she was, as he imagined, very pretty. Even the wrinkles, slight creases from her cheeks to her chin, seemed to fit.

'No, Mother, I would not. If there's one thing I do not wish upon myself it's to nurse you through the sickness of your declining years. I want you healthy for years to come. Are you still exercising regularly?'

'That's him. There.'

'Yes, I assumed that was why we're standing here in front of him.'

'Well?'

'Don't see the resemblance.'

'Take a good look, James. I know he's a little scruffy and his hair's longer and he's . . . older, yes. But take a good look: it's you.'

James took a good look. Perhaps if the man stood up he'd be about James's height, although he didn't really look like the type who'd ever have a need for standing. It was difficult to get a proper impression of his face; his head was tilted towards the ground and he remained expressionless. But he did have a rather noble forehead, all things considered, and a nice curl to his hair, which was flecked with silver around the temples. Like James, he had brown eyes and there was something to the bridge of his nose that seemed very familiar. Still, the clothes were all wrong. How could he wear so many heavy clothes on a day like today? And he wasn't even sweating. Not that he'd actually moved an inch in the time James and his mother had been standing there.

'I don't know, Mother. Perhaps there is a slight resemblance. But he's hardly my double. Now that I think about it, I fail to see what exactly I'm doing here.'

'Mpht near memoo npht nell noo.' Evidently not satisfied with the quality of the air, she'd slipped the mask back over her mouth.

'Mother, I will not continue to stand here while you mumble at me through that thing. That's it – I'm going back to the office.'

James turned abruptly and walked off in the direction of the train station. She stayed for another half minute or so, still looking down at him, before she too headed towards the station. At that pace, she'd catch up with him in no time.

When James walked past Betty Palmer's reception desk and into the offices of Sandler and Harris, his mother was only two steps behind him. She had kept that distance since catching up with him just outside the railway station. She stood to his left in the busy carriage and followed him off the train and through the city streets to Yeats' Towers. Betty Palmer's head came up sharply when she saw the woman in the mask approaching. She opened her mouth, quite wide, but no sound escaped as Veronica Bloomington stepped quickly and confidently past her desk. As James headed for his own desk he noticed that his mother had trailed off behind him and was heading for the Jeremiah Sandler Memorial Boardroom.

A few seconds after she went through the board-room door James heard his mother's voice. The mask was off.

'Excuse me,' she said. 'But I really must have a rather urgent discussion with my son. We shan't be long, I assure you. If you'd care to step outside until we're done I'd be very grateful.'

Two men made a hasty exit from the boardroom. One was Geoffrey Sandler, who looked as if he was unsure himself of why he had responded to the clipped authority of the woman's voice. His head was moving quickly from side to side, looking about the office for clues. The other was Stephen Hunt, editor of *Saddlery and Stirrups Monthly*. Hunt was much taller than Geoffrey Sandler, his thin frame clothed in an impressive tweed suit. He too looked baffled and was repeatedly running his right hand across the thick grey hairs of his moustache and down to his chin. His head remained largely stationary but his green eyes darted about. He was clutching two folded magazines in his left hand. James assumed that he and Geoffrey Sandler had been involved in some kind of editorial meeting. After a pause during which neither man said a word, Sandler walked off to the right and Hunt to the left, leaving James a clear passage to the boardroom.

James pulled the door closed behind him. His mother fixed her eyes on him as he came in.

'Well, what did you think?'

'Mother, I must insist that you stop harassing me in my place of business.'

'I asked you a question, James. What did you think?'

'That was my employer who you just turfed out of here, Mother. Mr Geoffrey Sandler. A very important man. How am I going to explain you to him? He must have thought you were some kind of mad woman. He may be calling for the police right now. In fact, I suspect that that is exactly what he is doing.'

'Do stop carrying on, James. What did you think?'

'About what?'

'About the man in the lane, James. Why else did we meet just now? Please, James. Try to concentrate.'

'What's to think about? I suppose he bears a slight resemblance to me. But I'm sure there are many people scattered about the globe who are similarly blessed. Perhaps even a Hindu holy man in Pakistan.'

'There's no need to be facetious, James. By the way, what's that horrible sound?'

'That's Mr Whitely-Smalls, my editor.'

'He sounds incredibly unwell.'

'Yes, I expect that he is. Still, you get used to it after a time. I find it quite soothing. He's very regular.'

'I find it unnerving. I'd hate to be placed in a secure environment with that man. I should have to insist on his prompt removal.'

'Yet you have no objection to staring at an apparently homeless man in a public street. You should be careful, Mother. Those men are often psychotic. Perhaps more so than you.'

'I hardly think so, James. But at least you're getting to the point. The man. His appearance means nothing to you?'

'No, Mother. Aside from being the best-looking beggar I've ever seen, his appearance means absolutely nothing to me. In fact, I fail to see why you dragged me out there.'

'Because we can learn from him, James. Isn't that much at least obvious?'

'What can we possibly learn from that man, Mother? That sitting on concrete for days on end does in fact give you haemorrhoids?'

'Really, James. Even if there is a Hindu holy man in Pakistan, try to think about why this particular man has been placed in your path.'

'He hasn't been placed in my path, Mother. I had to take an unscheduled break from my work and catch a train I would have much preferred not to have been on just to get to him.'

'Well, he *is* there, James. And it means something, I'm sure of it.'

'What has gotten into you, Mother? Will you listen to yourself? It's just a man, Mother. A man who may or may not look like I may or may not look one day. That's all. Now if you'll kindly excuse me, I really must be getting back to work. I've got a busy day ahead of me and I've already wasted quite enough of the company's time this morning.'

'Think about it, James.'

'Mother, I haven't the time to think about anything other than procedure and practice in Family Law right at the moment. Please, I have to get back to my desk.'

Her eyes did not leave his as she adjusted the straps at the side of her respirator. When the mask was securely in place she turned her back to him, opened the door and walked quickly past Betty Palmer towards the exit.

James was at his desk, trying to concentrate on 'Family Court Practice in Australia since *Kramer v. Kramer*'. It was impossibly dull but a likely candidate for inclusion in next month's journal regardless. There was a shortage of quality submissions at the moment. Most practising lawyers preferred to concentrate their writing efforts on developing scripts for television dramas and situation comedies, and student submissions, though often worthy of attention, were rarely up to the quality expected. He looked up to see Geoffrey Sandler zigzagging his way across the office floor. Judging from his path, he would almost certainly end up at James's desk.

'Bloomington. What are you doing?'

'Assessing a submission, sir. "Family Court Practice in Australia since *Kramer v. Kramer*".'

'Weren't you working on that yesterday?'

'Yes, sir, Unfortunately, my work has been some-what interrupted in the interval.'

'Jesus, Bloomington. If you were any fucking slower I'd need to shove a crank up your arse and wind you.'

'Yes, sir. Obviously I'd prefer to avoid that.'

'Hmmm. I'm not so sure you wouldn't enjoy it. Still, we do what we can to keep the workers happy here at Sandler and Harris. Was that your mother earlier? In the Jeremiah Sandler Memorial Boardroom?'

'Yes, sir. I'm sorry she disturbed you and Mr Hunt.'

'Striking woman, Bloomington.'

'Sir?'

'Your mother. Striking woman.'

'Yes, sir.'

'Her name is?'

'Veronica, sir. Veronica Bloomington.'

'Very striking. And your father, Bloomington?'

'I don't have a father, sir. At least not that I'm aware of.'

'You weren't one of those test-tube-baby disasters, were you? That would explain a thing or two. Sperm donations from around the country mixed into some sort of ungodly paste . . .'

'No, sir. I was the product of a natural conception. My father vanished when I was eighteen months old.'

'What do you mean "vanished", Bloomington?'

'Just that, sir. My mother says he vanished. He left the house for his evening walk – I understand he was a regular walker – and vanished. I assume he simply decided against returning.'

'And your mother has been alone for all these years?'

'Yes, sir. We had a German shepherd for a time. His name was Hans. But he returned to Germany after some trouble with one of the local farmers. He claimed Hans had interfered with one of his best sheep and was not a particularly good shepherd besides. The farmer informed the immigration authorities and they came to take Hans away. Mother was sad to see him go, of course.'

'Of course.'

Silence.

'Is there anything else, sir?'

'Er, no. Carry on.'

Sandler's little legs hurried away. James carried on, hoping the day would soon come to an end. Outside, the sun was slowly flattening pedestrians beneath it. Sitting at his desk, he could feel himself beginning to sweat through his shirt at the small of his back. He glanced at his watch. It was only twelve minutes past two.

Chapter 6

Oliver came to get him just before six. He was wearing a lightweight wool, dark-grey, single-breasted suit, a yellow shirt – James would never wear yellow, but it did look good on Oliver – and a maroon tie. He was smoothing the hair at the sides of his head.

'Jesus, Jimmy. You look like shit.'

'Thank you, Oliver.'

'No, I really mean it. You look like a pile of shit. Your face is all red and your hair is all . . . well, it's limp. Chicks don't dig limp hair, Jimmy.'

'I'm sorry to hear that, Oliver.'

'Maybe you can go and splash some water on your face or something? Make sure it hits the hair too. Get some life back into it. You know, just freshen up a little. If the toilets here aren't good enough, you can use my toilet up on the twelfth. Plenty of room in there to splash stuff around. Might even find some deodorant in there somewhere. Not that it's necessary.'

'You have your own toilet?'

'I have my own toilet. It's very nice. Plenty of room to splash stuff around. Here's the keys. Go ahead. Twelfth floor. Down the main corridor, third door on the left. My initials are on the door.'

'Your initials are on the door.'

'My initials are on the door. O. M. S. Twelfth floor. Come on, Jimmy. Snap to it. Just tell Sandy at the desk that I sent you up.'

Oliver steered James past the Sandler and Harris reception area and into the lobby. He pushed the 'up' button and waited with James by the elevators. An elevator arrived and unloaded a group of eleven people, workers from the various floors heading for home. When the last of them had cleared the elevator, a perfectly round man in a dark-brown cardigan and bow tie, James got in and pressed the button for the twelfth floor, Handley, Hanson and Short.

When he got out of the elevator, his nose – the left side – began to bleed. It was, he knew immediately, the heat of the day catching up with him, coupled with the sudden change in elevation and temperature (the twelfth floor, unlike the bottom floor, was air-conditioned). It was a problem he'd had since he was a teenager and he'd become adept at dealing with it under varying circumstances. He reached for a tissue from his inside jacket pocket, tilted his head towards the floor and began to pinch the bridge of his nose between his fore-fingers. He stopped just outside the elevator doors and waited for forty seconds or so, enough time to stop the bleeding.

Oliver had shown him the Handley, Hanson and Short offices before — crisp white walls, a circular plan leading forever inwards to the centre of the floor. Employees would begin their careers at the centre and work their way towards the edges. Oliver possessed one of the prized outer offices, a small window giving him a view, such as it was, of the city below him.

James made his way to the main corridor. There was an irregular ring of blood around the outer edge of his left nostril.

'Can I help you, sir?' A fragile voice.

'No, thank you, er, Sandy. I'm a friend of Mr McDonald-Stuart. I work at Sandler and Harris, on the bottom floor. Oliver sent me up to use the bath-room.' James dangled the keys out in front of him at eye level.

'Oh. It's the third door on the left, sir.'

'Thank you, Sandy.'

O. M. S. Oliver McDonald-Stuart. James tried the key and the door swung open. He had his own toilet. White porcelain bowl and white plastic seat. A small sink underneath an ample wood-framed mirror. A glass shelf below the mirror held soap, shaving cream, a few blue plastic disposable razors and a glass bottle of aftershave. Alfred Dunhill. There was also, as Oliver had mentioned, a roll-on deodorant. To the right-hand side of the sink lay a magazine. It was, James discovered, the Handley, Hanson and Short company newsletter, *Lawyers, Guns and Money*. There was a picture of Oliver on the third page. A towel rack on the back of the door held a small white towel.

James stood in the middle of the room, facing the mirror, and stretched his arms out straight by his sides. His hands didn't touch the walls. He rotated slowly, counterclockwise, arms straight, until he was looking into the mirror again. It wasn't good. The dark traces of blood simply made his nostril appear unnaturally large, distorted. His face was covered in a slick film, multiple layers of sweat. His hair was indeed limp.

He lowered his head towards the basin and reached for the cold water tap. Oliver had turned it tight, an old habit, but soon the water was flowing through James's cupped hands. He splashed it across his face, from forehead to chin, and rubbed his nostril between thumb and forefinger, watching the water turn pink as it hit the basin below and clung to the porcelain momentarily before more water washed its traces away. Finally he tilted his face down, bringing his eyes to his chest, and ran his wet hands through his hair. He looked up into his reflection, lingering on his face. It was a good face, of that he was sure.

The sound of the running tap had made him aware of his need to urinate, which he did, being careful to concentrate the stream straight into the centre of the toilet bowl. He shook himself slowly and methodically, zipped, and waited for the shock of the last errant splash of urine on the inside of his thigh. It soaked into the cotton of his boxer shorts as he reached for the towel.

When his face was dry he replaced the towel on the rack and opened the door. He pulled it shut behind him, locked it and headed for the elevator. Sandy had gone home. At least she was no longer at her desk.

Oliver was waiting for him when the elevator reached the bottom floor. James, who had been the first to enter the elevator, was the last to emerge.

'Hey there, Jimmy! Looks a lot better already. Like the toilet? I like what you've done with the hair. Brings up the curl nicely. Give me the keys. C'mon, let's go. We'll be late.'

They walked down the stairs and into the street, James trailing slightly behind Oliver. The sky had turned dark – heavy clouds were forming and rain looked likely. People looked up as they were walking, many hoping for the summer storm that looked certain to come. Raindrops were beginning to fall and the pace of the street's pedestrians picked up. Oliver's pace remained steady.

'We'll pick up the girls from the shop, OK? They can close up and then we'll head down Liverpool Street maybe, find a place to eat. There's a nice little Japanese place just after the park. Dark and cosy. We'll pop our heads in there, huh? They both live out in the eastern suburbs somewhere, so we'll be in the right spot when it comes to going our separate ways. You'll like Alison, Jimmy. Trudi says she's a great girl, a good friend.'

The rain was getting heavier as they approached the mall and the shopfront. There were mannequins, male and female, in the windows on each side of a wide glass door, all clothed in subdued leisurewear. The predominant colours of the season were khakis, browns and light blues, with the occasional splash of bright orange. James thought the whole arrangement tacky. The door was shut. A white cardboard sign on the glass read 'Closed' but James could make out two women standing together at the back of the store, almost on each other's toes, talking hurriedly. One, the dark-haired girl, was quite tall; the other was shorter, although by no means short, and blonde. Both were dressed in a similar style to the display mannequins.

Oliver rapped his knuckle on the glass and leaned his face, its broadest smile on show, close to its surface. The shorter girl stepped quickly to the door.

'Trudi!'

'Hi, Oliver. How are you?'

'Fine, Trudi, fine. You look great, by the way. Trudi, this is Jimmy.'

'Hi, Jimmy. Nice to meet you.'

'It's James, actually. James Bloomington.'

He held out his hand.

'Hi, James. Come on in, boys. We'll just get our things together and we can go. Oliver, James, this is Alison. Alison – Oliver and James.'

'Hi.'

She was long and slender, probably twenty-two or twenty-three, wearing a cream cotton shirt and a knee-length khaki skirt. She appeared to be wearing only a little make-up, eyeshadow and lipstick. Her hair, a dark brown, was pulled back from her face and held at the back with a plastic comb. She was not particularly pretty – her nose was too broad and her features were generally unremarkable – but she was pleasant-looking, her face dusted with fine freckles, and, as far as James could tell, she was not yet salivating.

'Hello,' he said, holding out his hand. 'James Bloomington.'

'Hi, James.' She took his hand. Her hand was warm and smooth and quickly gone. Her voice was surprisingly strong and clear.

'OK, Jimmy, let's get out of here. Everyone ready?'

They headed for the door. Trudi locked it behind her and began walking by Oliver's side, looking up at him, talking. James hadn't noticed when, but Oliver had taken Trudi's hand in his. James and Alison fell in a few steps behind, the voices in front of them muffled by the falling rain.

'Trudi tells me you're a lawyer like Oliver.'

'Yes. Well, no. I'm an editor at Sandler and Harris

Publishers. *Uncommon Cases and Commentary on the Common Law.* It's a legal digest.'

'Oh.'

They continued to walk but did not exchange another word until they reached the restaurant. The rain was still falling as they were ushered inside by a middle-aged Japanese woman in traditional dress. The restaurant was merely a narrow room with rows of wooden tables broken by a narrow walkway through the centre. A hallway at the end presumably led to the kitchen. Before they sat down Oliver ordered *sake* and Japanese beer for everyone. They took a table against the far wall, James and Alison facing the entrance, Oliver and Trudi opposite.

'OK then,' said Oliver. 'Let's get this show on the road. Don't pay too much attention to Jimmy, Alison. He'll talk your head off, given half a chance. Let's take a look at these menus . . .'

They ordered chicken and vegetable dumplings and skewers of chicken as an entrée, sashimi and a beef and vegetable hotpot – *sukiyaki*, the menu said – for the mains. Oliver picked the dishes as the drinks arrived; James remained motionless, staring beyond Oliver to the rain falling outside.

Oliver waved his hand in front of James's face, laughing. When James turned to look at Oliver he was holding out a small glass of clear liquid, motioning for James to take it. The *sake* felt hot on his tongue and all the way down his throat, right to his heart. It was necessary to follow it quickly with a few gulps of beer. He was surprised at how quickly his head began to pound, although it was not an entirely unpleasant sensation. The voices around him began to take on an abstract quality.

'Do you like your work, James?' It was Alison, looking up at him casually. Her face was still soured – lips pursed, one eye slightly closed – from her first taste of the drink.

'I beg your pardon?'

'Your work. Do you like it? It sounds interesting.'

'Does it?'

'I suppose so. What exactly do you do?'

'I read submissions, pass them on to my editor, edit copy, proof-read final layouts. It can be quite demanding.'

'Is it like being a lawyer?'

'No, not really. It's more of an academic pursuit. Occasionally the journal may be of help to lawyers, analysing case law and what-have-you, but mainly it's an exercise in elegance and logic. At least, that's the theory.'

'I work in the Polo shop. But you probably guessed that.'

'So you being in the shop when we came to get you, dressed identically to one of the mannequins – the third from the left, on the right-hand side of the door, if I'm not mistaken – was not the coincidence I assumed it to be?'

'No. I really do work there.'

'Fascinating.'

'We meet some nice people, don't we, Trude? I like it when they like to talk. They tell us about themselves, where they've been.'

James was again silent, looking at the rain falling outside. Meanwhile, a constant drone was coming from Oliver and Trudi as the food was brought and plates taken away. They were both laughing. James could not understand why. He continued to drink.

'So what do you do when you're not at work?' Alison again.

'Pardon?'

'What do you do to relax? What sort of things do you like doing?'

'What do you mean by that?'

'Nothing. I mean, what do you do at home?'

'Nothing at all. What makes you think I'd be doing anything at home?'

'You must do something . . .'

'Nothing at all. I go home to Mrs Salvestrin, eat, go to bed – to sleep – and wake up in the morning and go to work.'

'Who's Mrs Salvestrin?'

'My landlady.'

'Is she nice?'

'She grants me exclusive possession of a few rooms of her house at a reasonable weekly rate. She is my landlady. She doesn't have to be nice.'

'Oh. Don't you do anything at home, besides eat and sleep?'

'I read a little.'

'But isn't that what you do at work?'

'Yes, it is.'

'I like going to the movies.'

'That's lovely, I'm sure.'

'Anything funny. I like to laugh.'

'I'll try to remember that.'

James returned to his food. He had been picking at it intermittently. He was quite fond of the *sukiyaki*, although he was sure he didn't like the look of those large mushrooms. There was something menacing about them. He was feeling increasingly light-headed; it was probably the mushrooms. He continued to eat, chewing his food with a slow, hesitating rhythm. It was as if by slowing the pace of his jaw, he was slowing time itself. Laughter and conversation continued around him, without him.

Oliver had loosened his tie and had his arm firmly around Trudi, who appeared not to mind in the slightest.

'I want to make a toast!' he boomed. 'To my good friend Jimmy Bloomers. A gentleman. A scholar. A fine scholar, as it happens. A prince among men. But not much of a fucking dinner companion.'

Trudi and Alison laughed with Oliver. James did not. Inexplicably, Alison placed her hand around his and continued to laugh. Oliver looked casually at his watch.

'Well,' he said. 'Time to get moving. Trudi and I are

going to grab a cab. We'll see you two later. Don't worry about the bill, Jimmy. I'll pick it up on the way out.'

Alison was still holding his hand. Her eyes were red, her body heavy against him as they stood and left the restaurant. She too appeared to be under the influence of the mushrooms.

They made their way into the street and hailed a cab. Alison gave the driver an address in Bondi and settled her head against James's shoulder in the back seat. The cab driver, an Indian by the look of him, was looking at James in his rear-vision mirror as he drove. James could see the whites of his eyes, his pupils enlarged, merging with the blackness of his eyeballs. The streets were slick with oil and water, headlights dazzling.

'Is that permed or natural?'

'Pardon?'

'Your hair. Permed or natural?'

'It's natural.'

'It's very nice.'

'Thank you.'

'Are you French?'

'I beg your pardon?'

'Are you French?'

'Not that I'm aware of.'

'You look French.'

'I'd never noticed.'

'Do you like French?'

'What?'

'Do you like French? You know, you and the girl . . .'

'What on earth are you talking about?'

'You and the girl. Are you getting any French?'

'I'd like you to stop talking to me now.'

'C'mon, you can tell me about the French . . .'

'I'd like you to cease your talking right this second. Take us to the location we've asked and remain silent or I shall be forced to rap you across the back of the head with my knuckles.'

Soon they arrived. The moon was hidden behind dark clouds and the rain was constant. Alison led him by the hand up a short concrete path and inside a light-coloured-brick apartment block. Two floors up she unlocked a door and led him into a narrow hallway. She placed a finger to her lips to indicate he should remain silent. It was difficult for James to get his bearings in the dark but soon he found himself sitting on a bed in the centre of a small room illuminated by candle-light. He could just make out Alison's face in front of him, wet and soft.

'They told me you were an emotional cripple.'

'What?'

'A cripple. Emotionally. Underdeveloped.'

'A cripple?'

'Trudi says Oliver says that you've been hurt before and that you don't form attachments.'

'Not if I can avoid it.'

'That's fine with me.'

'Good. I can promise you that I will form absolutely

no bond with you whatsoever, no matter what depraved and senseless acts we may commit upon each other's bodies now or in the future. And I happen to have a few in mind . . .'

'Good. Let's fuck.'

'Yes. Let's. But I think you should know that if my penis should go flaccid during intercourse it's only because I really don't find you terribly attractive at all.'

'Oooh, James! That's just the kind of pillow-talk a girl likes to hear. Come here, big boy . . .'

Her mouth was covering his and he found himself tumbling backwards, wondering if anything would ever break his fall.

Chapter 7

Saturdays and Sundays were idle days for Veronica Bloomington. Not that her weekdays were particularly busy, but she had decided long ago that her weekends were to be spent, for the most part, prone. She was lying in the centre of her loungeroom floor, the soft pink carpet turning into light balls of fluff under her. The carpet was now four years old but it simply refused to settle.

She closed her eyes and concentrated on the hum of the central air-conditioning unit; the sound always relaxed her mind. She rolled her body up and into a seated position. Her legs, covered in a pair of navy leotards, were split wide apart, toes pointed. She stretched her body forward along her right side, moving her chest towards her right knee and her chin to the middle of her shin bone. Her hands grasped her right ankle, fingers overlapping, forearms resting upon the carpet. She held the position for forty-five seconds, released it, and began again on the left side. Her movements were slow and methodical, the product of years of repetition.

When she met Cecil Bloomington, James's father, Veronica Stroker was a dancer, a ballerina of some promise with the Muriel Lermentov Troupe ('refined young ladies all' read the standard program notes). She was seventeen years old, marked by Muriel Lermentov herself as a future lead, and visiting the English town of Cornwall as part of a cultural exchange program with her home city of Sydney. Cornwall was not exactly the romantic seaside port that she and the other girls had hoped for but it did contain, for Veronica, one attraction of note: Cecil Bloomington.

Cecil was, Veronica thought, perhaps the most handsome man she had ever seen, beside her own papa. He was the proprietor of the town's best fish and chip shop, Bloomington's Cod Basket, and despite spending much of his day surrounded by boiling oil, Cecil had a remarkably clear complexion and unusually thick, dark curly hair. When he smiled, which was not often, the left side of his face seemed to struggle with the effort. He was twenty-six years old and had, Veronica soon learned, no parents or ties of his own in Cornwall.

So began Veronica Stroker's battered-fish romance. In little over a week she was able to persuade Cecil to sell up shop and return with her to Australia. A month later they were married and Cecil used the profits from the sale of Bloomington's Cod Basket to begin a new trade in imports and exports. At first he concentrated on fish products and by-products (the market in cod-liver oil was particularly lucrative) but soon he was expanding his trade into fabrics, dyes, processed and preserved meats, pickled vegetables and, occasionally, livestock. Cecil was dour but somehow personable and, more importantly for Veronica, he managed to make a lot of money.

Three years after her marriage, Veronica fell pregnant. It was not an easy birth. While Veronica endured the four-hour process, Cecil, who could not be relied upon to maintain his dignity during childbirth, waited outside. When the child finally emerged it was almost dead. The umbilical cord was wrapped firmly around its flabby neck and its colour – it was quite literally black and blue – was hideous. It took four firm slaps from the doctor to encourage the child's first tears. Veronica then expected it to stop crying, but from that point on it never seemed likely.

Left alone in the hospital ward with her son, Veronica would search the child's face, hoping to find something of herself, or of Cecil. She was looking for some sort of recognition. She could find none. The child could have been anybody's. Regardless of the fact that she had seen it ripped from her own body, Veronica was struck by a deep distrust of the baby before her, and of its motives. What it wanted from her remained to be seen.

Cecil was of little help. Bloomington Distribution continued to grow at a rapid pace and he spent few of his waking hours at home. He did hire a nanny to tend to the child for most of the day, but it continued to voice its dissatisfaction long after the nanny went home to her own family, wherever and whatever that might be. When it did finally exhaust itself and fall asleep, Veronica would take the opportunity to further examine the child's face. Still there was no recognition.

Cecil insisted that the child be christened by the Church of England. It was to be called James, after Cecil's long-dead father. Veronica had no objection to this and began addressing the child by its given name. After ten months the crying began to subside, but the child, James, showed little willingness to do anything other than eat. According to the nanny he was not interested in crawling and he simply refused to walk. Speech was out of the question.

When Cecil disappeared, however, James was walking. He was not steady on his feet – in fact he showed absolutely no grace in any of his movements – but he could walk. As far as Veronica knew, he had not yet begun to talk, although the nanny insisted she had often heard him babble softly to himself and had on one occasion called out for her by name, whatever that was.

Cecil had also taken to walking. Mr Bloomington was a man of routine, sober habits. He would come home from work at 7.30 or thereabouts every evening. He would eat the dinner that Veronica had prepared for him, usually meat and vegetables of some sort, never fish, not of any kind. After dinner he would sit with Veronica and talk about the day's movements at Bloomington Distribution for a half-hour. Then he would stand, take his coat off the lounge chair he had placed it over when he arrived home, and set off on his evening walk. He was never absent for more than forty minutes.

Sometimes Veronica believed that the earth had opened up, quickly and violently, and taken him away, or that he was a victim of spontaneous (and unwitnessed) combustion. Sometimes she believed that he had come to some sort of harm. A man ahead of him looking up from the ground and asking for the time, another man behind clubbing him with a truncheon – a car jack, perhaps – when he stopped to look at his watch. A car waiting with an open boot by the side of the road. Another man with a knife, another with a shovel. At other times she believed what she suspected James had grown to believe: that Cecil just kept walking. In any case, he was gone. And he did not come back.

Veronica stood and stretched her hands towards the ceiling, palms up, fingers interlocked. Her floor routine over, she began looking around the room, searching for something to occupy her mind. The television in front of her, set into a black-stained wall unit, was not on (she had no desire to change this) and the paintings and prints on the plain white walls surrounding her had long since exhausted her interest. She walked to the sliding glass doors that led to the balcony, which extended across the front of the entire top floor of the house, and looked through the glass. The sky was blue and clear, clouds spread thinly across its surface. The sea below was still, a few single-masted boats passing slowly across her field of vision.

It was Saturday morning. The weekend newspaper would be waiting for her on the narrow path that lead to the house, split into two thick sections, tightly rolled, each wrapped in a thin plastic sheath. It was almost obscene.

She walked lightly across the carpet and into her bedroom. The room was not large, containing only a king-sized bed and matching side-tables, a set of drawers at the foot of the bed, a wall-mounted mirror in front of the drawers and a floor-to-ceiling walk-in closet to the immediate right of the door. The bed was covered by a quilted salmon bedspread, which matched the colour of the walls. The head of the bed was pushed against the far wall and there was barely enough room to walk around the bed's edges on the other three sides. Another set of sliding glass doors, which were never opened, led from the bedroom to the balcony. Veronica opened her closet and reached into the Safe-T Services box on the floor, bringing her hand out with a fresh particulate respirator for the day.

A short hallway led from Veronica's bedroom into a

large bathroom. The toilet, separate from the bathroom, was behind a door on the right-hand side of the hall. Veronica would don a respirator and heavy green rubber gloves and scrub the toilet with a solution of warm water and ammonia every three days. The floor tiles hurt her knees terribly, but coupled with the frenzied scrubbing, it was a sensation she found to be not entirely disagreeable. The next designated cleaning day was tomorrow.

She moved past the hallway and back into the loungeroom. A central staircase, also carpeted, led her downstairs and towards the entranceway to the house. She placed the mask of the STSC-720 N95 carefully over her face and tightened the two headstraps. The lower floor was not large. A hallway to the right led to a second bathroom, a second toilet and, facing the front of the house, a second bedroom. James's bedroom. At least it was James's bedroom up until five months ago. Before he went to work. Before he went to live with that cut-rate Italian whore. She was old enough to be his mother.

Outside, Veronica could feel the sun's warmth through her clothes, a loose white cotton overshirt and the leotards beneath. She held her arms out by her sides and breathed in deeply through the STSC-720 N95, closing her eyes and tilting her head towards the sun.

The mere act of donning the respirator (and the STSC-720 N95 had an effective donning time of under ten seconds and a doffing time of under seven seconds, less if the respirator was allowed to rest around the wearer's neck by its two durable, latex-free, pre-stretched and ultrasonically welded polymer headstraps), securing the adjustable metal nose-clip and inhaling the scent of the inner lining and the state-of-the-art, electrostatically charged, hypoallergenic filter media, filled her with a near complete sense of serenity and security. Inside the STSC-720 N95, each breath anticipated the next, lending a peculiarly meditative calm to any outdoor activity.

Veronica had never once regretted choosing the Safe-T Services Corporation (of Boise, Idaho) product over the market-leading and perhaps more aesthetically pleasing line of disposable particulate and irritant respirators manufactured by the Minnesota Mining and Manufacturing Company. Guided by an enthusiastic salesman, she had quickly decided that her needs would be best met by a disposable respirator (largely because such respirators were, by their very nature, maintenance free). The salesman, whose name tag had identified him as Gil Gerard, Sales Professional, had then encouraged his rather stern but handsome customer to make her selection from the recommended range based purely on the fit and comfort of the respirator. He, Gil Gerard, Sales Professional, was willing to stand behind (no pun intended, Mr Gerard assured her) just two quality products: the STSC-720 N95 and the 81105 N95 from 3M. Each complied with the United States Occupational Safety and Health Administration (OSHA) and National Institute for Occupational Safety and Health

(NIOSH) requirements (OSHA 29 CFR 1910.134 and NIOSH 42 CFR 84 N95); each had a minimum filter efficiency of 95 per cent against solid (0.3 micron) and non-oil based particles; each had two headband straps for a secure fit and an adjustable nose-clip to provide a snug seal and reduce the potential for fogging of eye-wear (not that she was wearing any eyewear but you never knew what could happen to your eyes in the future and besides which she'd look pretty nifty in glasses anyway); each had an NIOSH Assigned Protection Factor (which reflects the ratio of contaminant outside the respirator to contaminant inside the respirator, set by taking into account filter efficiency and fit factor, a measurement of the leakage that occurs between the respirator face seal and the face as determined by use of either a quantitative or qualitative fit test) of five; each featured collapse-resistant, double-shell construction to withstand hot and humid conditions; and each contained a built-in exhalation valve to reduce the build-up of warm exhaled air, prevent the filter media from moisture loading (which was not at all desirable), and facilitate positive pressure seal checks. After repeated fittings Veronica decided on the STSC-720 N95 because it 'just felt right'. It still did.

She exhaled and opened her eyes. She could see the two sections of her newspaper further down the path. One sat almost in the path's centre, the other was partially hidden behind the broad base of one of her potted palms. She moved towards the palm.

As she picked up the newspaper she saw that there were bugs – tiny black bugs with barely visible legs – walking across the leaves of the palm. Dozens of bugs, all presumably hungry. She bent to the ground and quickly found two elliptical rocks by the side of the path. The rocks' edges were sharp but both were easily grasped by each hand. Their weight and mass was excellent.

Veronica set her eyes on the bugs, watching their movements closely. She rested the rocks lightly on the palm leaves, one on each side of a particular bug's projected path. When the bug reached the target area she brought the rocks together, suddenly and fiercely, grinding the uneven surfaces together slowly and methodically. When one bug was gone she would move on to the next. It was a potentially endless process.

Chapter 8

James woke with a pain in his head, somewhere off in the distance. There was a girl, Alison, to his left, asleep and covered in dried blood from the top of her head to her chest, and probably below. Her hair, now extended past her shoulders, was also clotted. There were thick drops of blood soaked into the pale-green sheet that covered them. His nose. He could taste the blood deep in the back of his throat. He reached up and gently felt the inner edges of his nostril. He would have to explain this inconvenient abnormality to her when she awoke. It was all rather unfortunate.

The morning light was seeping into the room from behind thick orange curtains that hung above the head of the bed. Alison (he realised he did not know her last name) appeared to be sleeping heavily. Her chest (it was, he noted, ample) rose and fell evenly with each breath. She slept open-mouthed. Her jaw was somewhat slack. Her lips were parted wider than James would have liked and he could see the uneven row of her bottom teeth. There were tiny bubbles of saliva inside the corners of her mouth. Still, her face – a pleasing oval – appeared finer and more fragile than he recalled.

The room was small, taken up mainly by the bed and a large white built-in wardrobe with mirrored sliding doors to James's right. There was a black chest of drawers – cheap, prefabricated materials, probably from one of those Swedish catalogue shops – against the far wall. A burnished metal candle holder, tall and twisting, sat atop the drawers and held the remains of a candle in a shallow circular dish. The door, immediately to the left of the drawers, was shut. The narrow leather strap of a black handbag hung over its handle.

He had little choice but to lie there and will her to wake. The urgency was of his own making. It was Saturday morning and he was not required to be anywhere. But he wanted to be anywhere but here.

He could see his clothes strewn on the carpet by the door. They appeared to be mercifully free of blood. His face, however, was not. James propped himself on his elbow and glanced at the mirror and saw dried streaks of red across both cheeks and down the left side of his neck. There were dark circles under his eyes, emanating from the bridge of his nose, and his skin appeared porous and irritated.

Alison turned slowly onto her side, facing him, and opened her eyes. She was looking up at him.

'Good morning,' she said.

'Good morning.'

'There's blood on your face.'

'Yes, I know. It's from my nose. Left nostril. It's all over you, I'm afraid.'

'Is it?'

'Yes. It's in your hair.'

'It'll wash out, I expect.'

'Yes. You don't seem surprised or perturbed by this.'

'I'm not surprised. You look like a nose-bleeder to me. I may or may not be perturbed. I don't know what the word means.'

'Disturbed, troubled, upset.'

'It'll wash out.'

'That's a very mature attitude, Alison. What's your full name, by the way? For some reason I expected a degree of panic. Possibly an unpleasant scene. Very good. Except for the fact that, according to you, I look like a nose-bleeder. What exactly does a nose-bleeder look like?'

'It's Gately. Alison Gately. And anyone who wakes up covered in his own blood is either a self-mutilator or a nose-bleeder. You don't look like a self-mutilator.'

'I look like a nose-bleeder.'

'You look like a nose-bleeder.'

'And a nose-bleeder has certain facial characteristics?'

'None in particular. A certain something in the eyes.

A caution. They tend to hold their chins up higher than most.'

'And this was immediately obvious to you?'

'No. It's just that when I saw the blood I figured you for a nose-bleeder.'

'I see. Would you direct me to the bathroom, please? I must be on my way and I'd very much like to take a shower before I go. If that's not possible, perhaps I could wash my face in a sink? I have my own soap.'

'No, you can use the shower. You don't want to stay for breakfast or anything? We've got muesli and Corn Flakes.'

'Thank you, no. I really must be on my way. I've got rather a lot of work to do today. Papers to read. Papers to edit.'

'Sure. Whatever. Bathroom is down the hall, the second door on the right. Use whatever you like. We have soap, you know.'

'I'm sure you do. But I prefer to use my own. It's in my briefcase. No trouble at all, really. I would like a clean towel, however.'

'I'll get you one.'

'Thank you. And if you'd like, write your phone number on a piece of notepaper and leave it by the door. I'll pick it up on my way out. Perhaps we could do this again sometime?'

'You mean the sex or the conversation?'

'Primarily the sex.'

'I'll leave the number by the door.'

. . .

James could see little trace of last night's storm as he walked out into the street. The sun was climbing high and the heat only made him more aware of the dull ache in his head. It centred itself squarely between his eyes.

He began to walk along the street. He assumed he was heading west; he was not exactly sure where he was. Soon he came to a bus stop. There was no shelter from the sun but there was a metal bench on which to sit. A timetable encased in yellow plastic below the bus-stop marker indicated that a bus would soon pass and take him in the direction of the city, back to Central Station. He sat, crossing his right leg over the left, and waited. According to his watch the bus was running late. That was the problem with timetables: no one ever stuck to them.

Sitting in the direct sunlight, James knew it was only a matter of time before he would begin to sweat. His odour would betray him, revealing traces of last night despite his morning shower. It was the stench of alcohol, the stench of sweat, of shit and decay.

Another man was approaching the bench. The sun was directly behind his crown, casting his face in shadow. He was very large, a fleshy neck falling into a huge sphere of a body carried along on a pair of unsteady legs. As the man walked, his shoulders dipped suddenly from side to side. It was an irregular motion but James was soon caught up in its rhythm and he found himself watching the man's progress until he was seated, with a great deal of effort and a passing display of his huge rump, directly to James's right.

His hair, slick with oil, was thin and grey; his face was ruddy. The nose, a little squashed and slightly off-centre, was, James's mother had taught him at a young age, the nose of a drinking man. He must have been at least sixty years old.

'How ya going, son?' His voice was gruff, somewhere between a whisper and a hacking cough.

'Fine, thank you.'

'Where you headed?'

'Home.'

'You get some action last night, didja?'

'I beg your pardon?'

'No need to beg my fucking pardon, sunshine, it's given very easily . . . You look like you got some action last night. It's written all over your face, ya smug little cunt. Local girl, was she? Shit, girls these days will jump anything that moves. Not that you're not a good-looking boy, of course. It's just the tarts around here aren't fucking choosy. You want a smoke? You'll have to roll your own.'

'No, thank you.'

'Don't smoke? Don't blame ya. I've been a smoker since I was fourteen fucking years old. Look at my hand. Looks like I've just been sticking these three fingers up my arse, doesn't it? Fucking nicotine stains. But I'll let you in on a little secret: I just stuck these other three fingers up me arse!' The man erupted in laughter. He was soon gasping for breath, forming a fist with his left hand and bringing it heavily against his chest.

'Ah, shit. Only joking, son. Only joking . . . So tell me about last night. It'll pass the time while we wait for the bus. They're never on time on the fucking weekend.'

'I really don't see that it's any of your business.'

'Aw, don't be like that, son. I'm just trying to be sociable, share a little human kindness. Share a little tenderness. I'm not a young man anymore, you know, and it's not often I get much action myself, not without paying through the fucking nose anyhow. Would it kill you to share a tale with an old man? Come on, you'll be old and past it one day too. You won't be able to remember your own fucking stories so you'll be begging some young prick to let you in on his, too. What do they call it? Living variously through some-one else?'

'Vicariously.'

'What?'

'It's vicariously. Living vicariously.'

'Yeah, whatever you say. Just keep talking.'

'I'm sorry, but I'm really not about to tell you any-thing about last night. In fact, I'd prefer it if we simply ceased this conversation altogether.'

'You little fucking cunt. Come on, tell me about it. Tell me about the girl. You fucked her, son. I know you fucked her. It's in your fucking eyes. Tell me about it. All about it. How big were her tits? How was the bounce? An even bounce or a bit on the floppy side? Was she a big girl? Round and firm? I've always liked the round ones myself, gives a man something to grab on to. A nice, round arse. Nice and round. Come on, son, you can tell me. Tell me about her arse. Didja do the bitch from behind? Come on, tell me you did her from behind. Tell me how hard ya fucked her. How hard?'

The man was rushing his words by now; he was breathless and his face was sweating profusely. The sweat ran in thick streams from his forehead to his jowls. James glanced down and saw that he was playing with himself, grasping his withered old cock between the thumb and forefinger of his right hand and rubbing the foreskin back and forth as rapidly as he could. He had not been circumcised.

'Do you mind?'

'Mind what? Oh, shit. You're breaking my fucking concentration. The arse, the fucking arse.'

'Please stop that this instant.'

'Actually, son, I'm just at the point where I want to keep going. Give me a hand, will ya? Now don't look at me like that. I don't want you to fucking touch me. It's never the same. Never the right rhythm. Just talk to me. Tell me about the girl. Tell me how hard. How fucking hard . . . Didja fuck her up the arse? I hear girls these days'll let you . . . Oh, fuck. How hard? How hard?'

The man closed his eyes and tilted his head back.

He was mumbling to himself and it was obvious that James's participation was no longer required. James stood up and moved to the end of the bench. As he stood, a bus appeared and quickly came to a stop in front of him. Beside him, the man snapped his head forward and hurriedly zipped up his fly, stumbling to his feet.

James was mounting the first step before the doors had fully opened, reaching into his side pocket for the weekly travel ticket in his wallet. He took a seat almost directly behind the driver, two rows from the front. The fat man was a few steps behind, fumbling in his pants' pockets looking for change. When he paid the driver he moved quickly down the aisle to the rear of the bus.

There were only five other passengers and the fat man sat behind all of them. James hoped that he would finish his business in silence. He looked out the window and into the empty street as the bus pulled away from the curb.

He wasn't there. James had stepped off the bus as it terminated its journey at Central Station and had walked to the spot where he had stood with his mother the day before. The man in the lane, his mother's homeless man, wasn't there. But the man from the bench, the fat man, was. He had followed James from the bus and was now coming up behind him, sweating and panting.

James turned quickly and headed back towards the train station. He walked straight past the fat man, brushing his shoulder with his own as they crossed paths.

'Hey, son. Hold up. Where ya going, son?'

'I am not your son and I'm going straight to the police if you don't stop pursuing me.'

'Jesus, son, don't be like that. I'm not following you or nothing. Sure, we shared something back there but that's the be all and end all of it as far as I'm concerned. I'm just taking a stroll in the same direction as you, that's all.'

James stopped and turned to face him.

'I want you to listen carefully to me, old man. Fuck off and fuck off right now or I will hurt you, and I promise that I will hurt you to the best of my ability. You are a filthy old pervert. I am young and strong and this is my world. This is not your world. We do not share a world, we do not share breathing space, we do not share anything. I am going to carry on with my day and forget that you even exist. Now get the fuck away from me.'

James was walking away from him, making his way towards the station with deliberate steps when he heard the man call out after him, shouting violently into the hot air.

'You ungrateful little prick! You ungrateful fucking faggot!' he screamed.

But he did not follow.

Chapter 9

James was aware of the perspiration gathering under-neath his arms as he crossed the grass towards his lodgings. The shirt underneath his jacket would be stained with dark, wet circles.

He had stopped off at a corner store near the train station to pick up some lunch and was carrying his briefcase and a turkey and salad sandwich in a brown paper bag in his right hand and a plastic bag contain-ing a small glass bottle of apple and guava juice, a carton of milk, a green pear and a bruised banana in his left. As he mounted the steps to the front door he took the crumpled end of the paper bag between his teeth, switched the briefcase to his left hand and extended his right arm towards the door knob. There was lint — probably picked up from Alison's carpet —

on his jacket sleeve. The door was locked, forcing him to hold the paper bag in his mouth and reach across his body into his left pants' pocket for the keys. The effort was almost unbearable.

He pulled the door closed behind him and, after a little rearranging, made his way down the hall towards his rooms. The house was dark and quiet and he wondered if Mrs Salvestrin was at home – or worse, if he would stumble into her in some sort of state of undress or otherwise catch her unawares – and called out an uncertain greeting.

'Hello?'

He strengthened his voice and repeated the call.

'Hello?'

There was no reply.

He went through the doors to his rooms and placed both bags onto the kitchen table. He took out the bottle of juice, unscrewed the cap and began to drink, feeling the sweet, heavy liquid slide down his throat and into his empty stomach. He placed the empty bottle on the table and wiped the perspiration off his forehead with the palm of his right hand.

His suit would definitely need to be dry-cleaned. The jacket was crumpled and the pants were heavily creased. On close inspection he noticed a multitude of white fibres clinging to both the jacket and pants. The fibres were from Alison's carpet, possibly wool but probably a synthetic. Dry-cleaning was a matter of urgency. He hung the suit with his usual care and took off his shirt, socks and underwear and stuffed them into a blue laundry bag he kept below one of his clothes racks.

He pulled an old green t-shirt and a clean pair of underpants, dark blue Y-fronts, from his drawers. His jeans were on a hanger; he took them from it, folded them neatly in half and placed them together with the t-shirt and underwear at the end of his bed. His bed had been made and a clean white towel was placed on top of the pillow. Below the pillow was the manuscript to 'Hello, Sailor! Homoerotic Imagery in Herman Melville's *Moby-Dick*', face up on the bed.

James wrapped the towel around his waist and headed through his kitchen and up the hallway to the bathroom. He needed another shower to wash the morning's events off him; the smell of it was still with him.

The door was slightly ajar and he pushed it slowly inwards. Sunlight was coming in through the small, high window and its white lace curtains in thick, expanding shafts that spilled onto the pale-blue tiles of the floor. The light was bright and dazzling, reflecting off the gloss white ceiling and walls, filling the room with a neon glow. It was almost surreal. The bathtub, a pale-blue porcelain shell surrounded by shiny black tiles, was to his right. A shower head at the end of a flexible metal hose was attached to a primitive gas heating unit above the tub.

James closed the door and pulled the towel loose

from his waist, hanging it on the hook at the back of the door. It was then that he heard Mrs Salvestrin's voice.

'Where's my rent?'

She pulled the thick plastic shower curtain across her body with a sudden, unconvincing flourish and sat slumped on the far edge of the tub, half dissolved into the light in a white bathrobe held loosely at her waist. Her right breast was plainly visible. There was a bottle of red wine, nearly empty, at her feet. Another bottle was in her right hand. James could barely make out her features. They were both squinting through the sun's beams. Her black hair was tangled wildly about her head and James could see the thick streaks of silver at the roots. She was looking down at the floor, her shoulders and neck limp, and did not appear to notice that he was naked.

'The rent. Where's my rent?'

'Excuse me, Mrs Salvestrin. I didn't know you were in here.'

'I'm asking you for the rent, boy. Where is it?' She did not raise her eyes.

'I don't have it with me right now, Mrs Salvestrin, but I'll gladly fetch it for you if you'd care to wait a moment. I'll just get my towel . . .'

'Get back here. Sophia. It's Sophia.'

'Yes, I'm sure it is.'

'It's Sophia. Sophia. Where have you been, James? Where were you last night?'

'I spent the evening with my friend, Oliver.'

'I bet you did.'

'I beg your pardon?'

'The entire evening with your friend . . . He must be very entertaining. Probably got a few tricks up his sleeve that I haven't got. Is he good-looking, this . . . friend of yours?'

'I haven't really considered it, but yes, I suppose he is quite handsome.'

'I'm happy for you, James. I'm ecstatic. You're a nice-looking boy yourself, you know. You deserve to be with someone nice. Someone young and strong. Does he have a big harpoon? Is that what you people call it?'

'I'm not sure that I'm following you, Mrs Salvestrin.'

'Sophia. It's Sophia. I'm just trying to understand the mechanics of it, James. Of whatever it is that you and your friend do. Which one of you was the whale?'

'The whale?'

'Yes, the whale. If one of you is the harpoonist, the other must be the whale.'

'You read my manuscript?'

'Which one is the whale?'

'I'm afraid that you've got the wrong impression, Mrs Salvestrin. Oliver and I are merely friends.'

'It's all right, James. You don't have to pretend with me anymore. Having spoken to your mother it all makes perfect sense. I mean, it's obvious really.'

'You spoke with my mother?'

'On the phone when she rang for you, remember? We didn't talk for long but she was very overpowering.

I could sense it – a very overpowering woman. But not all women are like that, James. We're all different. You're such a young man, with so much to experience, so much to offer. It's foolish of you to close yourself off to others, James. It's only natural to be curious and I'm sure it's easier these days for two men to be perfectly happy and have some sort of a life together but, James, it's just not right for you to make a choice like that yet.'

'What on earth are you talking about? If you must know, Oliver and I spent the evening in the company of two young women.'

'Women? But James, that's disgusting. And besides, it's not hygienic.'

'Mrs Salvestrin, if you'd just listen to me and try to think clearly – here, give me the bottle – perhaps you'd understand. Oliver and I took two young ladies to dinner last night. After dinner, Oliver went home with one young lady and I went home with the other.'

'You went home with a girl?'

'Yes.'

'What was her name?'

'Alison. Not that it's any business of yours.'

'I cooked dinner for you last night, you know. It was a surprise. It's in the fridge. Chicken and vegetable risotto. I waited for you to come home and waited and waited. I thought we'd have a nice dinner together, some wine, just the two of us . . .'

'I'm sorry, Mrs Salvestrin, but I can hardly be expected to know what you have in mind of an evening.'

'But I made it for you, James.' She raised her eyes up from the floor, moving past James's waist, over his nearly hairless chest, and looked straight into his eyes.

'Well, I'm home now. I can have it for lunch. I'll soon be hungry anyway.'

'Will you, James?'

'Yes, I expect that I will. Now, let's get you into your room and see if you can't sleep this off.'

James turned his back to her and took his towel off the hook, wrapping it around his waist in the same movement. When he turned around he found Sophia struggling to rise from her seat on the bathtub; her arms were fully extended and her hands pressed flat against the tiled floor.

James reached down and placed his hands around her upper arms. He could feel the loose flesh dispersed beneath the terry-towelling of the robe. His grip was firm and he pulled her quickly to her feet. Her body leaned heavy against his, her face pushing into his breast bone. He was surprised at how easily she rested in his arms and at the looseness of her limbs as he pulled her through the bathroom door and backed his way through the darkened loungeroom and into her room.

He placed her gently onto the bed, where her body sank heavily into a quilted bedspread. The room was dark, only a few stray beams of light breaking through the gaps between the windows and the curtains drawn against them, but James could make out some sort of a

93

crude design on the bedspread. Blood-red roses on a black background.

A white vanity table lay to the right of the bed against the wall, which was papered with a faded gold fleur-de-lys pattern. James reached his hand out to touch one of the lines of gold thread that ran through the pattern in vertical stripes at regular intervals. Jewellery and make-up brushes rested on top of the vanity; a full-length oval mirror sat on a stand next to it.

James saw himself reflected in the mirror, naked save for a towel around his waist, hunched over the widow Salvestrin's robed body. The image was enough to give him pause; it was time to return to the bathroom.

He ran the shower hot, scrubbing at his body with one of Mrs Salvestrin's loofah sponges until it raised the skin, pink and patchy. As he turned off the water he was aware that he was suddenly very tired. It was a lethargy that sank right through his bones. He hadn't slept very well at Alison's house – the liquor had helped but it was never enough – and he knew he needed to make up for it in his own bed, now.

On the way to his rooms he stopped briefly in the kitchen, where he opened the refrigerator door and quickly located the risotto in a green plastic container. He snapped the lid and spooned as much of it as he could into a large breakfast bowl, making sure that he left clumps of the softened grains of rice scattered loosely around the kitchen bench. Other grains stuck to the outside of the container and covered the surface of the dessert spoon he had taken from a rack of clean dishes and cutlery next to the sink. He left the spoon in the middle of the bench and found the overall effect quite pleasing.

Not a masterpiece but it would have to do.

Only a few short steps remained.

He carried the bowl of risotto to his own small refrigerator and made his way to his bed, levering himself between the tightly fitted sheets and throwing Joost P. Sandal's manuscript to the floor.

As his head settled itself into the pillow he began to dream, inexplicably, of the sea.

Chapter 10

It surprised no one, least of all the waitresses who served him at the small city cafe where he took his breakfast every Sunday morning, that Geoffrey Sandler was agitated. He carried his anger with him wherever he went, whatever the circumstances, waiting for an opportunity to unleash it, and those who served him, indifferently or otherwise, did not soon forget his face. The constant movement of his eyes was, by all reports, particularly unsettling.

But this morning he appeared even more agitated than usual. His right leg was jiggling up and down at a furious pace and his undersized hands were grasping and quickly releasing anything within reach: knife, fork, spoons, sugar bowl, the thin, cylindrical packets of sugar inside the bowl, plates, napkins, a woven bread basket, the plastic-coated menu. What's more, he had yet to insult anyone who had approached him, dismissing a succession of waitresses with a disinterested grunt and a wave of his tiny hand. Everyone was on edge.

He was wearing a pale-yellow Polo shirt, navy pants sharply creased along the seams and brown leather boating shoes with matching leather laces. He was not, according to at least one waitress's observation, wearing any socks. His leg continued to betray some sort of fever in his mind.

Geoffrey Sandler lived two blocks away in a large and fashionable apartment building in the middle of the city's central business district. He had a corner apartment on the tenth floor, the livingroom window looking out upon Hyde Park and the busy streets below. It was expensive but convenient, allowing him a brisk walk to and from the Sandler and Harris offices every morning and affording him a sense that he was caught up in an energy and restlessness that matched his own.

He had moved to the apartment after his divorce, bringing with him only a few sets of clothes (suits mainly), four pairs of shoes (three dress, one casual) and his own sense of intolerable injustice. That was nearly five years ago. She didn't love him, she said. Of course she didn't love him – he didn't expect her to. He hadn't loved her, by his own reckoning, since July of the year 1983. In fact, he wasn't entirely sure that he had ever loved her. If he had, he certainly couldn't remember it clearly.

What was it about Anne that had originally appealed to him? It was all so hazy. They had met through mutual friends soon after he had started at Sandler and Harris. His father had voiced his approval and she was amiable and pretty, there was no doubting that. Her face was almost perfectly symmetrical, with the notable exception of a bump high on the left side of her forehead, the legacy of a childhood fall from a ladder. Full lips surrounded two rows of very white and very prominent teeth. As Geoffrey remembered it, her mouth had two natural and constant states: wide open in a dazzling smile or drawn down at the corners in a delicious pout. Her cheeks were high and round, usually flushed with colour, and her blue eyes were remarkably clear and, to Geoffrey, unusually calm.

Often as he lay asleep at night the face would come to him, floating, disembodied, through his dreams. Sometimes it happened if he closed his eyes for a second or two, which he regarded as due punishment for a bad habit. But something had happened to Anne's face. It wasn't just the extra lines and creases: he had accumulated plenty of those himself over the years. It was if the calm in her eyes somehow gave way to abandonment, abandonment of caring, abandonment of feeling. He would look at her and wonder what she was thinking. Usually, he guessed, she was thinking of absolutely nothing. Her mind, as it turned out, was a complete blank. They had never really talked much but that hadn't bothered him. Suddenly it did. He started to notice that she was changing physically. Her hips had grown larger while, perversely, her lips had grown thinner. Her back and shoulders had broadened to match her middle. She said nothing, she did nothing; she was an entirely slothful, useless creature.

And she had the fucking nerve to tell him she didn't love him. That she wanted a divorce and would appreciate it if he could leave the house as soon as possible. That she had met someone else – how the fuck she managed that without shifting her ever-growing bulk off the couch was anyone's guess – and wanted to see if she could start her life again. New and fresh. With that arse?

The formalities were uncomplicated. Their daughter, Imogen, was at boarding school. 'Imogen all the people, living in harmony.' Anne had been a John Lennon fan and somehow he had let his daughter be named in this ridiculous fashion. Fucking hippy. There was the house they lived in and a seldom-used holiday house. There were two cars, his Mercedes and her Volvo. There was Sandler and Harris. There was money, and a lot of it. He let her have everything she wanted except for a share of the company. His father would have rolled over in his grave.

Imogen was now at university, in her first year of a Visual Communications degree, whatever the fuck that was, living in the inner-city suburb of Paddington in a shared terrace house on which he had taken the lease. And here she was, late as usual. She was approaching the table, dressed in a pair of loose khaki pants (they looked to Geoffrey like combat fatigues although he was sure they would have cost far more than army surplus prices) and a plain white t-shirt.

As she grew older Imogen was beginning to look more and more like her mother, although she wore her brown hair cropped close, almost boyish, a style Anne had never adopted. She had also inherited her mother's height (others would not describe her as tall but she was taller than Geoffrey). She did not have a bump on her forehead, although Geoffrey had been tempted to give her one on several occasions over the years.

She walked with an easy, careless grace, shoulders squared and toes pointed outwards. The walk of a child who has never wanted for anything, thought Geoffrey. The walk of a mindless, idle fool — more like her mother than even the physical resemblance would suggest.

'Hi, Daddy. Sorry I'm late.' Already her voice suggested boredom.

'You're always fucking late, Imogen. Why apologise for it now?'

'Jesus, Daddy. It's just an expression. You know I'm not really sorry. I just wanted to lie in bed a little longer.'

'And that's supposed to make me feel better? That you're not genuinely sorry?'

'No, it's not supposed to make you feel better. Next subject. Show me the menu. I'm starved.'

'Starved? With the money I give you every goddamned week, you're starved? What the fuck do you spend it on? Clothes? Drugs? Shipments of herbal fucking tea?'

'No, Daddy. I spend it on food. And books, paints, paper, brushes. It's not a cheap course.'

'Of course it's not. Why else would you be doing it?'

'It's what I want to do, Daddy. Why can't you just support me on that?'

'I am fucking supporting you, aren't I?'

'Emotionally, Daddy. Why can't you give me your emotional support?'

'Which would you prefer – my financial support or my emotional support? Take your pick. You're not getting both.'

'You're especially grumpy today, aren't you?'

'No, not especially.'

A waitress approached tentatively, pen and pad in hand.

'Are you ready to order?'

'Ready? Do we look ready? My daughter's just sat down. Give us some time for fuck's sake . . .'

'I'm sorry, sir.'

'Everybody's fucking sorry this morning.'

'Actually, I am ready to order, Daddy. I'll have a bowl of the Irish oatmeal, the blueberry pancakes, an orange juice and a flat white.'

'Jesus fuck. Don't let youth fool you into thinking you're going to keep your figure forever, Imogen. Just look at your mother if you need a scare.'

'Please, Daddy.'

'Bring me some toast and coffee. Black.'

'Yes, sir.'

The waitress walked away stiffly, as if the blood in her veins had suddenly solidified; she clutched the order tightly in her right fist.

'Do you have to be so rude to everybody, Daddy?'

'No, I don't have to. But it sure as hell helps to release the tension.'

'You're always so full of tension, Daddy. Maybe it's time you got yourself a woman. You know, a girlfriend? If you could try to keep your face from turning red and hold yourself still once in a while I'm sure you'd be a very nice catch for some nice older woman.'

'I'm not that fucking old, Imogen.'

'Of course you're not, Daddy. You're still quite nice-looking, too. Distinguished.'

'Yes, well . . . In any case you might be right. I think it might be time for me to settle down again. Christ, even your mother's not alone. Is she still seeing that prick, what's his name?'

'Gavin, Daddy. His name is Gavin. And unfortunately he is a prick. But he makes Mummy happy.'

'I certainly don't envy him the job. There's a lot of acreage on that woman to cover these days. I wouldn't even know where to begin.'

'Well, I'm not about to give my own father sex education lessons.'

'What the hell are you talking about? Your mother,

Imogen — I wouldn't know where to begin with your mother. Give me a woman of lesser bulk and I'm sure I'll be fine. It's like riding a bicycle, or so they say.'

'Charming comparison, Daddy. Boys never really grow up, do they? Obsessed by their fathers and their dicks until the day that they die.'

'Are you taking philosophy classes on the side? I'm not sure I can afford extra lessons, you know. Just stick to the finger painting, please.'

'Fuck off, Daddy.' Her eyes looked quickly to the left, away from her father's face; her mouth fell into her mother's pout.

'Imogen? Stop that. Look at me when I'm talking to you. Fine. Don't look at me. Just sit there. Oh, fuck it. Look at me, Imogen.'

'What?'

'Look at me.'

'I'm looking.'

'I'm sorry.'

'So you should be.'

'I am.'

'Good. Now tell me about this woman.'

'What woman?'

'The woman, Daddy. The woman that's making you think that it's time to settle down again. The woman that's responsible for your leg jerking up and down like that, like some sort of dog on heat. The woman that's putting the extra colour into your cheeks. My God, you're almost purple. You look as though you're going to burst.'

'It's work, that's all. I'm tired. Agitated. No more than usual. There's no woman.'

'Are you sure, Daddy?'

'Yes, I'm sure.'

The waitress who took the order returned with their food on a silver tray. Her mouth was fixed in a tight, straight line and her eyes stared dead ahead. She placed the tray on the side of the table and began to serve. Imogen immediately took up her spoon, waving it in circles over the oatmeal before placing it on the table and selecting a fork for her pancakes. She sensed a danger about the oatmeal — there was an unnatural amount of steam rising from the bowl — and she thought it prudent to let it sit.

Geoffrey sat back in his chair and watched his daughter begin to eat. The waitress had almost finished unloading the tray. She placed a white china cup and saucer before him and began to pour coffee from a small silver pot she took from the tray. Her waist was just above Geoffrey's eye level and he noticed the outline of her hip bone, hard and strong, against her tight black skirt. His eyes moved up along her torso, over her narrow shoulders, and began to search her face.

She was young, probably only a few years older than Imogen. Her skin was pale and clear, her lips pursed tight, almost colourless. She looked down at him and, quite suddenly, her eyes locked onto his. They stared at each other in silence. He saw her nostrils expand and contract for two short, sharp breaths. Then her lips began to part. She kept her teeth clenched and the movement of her lips was barely noticeable but he knew the word she had mouthed was for him alone.

'Cocksucker.'

Chapter 11

There was no rhythm to the cough this morning, which James found especially unsettling for a Monday. Mr Whitely-Smalls (for James, like everyone at Sandler and Harris, assumed that the owner of the cough was Mr Whitely-Smalls) was usually reliable, so much so that James had come to depend upon his soothing rasps and rumbles as an indication that another week in his life had begun. If the week did not begin in the usual manner, what would become of it?

James sat at his desk and tuned his ears to the silence, blocking out the extraneous noises of the office and the steady hum from the internal fan of his computer. He waited. Nothing. And then a low, deep cough, rising from the pit of a no doubt massive stomach and forced finally over a swollen tongue, past yellowed teeth and into the air. He could feel its wetness surround him. The cough subsided into a wheeze, the summoning of phlegm and then, again, nothing. James counted the seconds. Fifteen. Twenty. Twenty-eight. Thirty-two. Thirty-six. A sharp expulsion, strangled in the throat almost before it started. A mere nine seconds later, a series of coughs of a duration long enough to be considered a fit. Then silence. The next outburst could come at any time. It was the uncertainty that commanded his full attention. He was becoming agitated.

A short, high-pitched tone announced an incoming email message on his computer. It would be Oliver. It was always Oliver. James was not fond of email. Yes, it encouraged the use of the written word, which was commendable, but inevitably any ongoing email exchange deteriorated into a series of short questions and answers, with one party quoting the other's message back at the other, adding a new query or topic and returning it for comment, always keeping the original message in its entirety in the reply. The result was an unwieldy, inelegant mess; the history of a discussion reduced finally to the monosyllabic essentials. It was not something James cared to be a part of. Still, Oliver was nothing if not persistent.

James turned his eyes to the monitor in front of him and reached for his computer's mouse. The office had fallen silent, anticipating Mr Whitely-Smalls' next eruption. James clicked on his email window and double-clicked on the message. It was Oliver. The subject line was left blank. Oliver never did like to be restricted to a single subject. The message started, as usual, with a joke.

A well-dressed English taxidermist walks into an outback pub. Everything in the pub – the bar, the bar stool, the tables, the customers – is covered in a thick red film of dust. Outback dust. The taxidermist is spotlessly clean. He doesn't fit in, everyone can see it. The locals send him a few hostile glances. He looks around a bit nervously, aware of the sudden change in atmosphere his appearance in the pub has caused. So he walks up to the bar and orders a drink from the barman, a big bloke with an unpleasant sneer on his face. 'I'd like a gin and tonic, please,' says the Englishman. His accent attracts the attention of a tough-looking bunch in a corner. They look at each other, puzzled, then one of them approaches the bar, and looks the stranger straight in the eye. 'Gin and tonic?' he says. 'What sort of a poofter drink is that, mate? You're not some sort of queer, are ya?' The guy stands there shaking, fearing for his life. 'Actually,' he says, 'I'm a taxidermist.' The locals are puzzled. 'A taxidermist?' says the barman. 'What the fuck is that?' He hesitates. 'Um, well . . . I mount dead animals.' The locals all heave a sigh of relief. 'It's all right,' says the barman. 'He's one of us!'

Hey Jimmy! Thought you'd like that one. Just remember, you've got to be a taxidermist to mount dead animals legally. And speaking of mounting dead animals, Trudi turned out to be a bit of a dud. All the time and effort I spent on that one was hardly worth it. But you never know until you try. And

*even when you do know you wanna try again:-) Hope you
had better luck. Cya.*

Oliver

*Oliver McDonald-Stuart
Litigator
Handley, Hanson and Short
61 2 9214 5486 Ext 13
oms@handleys.com.au*

It was only after he finished reading the message that
James noticed there had been no cough in the interval;
in fact, during the time he had been occupied indulging
Oliver, there had been no sound at all that he could
recall. He kept his head still, chin raised, and listened.
Still nothing. Perhaps the last cough was indicative of
Mr Whitely-Smalls' final breath; a man with such a
persistent problem could surely be expected to meet his
end from it.

Today could be the day. It would begin as Mr
Whitely-Smalls was wheeled out of his office on a
narrow metal stretcher, a dirty white sheet sitting atop
his stomach and pulled over his face, his bulk hanging
over the steel frames on all sides, the fat knuckles of
one hand dragging along the floor for all the Sandler
and Harris employees to see. To gawk at. They might
be surprised. Perhaps he would not be large at all.
After all, who really knew? He might be a small, neat

man with silver hair and a neatly trimmed moustache stained, like his teeth, by excessive consumption of nicotine. His finger nails would be stained too, yellow from the nicotine and red from the ink of his ball-point pens. He might be a one-legged midget, a self-educated former circus freak who no longer sought the public's gaze and found sanctuary as the editor of a well-regarded but not widely read legal journal.

Of course, James knew that Mr Whitely-Smalls' coughing fits often simply ended, as if he had expelled everything he could possibly expel for the time being and had determined to expel nothing more. That was more likely. That's what had happened. Or perhaps he was sucking on some sort of lozenge. Who knew? James was simply bored and needed his mind to be occupied. It was obvious. But there were no submissions to look at and there would be nothing to edit until tomorrow at the earliest. He began to think of Alison. Unfortunately he couldn't remember exactly what transactions had taken place between them, which would make masturbation difficult. He would have to see her again soon.

He was searching his desk for something that would at least afford him the illusion of being occupied – an old submission, a previous issue of *Uncommon Cases and Commentary on the Common Law*, anything. He found one of his old textbooks in his top drawer, *Fleming on Torts*, and opened it to a random page. Sections of the text were underlined in pencil, a 2B if he remembered correctly, and there were tightly written notes in his own hand in the margins. He sat and stared at the pages, watching the words swim on top of them.

'Bloomington!' It was Mr Sandler. Somehow he was now standing behind James, looking over his left shoulder. James wondered how he had failed to notice the hurried clips of Mr Sandler's elevated heels as he crossed the polished wooden floor. He swivelled his chair to face his employer, laying the textbook open across his lap.

'Good morning, sir.'

'Yes, good morning. Busy, Bloomington?' The tone was uncertain. James could not tell if this was an accusation or simply a question.

'Yes, sir. I'm just catching up on some background reading.'

'Very good . . . How are you finding things here, Bloomington? Everyone treating you well? Anything at all you're having trouble coping with?'

'No, sir.'

'Nothing? Nothing at all?'

'No, sir. I'm very much enjoying the challenge.'

'The challenge, eh? I hadn't thought of it like that. Well, if there is anything I can ever help you with, anything at all to do with the company or, erm . . . otherwise, you know where to find me.'

'Yes, sir. I do.'

Then, nothing. He stood there, looking straight into James's eyes. There was movement – hesitant, but movement all the same – at both corners of his mouth. James was sure he was attempting to smile. It was awkward for both of them. But he kept standing there, his face quivering, eyes darting about madly. The space between them seemed infinite. A sharp, sudden cough from the central office of Mr Whitely-Smalls was enough to break the spell and Mr Sandler fled as quickly as he had arrived. Startled, James decided it was time for an early lunch.

James could feel the heat rising from the asphalt below him. He crossed the street and began a steady stride. He had no particular destination in mind but knew that he wanted to remove himself from Yeats' Towers and the possibility of a lunchtime assault from Oliver. The air he sucked into his lungs was thick with pollution; he could taste it as it gathered at the back of his throat. No wonder his mother insisted on wearing that ridiculous mask.

The sun was relentless at this time of year, becoming almost unbearable before the day could properly begin. It was 11.06 according to James's watch and yet he was still forced to squint as sunlight reflected off the windscreens of passing cars. He could never bring himself to wear sunglasses so he simply shielded his eyes with his raised right hand and continued walking, ignoring the shoulders of those who clipped him as he made his way through the crowds. Why did people insist on walking in both directions on both sides of the street? Surely it would be more sensible to make a clear distinction between the two sidewalks. One side could move uptown, the other downtown, north, south, east or west, in much the same way as automobiles were separated and directed on roadways. Rules and demarcations, codes of conduct. Why had not civilised society developed to a point that it directed, even sub-liminally, the flow of orderly pedestrian traffic?

James concentrated his eyes upon the oncoming rush directly in front of him and the backs of people walking in the same direction as himself that he intended to pass. To move quickly and efficiently required that his total concentration be given to an area of no more than three feet in front of him. As a consequence, he couldn't really tell where he was. The shopfronts in his peripheral vision were all part of the same blur, the faces of the people coming towards him bore the same blank and oddly hostile expression, and the sounds assaulting his ears – street spruikers, traffic noises, incessant chatter from those passing around him – had the same numbing effect.

When he stopped to check his bearings James found that he was standing by the entrance to Town Hall rail-way station. He had walked for nine or so blocks. It was well past peak hour but people were still descending in a steady stream down the flights of tiled stairs and into the underground arcade. Others were emerging from below, raising their heads instinctively towards the light of the morning sun and squinting at the glare.

The scene reminded him of a movie he had enjoyed as a boy, an adaptation of H. G. Wells' *The Time Machine.* He had never read the book but the movie was certainly colourful. In it, an impossibly good-looking race of very pale-skinned, blond-haired and blue-eyed humans or humanoids was subjugated by a particularly nasty and distinctly reptilian species. The humans were kept in darkness underground, forced to mine for a presumably valuable mineral. Hence, when the hero, an aging but virile Rod Taylor, rescued them it took their weakened blue eyes some time to become accustomed to the light. At least that's how James remembered it. He also remembered the very short white smocks that barely covered the pretty human girls and the suggestion that they were forced to endure terrible things at the hands of their reptilian masters. All of which was sure to titillate any young boy.

James was titillated by the memory. He found himself with a growing erection, following the swaying buttocks of a young woman in a short skirt of uncertain but very sheer material as she walked down the stairs and into the station below. Her shoulders were bare, covered only by the straps of a white cotton tank top, and her legs were uncovered. She wore high-heeled sandals, thin black straps crossing at her ankles, and she swung her hips from side to side in a manner that suggested a dizzying defiance. 'Look at me,' her buttocks seemed to be saying to him. 'Follow me, but know that I am forever out of your reach.' James followed them through the ticket turnstiles and down one flight of stairs onto the platform below.

The platform was narrow and dirty, covered in a thick coating of black dust. People milled about him on all sides but James managed to keep behind the girl, all the while eyeing her buttocks and the seemingly endless possibilities to be found within. Even on the dusty, crowded platform, there was a strong fragrance, probably from her neck or behind her ears, of vanilla. He tried not to inhale too deeply.

James could hear the sound of an approaching train and sure enough a train of eight silver carriages emerged from the darkness and came to a stop in front of him and the girl. He followed her through the nearest carriage door, pushing past people as they exited, and into the compartment.

Faced with the choice of going up or down to the seated sections of the carriage she chose to remain in the compartment where she had entered, holding onto a thin metal pole that ran from the ceiling to the floor by the far set of doors. She spun around on the pole and was suddenly facing him. Her brown eyes were slow and lazy, moving about the carriage without looking at anything at particular, including James. Her hair was a light brown, streaked with blond, and her eyebrows were rounded and very dark. She was younger than James had anticipated, her chin soft and round. Having spent so much time looking at her buttocks he felt uncomfortable looking at her face.

He turned away and pressed his forehead against the window of the carriage door and stared into the darkness of the tunnel rushing by. He left a thick smear of sweat across the glass. When the train came to a stop at the next station and the doors opened he stepped hurriedly onto the platform and walked towards the exit.

Chapter 12

It was now almost midday and the sun had risen to its full height above him. James was aware of the sweat gathering under his arms and at the base of his back where he was beginning to develop a patch of hair that burrowed down towards his anus. If he could do anything to rid himself of this new-found growth, short of waxing or shaving himself, which was simply unseemly, he would.

He knew if he removed his suit jacket that anyone passing by who cared to look would see the signs of his discomfort through his white cotton shirt. Still, he was not inclined to remove his jacket under the best of circumstances, believing what his mother had once told him to be an unbreakable principle of style: if you are going to wear a suit, you wear the whole suit; you may unbutton your jacket if seated, but you must never remove the jacket.

He continued to walk with a sense of purpose (apparent to all those around him), but without direction. He had walked two blocks when he stopped to consider his position. When he raised his head to the sky he was suddenly aware of his exact location. He was standing in the shadow of a concrete tower in the middle of a one-way street. Standing perfectly still. People were brushing past him in both directions. Looking to his left, he saw a man sitting at the base of the concrete building on a dirty square of cardboard. The man in the lane.

The man was sitting motionless, his head tilted down and his eyes fixed on the space in front of him. He appeared to be wearing a new, or at least a different, set of clothes: a pair of scuffed blue running shoes, chocolate-brown corduroy pants and a navy-blue, heavy cotton work shirt, the collar and cuffs of which protruded through the neck and arm holes of a dark-green cotton pullover. The crew neck of a soiled white undershirt was also visible.

James stepped from the asphalt of the road onto the concrete sidewalk. He stood there, staring down, searching the top of the man's head and shoulders for a sign. But the man remained perfectly still; he was not bothered by James's presence. In fact he had yet to indicate that he was even aware of James's presence. James wondered if the man was in some sort of drug- or alcohol-induced trance. It wasn't unheard of, for people like this – street people – to be of less than sober habits. Still, there was nothing about this man that James feared, nothing at all, and the coolness of the concrete so close below him held out an almost irresistible promise.

He moved a few steps closer to the man and got down on his haunches, balancing himself with the extended fingers of his left hand. He could feel the concrete's porous surface through his fingertips. It sent a pleasant chill all the way up his arm, which soon spread itself through his shoulders and back. James realised the danger he was placing his trousers in but he felt a strong desire to bring his remaining hand and both of his buttocks into contact with the concrete without further delay. It was the same sensation as lowering oneself into a shallow bathing pool and James, for a sweet, brief second, imagined himself by the sea. He could hear the waves rolling gently onto the shore and feel the ocean's spray.

When James opened his eyes the man in front of him was looking straight at him.

'Your mum dropped by today.' The voice was low and measured, which surprised James immediately.

'What did you say?'

'I said your mum dropped by today. Earlier this morning. She comes around the same time most every day.'

'How did you know she was my mother? Has she spoken to you? What has she told you?'

'She's never said a word to me. Just stands there and looks at me. I don't mind it, don't get me wrong. She's a pretty woman. Her ankles are real nice. I heard her talking to you the other day. You called her "Mother" so I figured she must be your mum. All the signs were there.'

'You heard us talking?'

'Yeah. It's funny. Most people figure just because you're sitting out here and trying not to look at anyone too much that you mustn't be paying any attention to what's going on around you. But I mean I'm not deaf, am I? If two people stand in front of me and start talking, especially about me, I'm bound to take notice, right?'

'Certainly.'

'And you and your mum just went right on talking as if I didn't exist. Let me tell you, mate, it's hard enough trying to concentrate out here sometimes without two people carrying on like that in front of you. And you really should show your mother a bit more respect, you know. I mean, I know she can be a bit of a handful, but she is your mother after all. And she's all that you've got.'

'How do you know that she's all that I've got?'

'I don't. I mean, it's just a guess, I suppose. Call it a feeling. Is she all that you've got?'

'If by that you're asking me whether or not I have any other immediate family, the answer is no.'

'What?'

'She's my only parent. My sole relation.'

'Oh, right. Just you and her. I lost my own mother about seven years ago, I think.'

'Where did you lose her?'

'What?'

'Where did you lose her?'

'I didn't lose her, mate. She died. That's what I meant. She died. Breast cancer. Ate her up from the inside. By the end of it she wasn't even there any more, in her own body and all. I'd look at her, just a bag of bones and loose skin, and I couldn't see my mum in there anywhere. She'd make these noises, these cries, painless cries – she was doped up and couldn't feel a thing. Morphine. Her eyes looked like the eyes of a dead fish, lying there in the bottom of a boat after it's finished flapping around and struggling for its life. She was in there somewhere though, waiting to go. And then she went.'

'I see.'

'Yeah, well. That's what happens with life, you lose it or it's taken from you. It just stops.'

'Yes, I suppose it does.'

'My dad went a long time ago, when I was only little.'

'Where did he go?'

'He died too, mate. Euphemisms. I'm using euphemisms. Surely a bright boy like you knows what a euphemism is? I "lost" my mum. My uncle Ted "went" soon after. My dad went a long time before that.

"Passed away". Or maybe he "passed on". To "heaven". To a "better place". Death, mate. It's all death.'

'How old were you?'

'When my dad died? Must've been eleven or twelve. Let me see . . . Yeah, I was eleven.'

'So you knew him?'

'Knew him? As much as a kid can know a man. He was my dad. My memory's not too great but I can remember his face. Photographs help, of course. He used to bring us little paper bags full of lollies when he'd come home from work. Not all the time – only when he was in a good mood or if he'd made a good sale that day. He was a salesman. A big man with a crooked grin. His teeth were shockers. Sold prefabricated steel, not sure what for. I just remember he sold steel. That's what we'd tell the other kids, "My dad sells steel." You know how it is with kids, always talking about their dads. Measuring them up. Comparing. Boasting. I've never been a dad myself but it must be great to be loved like that.'

'Yes, I imagine so.'

'Anyway, he had a heart attack one day and died. Thirty-three years old and he has a heart attack. Congenital condition, apparently, which I've always felt fucking great about. Happened at work. They thought he was kidding around at first, but he wasn't. So then it was just the three of us: Mum, me and my sister, June. She's a few years older than me. Married an insurance guy or something. Frenchman. They live in

New York now. Haven't seen her for a while. I don't get to New York much.'

The man was grinning. James did not grin back.

'My name is James Bloomington,' he said.

'Yeah, I know. Well, I know it's James, anyway. I heard your mum call you that. As for the other part, what was it, Bloomerton? I'll just forget that sooner or later anyway. James'll do just fine. Pleased to meet you, James.'

'And you are?'

'Byron.'

'Byron?'

'Yeah, I know, it's a fucking stupid name, but what can you do? My mum took a shine to it somehow and that's the name she gave me. I've always called myself Brian. Shit, people always called me Brian anyway. Even if you tell 'em your name is Byron they call you Brian. So I just started telling 'em it was Brian. Eventually even Mum came around. You should call me Brian.'

'Brian what?'

'Brian Jones. Like the guitar player.'

'What guitar player?'

'The dead one. From the Rolling Stones. Nice blond hair. They found him floating in his pool. Hair probably still looked good, all spread out around him in the water. They reckon maybe the builder killed him. As opposed to the butler. Anyway, he's dead. Died ages ago, in the sixties. Played guitar.'

'I see.'

'Played guitar once myself. Figured I should, being Brian Jones and all. But I guess I really am Byron Jones after all. I couldn't strangle much of a tune out of anything. Took lessons in high school and everything but it was useless, my hands just wouldn't do it. Those goddamned barré chords were the end of me.'

James sat on the dirty concrete staring into the face of the man in front of him. He was very familiar with the face because, as his mother had insisted, it was his own. Except that it wasn't. The colour was wrong; deeper, more pink than pale. There were lines at the outer edges of the eyes. Crows feet. The nose appeared to have been broken high on the bridge and had never properly straightened. The jaw was covered in stubble, flecked with grey, and there was a small scar noticeable directly underneath the chin.

The man – Byron? – stared back at him. A smile began to take shape at the left corner of his mouth.

'Yeah, I reckon we do look a bit alike.'

'Perhaps.'

'Yeah, well, you're not such a bad-looking boy, so I can hardly complain.'

'Who are you?'

'I've told you. Name's Brian.'

'Byron. I don't care what other people call you, I'm going to call you by your given name.'

'Are you now. Well, you'll have to do it tomorrow. It's getting late.'

'Late?'

'Lunchtime. I have to go home for lunch.'

'Home?'

'Yep. See you tomorrow.'

The man rose quickly, shaking each leg in turn and curling and uncurling his toes rapidly within his running shoes. He straightened the bottom of his pullover, bent at the waist and picked up the flattened cardboard square he had been sitting on. As he walked off in the direction of the train station, the cardboard folded and tucked under his right arm, he turned to give James a farewell smile. James remained on the concrete, feeling its cool surface seeping into his buttocks, and watched as the man moved into the oncoming crowd.

Chapter 13

James was sitting at his desk at Sandler and Harris. His head was still; three deep creases were set in his forehead. Casual observers would assume he was staring at a document displayed on the screen of his computer's monitor, fixated on a particularly vexing problem, legal or otherwise. In fact the screen was blank and James was looking past the top right corner of the monitor, eyes focused on a stained patch of the office wall beyond it. He had not changed the position of either his body or his head since he had returned from lunch and seated himself at his desk an hour or so ago.

To Betty Palmer's dismay he had rushed in off the street and straight past reception without so much as a hello. His movements had been quick and vaguely threatening, much like those of the woman in the mask, his mother. Betty had yet to regain her composure at the desk, a fact she tried to disguise by ensuring the constant movement of her hands across her keyboard and desktop, and those that passed her by could not fail to notice that her face had taken on a particularly violent shade of red. The summer heat only added to her general discomfort. She could feel the immense weight of her hair, much of which was trapped in thick, sweat-soaked curls by the edges of her face.

The offices of Sandler and Harris were unusually quiet, as if everyone within had simply decided that although victory over the heat was impossible, a reasonable detente could be maintained by keeping as still and as silent as possible. No sound had issued from the office of Mr Whitely-Smalls since James had returned and Geoffrey Sandler was nowhere to be found. Was it possible that even he was sitting rigid in his office, conserving his energy against future attacks?

James concentrated on maintaining the focus of his thoughts: the man in the lane. It was true there was a resemblance, that much was undeniable. But there was no other relationship between he, James Blooming-ton, and the man in the lane, Byron Jones, than that. It was an odd coincidence, yes, but that was all it was. One of nature's many tricks. Someone's idea of a joke, perhaps, if you believed in that sort of thing. Sheer chance. That was all that had led him there. Besides his mother.

His mother. An image began to form in his mind. If

indeed this was some kind of a joke, it was not out of the question that his mother was the one playing the joke. She had, for all practical purposes, been genuinely insane for as long as James could recall. Perhaps this was her doing, a plan of indecipherable motivation: to hire a man who looked somewhat like her son to sit in a lane; to reinforce this supposed resemblance herself; to lead her son to this man and then to step back and watch the hilarity that ensued. 'Byron Jones' was a fabrication, an out-of-work actor – weren't they all? – with a talent for impersonating the future. His future.

He was being ridiculous. He knew it. Still, he liked the process of allowing his mind to concoct connections where there were none. The man was Byron Jones and he appeared to be perfectly . . . affable. Not to mention genuine. To his surprise, James found himself wondering about where Byron Jones had gone when they parted. About his home. About what he did there and who he did it with. It was not like James to waste his time and his imagination thinking about people other than himself. He was not a curious person, quite the opposite: he did not care to know any more about other people and their lives than was absolutely necessary. It was true that being a unit of a society implied a minimum amount of social interaction. But anything beyond that had always struck James as vulgar. He closed his eyes in an attempt to bring his mind back to the task at hand.

. . .

There was a plumber in the house. At least there was a plumber in the house when James had left for school. The plumber wore stained green overalls over a black jumper. He was tall, much taller than James's mother, and broad shouldered. He had smiled at James when he arrived and James had noticed that his face was covered with dark stubble. He had asked James how old he was and James had replied that he was ten years old, so far as he was aware. The plumber had smiled a crooked smile.

His mother was having a new kitchen installed and it required the services of a professional plumber. Another man had installed new white cabinets, smudged with his own careless, dirty fingerprints, the previous day. Thin trails of sawdust were scattered across the linoleum of the kitchen floor as a result of the drilling. His mother would have swept the floor during the day, taking a dustpan and brush to every corner.

When James came home from school the front door was unlocked. He could feel a strange presence as he ascended the stairs: there was a plumber in the house. As James reached the top of stairs and stepped into the loungeroom, however, he realised that the presence he had felt was his own. He was the intruder.

There were noises coming from the kitchen, a cup rattling on a saucer, hard flesh against soft flesh, his mother's wordless voice gently coaxing a partner to greater exertion.

James stood in the kitchen doorway and saw his

mother bent over the new kitchen counter, arms stretched wide, her grey woollen skirt hitched over her hips. Her hand was clutching the handle of a tea cup that rested on a saucer. The plumber was hunched over her, his overalls around his ankles, his white, unusually hairy arse cheeks squeezing and releasing in a steady, forceful rhythm. The plumber's face and neck were red with effort. He was still wearing his jumper and beads of perspiration ran across the stubble of his face, falling from his chin and onto the shoulder of James's mother's white blouse, soaking the fabric through. The floor was still covered with sawdust.

James took a step forward into the kitchen. His mother turned her face towards him, looking over her left shoulder and fixing him with an annoyed stare. The cup continued to rattle in her hand.

'Go to your room, James. Right now.'

The plumber looked up momentarily, glancing at James without actually looking at him, then dropped his head and continued with his motions.

'I'd like a glass of orange juice, Mother.'

'James, go to your room.'

'I need to get to the refrigerator.'

'Did you hear me, James? Go to your room. Now, James! I'll bring you a juice in a moment.'

James held his mother's stare until she slowly turned her head away from him, dismissing him from the room. He went to his room and waited for the orange juice.

· · ·

James closed his eyes and saw his mother fucked over a kitchen bench by a tradesman. Over and over.

'Bloomington!'

It was Geoffrey Sandler. For the second time in the day he had somehow managed to sneak up on him. James opened his eyes and snapped his head around to face the direction of the voice.

'Sir!'

Sandler was standing to James's left, slightly behind him. His legs were twitching and he was holding a large bunch of flowers, wrapped in a silver sheath, in his right hand. He held the flowers out in front of him.

'Caught you having a bit of a nap, eh?'

Again, James was uncertain of the tone. He was beginning to suspect that Mr Sandler was equally uncertain.

'No, sir. A momentary lapse of concentration.'

'I've been thinking about your mother, Bloomington.'

'Yes, sir. As it happens, so have I.'

'Yes, well. As I say, I've been thinking about your mother. I want you to know that it is my intention to court her, Bloomington. To woo her, if you will.'

'If I will?'

'I'm not asking your permission, Bloomington. Don't get me wrong. I just want everything out in the open. Where everybody can see it, so to speak. I think it's important for you to know that I don't expect this to have any affect on our working relationship. I won't be giving you any special treatment. But I do hope we can be . . . friends.'

'Friends?'

'Well, no, not really. I meant that metaphorically, of course. Mutual tolerance is the best we can hope for, I suppose.'

'Yes, sir.'

'Please, call me Geoffrey.'

'If it's all the same with you, sir, I'd rather not. I would regard that as an unwelcome change in our working relationship.'

'Well, James . . . May I call you James?'

'You may. But I'd rather you didn't, sir.'

'Very well, Bloomington. Jesus, you're an uptight little prick. But I don't want to make you uncomfortable. I'll do my level best to forget that you are your mother's son.'

'That would be lovely, sir.'

'These flowers are for your mother.'

'They're very nice. I'm sure she'll be pleased.'

'Are you? That's valuable input, Bloomington. Very valuable indeed.'

'I'm glad you think so, sir.'

'Oh yes, I do, Bloomington. Very valuable information indeed. Perhaps you can be of further use to me with this matter. You see, I haven't actually called your mother yet to . . . erm . . . to make my intentions clear.'

'Would you like me to give you my mother's phone number, sir?'

'No, no, no. That's not necessary. I had someone look up her phone number for me already. I have the number.'

'But you haven't used it?'

'Right. I haven't used it. Just waiting until I can come up with the right approach.'

'Have you spoken to my mother at all, sir?'

'You mean ever?'

'Yes, sir.'

'Technically, no. But she has spoken to me. "I really must have a rather urgent discussion with my son," she said. "We shan't be long. If you'd care to step outside I'd be grateful." Her voice has quite a musical quality to it, doesn't it?'

'If you say so, sir. I really hadn't noticed.'

'Hadn't noticed? Yes, well, I suppose that's possible. Still, she's a very handsome woman, your mother. You must have noticed that. Very handsome indeed.'

'Yes, sir. So I've been told.'

'Who by?'

'Pardon?'

'Who told you she was handsome?'

'You did, sir. Just now.'

'Who else?'

'Oh, just . . . people. Over the years.'

'Other men, Bloomington? Is that what you're trying to tell me? That there are other men seeking the attentions of your mother?'

'No, sir, not that I'm aware of.'

'Because she's a very handsome woman, Blooming-ton. Very fucking handsome indeed.'

'Yes, sir.'

'Does she . . . prefer a particular type of man, Bloomington?'

'I'm not sure that I understand you, sir.'

'Well, she is your mother after all. Surely you've seen her with other men.'

'Once or twice.'

'And what were they like?'

'I really can't remember clearly, sir. I've never paid much attention.'

'That's not much use to me, is it? You never paid much attention. Too caught up in your own arsehole, I expect. Fucking hell.'

'I'm sorry, sir.'

'Forget it, Bloomington. Just tell me what you can remember.'

'Well . . . she seemed to be fond of unshaven types.'

'Unshaven?'

'Yes, sir. Swarthy.'

'Hmmm. Swarthy, eh? And were these men particu-larly . . . tall, for instance?'

'No, not always.'

'Not always. But some of them were tall?'

'Yes, some.'

'How tall?'

'I'm not certain, sir. Taller than my mother, I expect.'

'But some of them were shorter?'

'Shorter than my mother? Perhaps. Well . . . actually, no, now that I think about it. I suppose they were universally tall after all.'

'Universally tall? Shit.'

'Yes, sir. I suppose it might be said that my mother prefers the company of men somewhat taller than herself. In fact, all the evidence I can recall seems to support that very hypothesis.'

'Oh, shut the fuck up, Bloomington.'

'Yes, sir. I do believe it's best that I do . . .' James let his words trail off into silence. Geoffrey Sandler had already turned his back on him. The flowers hung limply from his hand as he walked away.

Chapter 14

Veronica knew that the neighbourhood children had christened her 'The Dragon Lady'; it was part of the terror she held over them, that she knew all their dirty little thoughts. The name was not based entirely on her demeanour but derived mainly from the fact that she was often seen in her favourite pair of leggings, white silk tights with printed Chinese dragons winding from the hip to the ankle of each leg. Like Veronica herself the dragons were beautiful but somehow sinister, and the children knew of the danger instinctively. Stories circulated about those unfortunates who had inadvertently strayed into her gaze. Survivors gathered hushed circles around them and told of the ordeal. Invariably they would all claim to have been overcome by an irrational, overwhelming fear, a fear that rose silently within them, and it was understood by all that in the event of an encounter even the toughest among them would be incapable of withstanding the force of her terrible eyes. It was generally agreed that in the event of such a confrontation, the best course of action one could take was to remain rooted to the spot and to cry and wail as loudly as possible until The Dragon Lady went away.

When Cecil disappeared, Veronica was left with a modest single-storey red brick home and a thriving import/export concern. She was also left with James, who was often disagreeable even at such a young age. As James grew, the neighbourhood was increasingly populated with other objectionable children, many of whom insisted on running across Veronica's small front lawn and committing various acts of trespass against her property. The parents of these children often proved to be even more objectionable than their offspring. But if Cecil was to return, this was the house that he would return to, and Veronica was content to remain exactly where she was.

James was not encouraged to bring friends home from school. (It would not have been an easy task for him to have found a child who would voluntarily submit to the terrors that were rumoured to lie within the Bloomington house, in any case.) He did not suffer because of this. Unlike other children Veronica had observed, her son demonstrated no great desire for the company of others of his kind. This neither distressed or pleased her; it was simply a fact.

Cecil's disappearance was, of course, somewhat inconvenient. Veronica would have preferred to have kept her husband's departure a private affair but if she was to exercise control over Bloomington Distribution and its property then the authorities had to be informed and the relevant procedures completed. Veronica struck those strangers around her at this time, mostly bureaucrats and detectives, as remarkably single-minded. She accepted her husband's unexplained disappearance with a stoic resolve quite unlike anything they had ever encountered (in fact her stoicism was such that, for a time, a certain detective made it known that he suspected that she and she alone knew the precise whereabouts of her exceedingly 'late' husband) and it was clear that she intended to waste no time ensuring that Bloomington Distribution remained a profitable concern.

It had been Veronica's habit to pay absolute attention to her husband's business affairs and she was now being rewarded for it. When Cecil talked after dinner, as he always did, he talked about the company, and Veronica listened to every word he said. She knew which employees could be trusted and which could not. She could separate the lazy from the industrious on the basis of surnames alone. She knew which lines were becoming increasingly profitable and which lines had not delivered the expected returns. She knew where opportunities for expansion existed and she knew how to take those opportunities without exposing the company to undue risk.

Still, she found even the idea of running the company on a day-to-day basis tiresome. It was never her intention to take Cecil's hands-on approach. Cecil had grown Bloomington Distribution to a stage where the company could, quite comfortably, run itself. All that was required was somebody to oversee the company's operations and ensure its continued profitability.

Shortly before his disappearance Cecil had appointed a dependable, church-going South African by the name of Cronje (whose merchant roots could be traced as far back as the Dutch East Indies Company) as General Manager of Bloomington Distribution. Taking her absent husband's counsel, Veronica could see no reason to displace Mr Cronje from his position. She would meet with him on Thursday afternoons and inspect the company books every two months.

All that was left for Veronica to do was to take a bookkeeping course at the local technical college, which she attended on Wednesday and Friday evenings for two semesters. Usually the nanny would extend her stay on these evenings to look after James. At the end of the course Veronica was encouraged to seek a full-time career in the bookkeeping field, her teachers expressing the opinion that she would make a valuable contribution to the profession. The thoroughness of her approach — taking every column on every page on its merits – was particularly noteworthy. The neatness of her handwriting was an obvious bonus as, of course, was her appearance.

Cecil's judgment of Mr Cronje proved sound. Cronje was a careful, capable man who kept Bloomington Distribution growing at a steady rate, diversifying the company's markets only when it was safe to do so. He considered it his solemn duty to protect the interests of Veronica Bloomington, a handsome, abandoned woman, and her small son. Although both mother and child could sometimes be less than pleasant company, Cronje was convinced that God had placed their financial security in his care. It was a charge he intended to acquit himself of to the best of his ability, and he had been doing so now for over twenty years.

Veronica was aware of Mr Cronje's devotion to the Lord, which was all well and good if it helped him to maintain his devotion to Bloomington Distribution, but she trusted her own watchful eye far more than she trusted that of any omniscient being. To date her scrutiny of the company books had not found any irregularity that could not be traced to error, oversight or a wayward employee. She expected Mr Cronje to deal with such despicable people swiftly and, taking it as an affront to his own sacred duty, he did so without fail, dispatching the amoral and the godless with a separate, violently unpleasant curse for every dollar of their severance pay.

. . .

Veronica was lying on her bed, flat on her back, arms folded across her chest in imitation of an ancient sarcophagus. A damp white flannel, folded into three equal sections, lay across her eyes. Taking deep, regular breaths through her nose she tuned her ears to the hum of the air-conditioning around her and soon imagined herself floating free in the Red Sea. The heavily salted water surrounded her, finding its way into all of her openings. She was wearing only a loose white robe tied at the waist, but in the sea she was naked. She began to shift the weight of her thighs, contracting and relaxing the muscles to the rhythm of the gentle waves beneath her. The air was pure and the warmth of the water matched the temperature of her blood, which flowed in strong, circular patterns from her heart to the tips of her fingers and toes.

She was sinking, the water slowly rising above her chin, lips and the tip of her nose, but the air continued to flow to her lungs and her heart continued to pump oxygenated blood through her body. As the water rose higher and higher Veronica began to feel herself dissolving into the sea, her flesh, blood and bones mixing into the salt, rising quickly to the surface to meet the sun's rays and evaporate into the air. This, she knew, was the process that would one day lead her to Cecil.

But something was wrong, something was pulling her back. The ring of a telephone. The telephone on her bedside table. It continued to ring and Veronica knew there was no going back to the sea. She was lying on her bed, arms folded across her chest, covered in her own sweat, her own salt. She opened her eyes. The sunlight coming through the glass doors filtered through the cotton of the flannel, which she removed from her face and placed beside her.

The telephone was still ringing but the anger rising within her prevented her from answering it. Let it ring, let it ring until it dies. But of course it would not. She heard the click of the answering machine and then her own voice, distant and small, far smaller than she would have liked. 'Hello. You've called Veronica Bloomington. Please leave a brief message after the tone.' But the caller was not leaving a message. Nor was he (Veronica was certain she could hear a man's breathing) hanging up. The silence was suspended between them until the machine reached the time limit it would allow for each message and dropped the line.

It was not a dirty phone call. Veronica knew about dirty phone calls; she had been receiving them ever since Cecil disappeared. She had sold the house Cecil had left her in exactly twelve years after his departure, moving, with James, from the noisy, child-infested outer suburbs to her current home on Sydney's inner harbour. The phone number changed but the calls continued. They varied in frequency – in fact they were sometimes separated by a period of years rather than days – but the content was remarkably consistent: silence, followed by a series of increasingly hoarse and rapid breaths, which, usually rather quickly, came to a sudden stop as the caller hung up. Obviously the man was masturbating. Veronica was sure it was always the same man.

At first she would hang up, but the telephone would continue to ring until she answered and the caller brought himself to satisfaction, so it was easier to simply let him finish within the one call. They had reached an understanding over the years as to the correct protocol. She would answer the telephone, say 'hello' once and once only, and remain silent until the call was completed. She would then wash her hands and continue with what she had been doing.

At first she thought it was Cecil, calling because he still wanted to be with her, wherever he may have been. Either he did not wish to or could not talk, but he needed her to be there on the other side of the telephone. But it was not Cecil. Suspicion then fell on Mr Cronje, where in fact it remained. Something in the way he looked at her suggested his complicity. Still, she found it hard to picture him on the other end of the telephone. And what would he tell Mrs Cronje he was doing? It didn't matter. Veronica didn't care who the caller was; his identity was not important. The calls were simply a part of her life, part of a shared routine. They would end one day.

She sat up on the bed and looked outside. The sky appeared to be a deep blue but the more she looked at it, the more obvious the stain of impurity grew. It was a sick brown haze on the horizon and it reached higher into the atmosphere every single day. Veronica could see it; others chose to ignore it. She closed her eyes and lay down again on the bed, reaching for the damp flannel by her side.

Chapter 15

James had not moved from his chair. The Sandler and Harris offices were empty except for the busy hands of Tom, the company's cleaner. James did not know Tom's surname, nor did he care to. Tom was a small, wiry man with silver streaks through his hair and a thin mouth that barely opened when he talked, which was not frequently. Tom was Korean by James's guess, although he couldn't be sure. He wore a sky-blue and white horizontally striped rugby jersey and matching blue shorts. He set about emptying bins and sweeping the floor, content to work around James, sweeping the broom under his legs and moving past him as quickly and silently as he could.

    Mr Sandler's outburst had unsettled James. He was comfortable at Sandler and Harris and he did not want his employer's infatuation with his mother to jeopardise his position or his comfort. More importantly, he simply did not wish to play any part in the proceedings, as an observer, commentator or participant. He wished for no knowledge of the affair whatsoever. But it was already too late: he knew. Mr Sandler had declared his intentions and James was now involved. Damn his mother.

It was the darkness that roused him. The sun stayed high in the sky well into the evening and James realised it must have been past eight for the light outside to have disappeared. He looked at his watch: it was sixteen minutes past eight. Time to go home. Mrs Salvestrin would be wondering where he was. He shut down his computer, stood up, buttoned his jacket, picked up his briefcase and walked towards the door. Tom was hunched over the rubbish bin by Betty Palmer's desk, fitting it with a new plastic liner.

'Good night, Tom.'

Tom lifted his round face to James and nodded, forcing his lips to form a polite smile. James returned the smile as best he could and continued walking.

A steady trickle of office workers, all, like James, with their heads bowed and pointed in the direction of their homes, headed towards Wynyard Station. The sun was gone but the heat remained. Most of the men had loosened their ties. Some had slung their jackets over a shoulder. James did not join them. His steps were slow and heavy and he felt the blood rising from his chest to his head, pulsing at his temples. He checked his inside jacket pocket for a handkerchief.

When he lifted his head he found himself on his platform; the route from the office was by now automatic. He could not measure the time it took him to get there, nor could he be sure that any time had in fact passed. He was simply there, standing behind the painted yellow line, waiting for the train that would take him home.

The train came quickly. Inside the carriage James felt a chill from the air-conditioning. Who was in charge of setting the temperature? The driver? The train guard? Whoever it was had little sense of moderation. It was unnaturally cold. James could never understand the impulse to control one's environment in such a manner. If the air is hot, make it cold, so much so that it too becomes uncomfortable. If the air is cold, make it hot. No wonder the blood vessels in his nostril were in such a fragile state.

He kept his eyes closed for most of the short journey, wrapping his arms tightly around his chest, hands nestled in the pits for warmth. He could feel each lurch of the carriage on the tracks below and noted the stops, one brief and unscheduled, probably waiting on a signal, and two at the stations before his own. When he opened his eyes the neon lights of the carriage dazzled him and for a moment he forgot where he was. He saw his image reflected on the window beside him, his face and lips colourless, and remembered. The train came to a stop again and he picked up his brief-case and walked onto the platform.

The heat was upon him quickly and he felt inclined to stagger. Of course he did not. His hand reached up for his nose but there was no blood. The light-headedness was not the result of a nose-bleed. Soon he would be home and he hoped Mrs Salvestrin would leave him in relative peace. He was confident she would not seek him out; they had not spoken since he had discovered her (or she had discovered him − James was still unsure how a third party would inter-pret the situation) in the bathroom.

As he walked he was aware of his hunger and, more so, of his thirst. He thought of the risotto in his refrig-erator. But there was nothing to drink. He needed a drink. He thought briefly about turning around and heading for the corner store by the station, but he knew it would be closed. If he could ignore the taste of the rust and God knows what else from those old pipes, there was always water. There was little alterna-tive but to keep walking, past the post box and the public telephone booth at the bottom of the hill and on to Mrs Salvestrin's.

James marked his route by a series of familiar junc-tions. The post box was just up ahead. There was a cardboard pizza box, printed in red, black and yellow, resting on top of it. Pizza? James came to a stop and lifted the lid of the box. There were four slices of pizza in the box; dark, oily stains filled the remaining spaces.

The pizza appeared to be pepperoni and it appeared to be hot, or at the very least warm. Melted cheese — it had not yet solidified — flowed from the topping and onto the cardboard below the crust.

James held an open palm over the pizza for a few seconds and breathed deeply through his nose. Yes, it was warm. He looked around, moving his eyes in every direction, seeking out the pizza's owner. The moon was bright and the streets were well lit but he could see no one. There was no one in the frontyards that merged with the footpath. There was no one across the street. There was no one further along the street, at least that he could make out. No one.

He stood and gazed at it, soaking up the smell of the spiced meat and the sweetened tomato, but he would not eat the pizza. The possibility occurred to him but not as a serious option. He knew nothing of the pizza's origins or its current condition. Who had left it? How long ago? What had happened to it during that interval? It was rubbish regardless, and James was disgusted at both the brazenness and the thoughtlessness of its owner. Was it really that difficult for people to take responsibility for their own waste products?

He resumed his walk, training his eyes on the telephone booth ahead, the neon light spilling through the glass walls onto the grass that surrounded it. The telephone booth was built on a small concrete square but the grass rose boldly, green and vital, at its edges. James always checked the booth for evidence of recent acts of vandalism. Every time he found the handset intact, the glass unbroken and the walls free of graffiti, it gave him an almost overwhelming sense of neighbourhood and civic pride. He knew it was only a matter of time before some aimless, listless adolescent, perhaps alone, perhaps as leader of a gormless trio, decided that the destruction of the telephone booth was an important and, of course, achievable goal. An act of unfettered free will, the purest form of self-expression. I break shit, therefore I am.

As he got closer to the telephone booth he could see that, for now, it remained intact. He glanced through the glass: the receiver was fine, as was the dialling mechanism and the coin slot and return areas. A few cigarette burns, but nothing new. He came to a stop. Sitting on top of the weathered phone books, which lay on a metal shelf underneath the telephone, was a clear plastic bottle of orange juice. Half a litre of orange juice. Five hundred millilitres. No added sugar, one hundred per cent juice. He knew the brand. The bottle was full; it was, in fact, unopened. The seal of the green plastic lid had not been broken.

James pulled back the glass door of the booth, stood his briefcase on the concrete square and looked at the bottle. Someone had left an unopened bottle of orange juice in the phone booth. Was it a mistake? Was it the same person who had left the pizza on the post box? Would they return for the juice once they realised the mistake? Would they remember where they had left it?

He looked around for any sign of movement in the darkness. Again there was none. He measured his thirst against the chance that the bottle had been in some way tampered with. But the seal had not been broken. James picked up the bottle and examined it. Nothing unusual. The bottle was cool and the condensation from its surface left his palm wet. He put the bottle into his left jacket pocket with one swift movement, picked up his briefcase and continued his walk, quickening his pace against the shadows around him until he was home.

Chapter 16

When Brian Jones arrived with his folded cardboard square, James was waiting for him, wearing the same suit he had on the day before, only this time with a different shirt (white) and tie (black with very thin red and white stripes). James, who had been occupying himself by staring at his own feet, looked up as Brian approached. Brian walked with a slight stoop and seemed to shuffle his feet softly as he approached.

'Hello, Byron.'

'Brian. It's Brian. Don't call me Byron. I can't fucking stand it.'

'Nonsense. It's a fine name.'

'A fine name? You've got to be joking. Like I said, it always ends up as Brian sooner or later, so just call me Brian, OK?'

Brian bent from the waist and unfolded the cardboard square, which he placed gently onto the concrete below him. He lowered himself slowly onto the square and let out a deep breath as he crossed his legs beneath him and began to make himself comfortable. When he was settled he lifted his head to look at James.

'So?'

'I've been waiting for you.'

'I gathered that, mate.'

'I enjoyed our talk yesterday and I'd like to continue it today.'

'Would you.'

'Yes, I would. Very much.'

'What if I said I'd prefer it if you just left me alone? What do you think I'm doing out here every fucking day anyway?'

'I don't know. What are you doing?'

'What am I doing? What am I doing? Absolutely nothing. Sitting. Minding my own business. Watching. Thinking. I do a lot of that. It's very peaceful out here, once you get used to it. Looking at people's feet, I do that a lot too. Sit right out in the open and people leave you well alone. Don't even see you, most of them, even if you look 'em straight in the eye. Especially if you look straight into their eyes. As long as you don't stand out, pick a nice, plain bit of cardboard, no one bothers you. Until now, that is. And maybe I don't want to be bothered. Did you think of that?'

'No, I didn't. Perhaps it's best if I left.'

'Ah, fuck it. It's all right. It'll make for a change, having someone to talk to. For a little while, at least. But it never hurts to try and think about what other people might want in any given situation, right? You can't just go through life doing what you want to do without taking anyone else into consideration. It's just plain rude.'

'I'm sorry.'

'Don't mention it. Just don't be surprised when I tell you to fuck off, OK? Now, what's on your mind?'

'On my mind?'

'Yeah, what are you doing here?'

'I'm not quite sure. To be perfectly honest I should be at work. It's just that I wanted to be here more.'

'Planning on meeting your mother here?'

'My mother? No, not at all. I didn't expect she would be here.'

'She's here every day, mate. Or nearly every day, I reckon. Weekdays, at least. I don't work weekends.'

'Work?'

'Well, you know what I mean. I'm not here on weekends. Spend them at home.'

'You really do have a home?'

'Of course I've got a home. You thought I was just another homeless bludger, right? Just another piece of shit left on the street. Not me, mate. I want to be here. Like I said, it's a great place to think. I leave people alone, they leave me alone. As long as you fit in and mind your own business, everything is fine. Nothing out here but time.'

'What about the money they throw at you?'

'I don't ask them to throw it, do I? It's just a reflex action for most people — throw them some coins and they won't follow you home and rape your wife and children. Most days no one throws any money, which is the way I like it. But once some dickhead starts it off, other dickheads feel compelled to follow. I just leave it here. It's always gone by the next morning.'

'But why aren't you at work?'

'Why aren't you at work?'

'Yes, but that's not what I mean. I have a job to go to. You should have a job to go to. You're not an old man.'

'I'm thirty-five.'

'Well?'

'What?'

'Why don't you have a job?'

'Maybe I don't want a job.'

'Don't be absurd.'

'What's so absurd about not wanting a job?'

'If, as you say you do, you have a home, then you must also have expenses. You must pay for that home and for its upkeep at a minimum.'

'I'm an heiress.'

'What?'

'I'm an heiress. I inherited my land from a rich uncle. He was always partial to me.'

'That's not true. Besides, you can't be an heiress — you're not a woman.'

'Who says so? Mate, you sit out here long enough, you're bound to think you're a woman some of the time. Shit, I can be a rubber tree if I like. You're right though, I'm not an heiress. But I don't need a job.'

'Why not?'

'I've got a wife.'

'A wife?'

'Maureen. She's paying the bills for a little while. She's a nurse, working a couple of extra shifts to make ends meet. You know how it is. As long as I keep the house clean and look after the garden she doesn't mind me having the time off. Sometimes she comes home for lunch, like yesterday, which is nice.'

'She knows you come out here every day?'

'Nah, she thinks I'm sitting around at home, moping most likely. I would, but the television is too distracting. All that noise. And the walls. It's just not the right place for thinking. If you want to think right, you have to come out in the open to do it.'

'Perhaps you could turn the television off.'

'I could, but it'd still be there. If it's still there, the distraction is still there, understand? Much better off out here.'

'And what do you think about?'

'What do you mean, what do I think about? Stuff. Lots of stuff. It's different every day. Sometimes you just think nothing, which is the hardest thing to do, making everything stop. Nothing at all in your head. You're just there, empty. Takes patience. It makes everything like waiting. Usually I'm not patient enough so I just go with whatever's in my head. Growing up, Mum and Dad, old girlfriends, that sort of thing.'

'Mother was right, you know. You do look like me.'

'Well, technically speaking, since I was here first, you look like me. Yeah, I can see it, but so what?'

'Mother is convinced it must mean something.'

'What can it mean? It's a coincidence, mate. That's all it is. It's funny enough when you think about it but there must be hundreds, maybe thousands of people out there who look the same. We all like to think we're special but there's only so many combinations of nose, eyes, ears and mouth to go around. Sooner or later you're bound to find someone with your face. Maybe they're making better use of it than you; maybe they're not. Hardly bears thinking about, really.'

They stopped talking, each looking at the other's familiar features, into the eyes and beyond, each uncertain of what they expected to find. James was the first to move, stretching his head towards the sun and raising his hand to shield his eyes from the glare.

'It's getting late,' he said.

'Yep. Your mum'll be here soon. You want to wait for her?'

'No. I'd prefer not to. As a matter of fact I'd prefer it if she didn't know I was here.'

'I'm not about to tell her, mate. She's not about to

ask either. Never says a word to me. Just stands there and looks. Not that I mind. Look forward to it really.'

'All the same, if for some reason she does ask, please don't tell her I was here.'

'You're asking me to lie?'

'Only if it's required.'

'But you're telling me it's required?'

'If the situation arises, yes.'

'And why should I lie for you?'

'Because I'm asking you to. Please.'

'Well, since you said the magic word, your secret is safe with me.'

'Thank you.'

'Don't mention it. You best be off.'

'Yes. Goodbye.'

'Bye.'

Brian lowered his eyes to focus on the patch of concrete in front of him. He relaxed his shoulders and let his hands fall limply in his lap as he prepared himself for the hours ahead. As James walked away, his outline turned slowly into a blur at the edge of Brian's vision. Soon the shape was gone. All that was left to do now was wait.

It was not like James to be late for work. Totally out of character. Betty was worried. He had not called (the unofficial Sandler and Harris policy, as instituted by Betty some eleven years ago, was that any employee who could not be at the office before 9.30 should call ahead with an approximate time of arrival or a claim for sick leave). It was reasonable to expect the worst. An accident of some sort. A car, sleek, black and European, mounting a curb and crushing pedestrians in its path, James among them. A gang of teenagers in loose-fitting clothing, hair filled with grease, one of them with a knife, threatening an elderly lady in a floral print dress and cardigan at an autoteller. James would intervene and the knife would find its way into the soft flesh of his abdomen.

Betty had begun to chew the red and black enamel off the end of her pencil, a habit she only fell into in times of increased anxiety. She could taste the paint flakes mixed with fine, moist chips of wood. Soon she would be down to the lead of the pencil itself and her tongue would begin to blacken. Instead, she forced herself to focus on her work and began searching her desk for a suitable place to start. She found a tape from Mr Sandler's dictaphone marked 'Urgent!' and decided to transcribe it. She placed the tape into her own playback machine and positioned the earphones over her head, where they were quickly lost in a mass of hair.

Mr Sandler's words were sounding in her ears and coming out of her fingers. She had long since mastered the technique of becoming a mere conduit for the words and was oblivious to their meaning. Words began to form quickly (Betty's speed was rated at fifty-five words a minute) on her monitor.

Date open

Mrs Veronica Bloomington
address to follow

Dear Mrs Bloomington,

*My name is Geoffrey Sandler. Your son James is currently in
my employ. I say this only to remind you of the circumstances
under which we happened to meet. You had come into the
offices of Sandler and Harris (my publishing company) to
meet with your son and graciously requested the use of our
boardroom. We met as I was on my way out of the boardroom, although due to the speed of events we were never
formally introduced. I trust, however, that you recall me as
well as I recall you.*

*I am not a great believer in wasting words or actions so I'll
get straight to the point: you have captivated my heart and I
feel it necessary to pursue you. My intentions, I should point
out, are entirely honourable. I wish to make you my wife,
although at this point I feel compelled to disclose that you
would not be the first Mrs Geoffrey Sandler. I am divorced,
through no fault of my own, let me assure you, but divorced
nonetheless.*

*I would like to initiate a courtship period of a length to be
determined at a future date. I propose to begin the courtship
with a series of dinner engagements. Should you feel it necessary, I have no objection to you having your son present at the
first of these engagements. If you like, I can also arrange to*

have my daughter, Imogen, present. However, I would prefer that we dined alone.

Please accept these flowers as a token of my esteem and respect. If they are not to your liking please advise and I will have replacement flowers delivered immediately.

Should you not feel disposed to accept my offer, or feel it necessary to discuss the matter further, please advise.

Respectfully yours,
Geoffrey Sandler
Sandler and Harris etc. etc.

As she was saving the document she had just created, Betty looked up to see James walk slowly through the entrance of Yeats' Towers. He appeared to be affected by the heat of the day but otherwise suffered no obvious restrictions to his movement. His back was slightly bent and his eyes were directed towards the ground in front of him. He did not look up as he passed Betty's desk. And he did not stop to wish her a good morning.

'Bloomington!'

It was Mr Sandler, standing to James's left, looking down at him in his chair.

'Good morning, sir.'

'Is it?'

'Pardon?'

'Is it. I said, "Is it."'

'I'm sorry, sir – I'm not sure I follow.'

'I'll break it down for you then, shall I, Blooming-ton? Let me see . . . First, is it morning? Let's look at my watch. My sweet Lord! It's almost midday. Hardly morning at all, really, is it? Technically, yes, it is still the morning, in that it is not quite the afternoon. But colloquially I think it's accepted that we use the ex-pression "good morning" as a greeting at the start of a new day, and it's hardly the start of a new day, is it?'

'No, sir.'

'Let's move on to the next bit then. We've estab-lished that it's no longer morning, by which I think it clearly follows that it also cannot be a good morning.'

'No, sir.'

'Glad to see you can still follow a logical argument. Now listen closely to me and try to follow this: you're abusing your position, Bloomington. Don't think I can't see it.'

'I'm sorry, sir?'

'Your position. You think that just because I'm in a relationship with your mother that suddenly the rules – the very rules of employment themselves, Bloom-ington – these rules no longer apply to you? That you can turn up for work not only late but dishevelled? I mean, shit, look at you.'

'I'm sorry, sir. I tend to be badly affected by extreme weather conditions.'

'I can tell that by looking at you, Bloomington. And it's not exactly a surprise to me. But today is no hotter than yesterday, or tomorrow will be, for that matter.

You've got to pull yourself together, get to the bathroom and take a good look at yourself in the mirror. If your mother could see you, I'm sure she'd be shocked at the state of you. Here, I've got something that'll help.'

Mr Sandler moved closer so that his stomach was brushing against James's shoulder. James shuddered at the contact. Sandler inclined his small, circular face towards James's own and pulled a small, cylindrical metal can from his right jacket pocket. It was a white can topped with a pink plastic lid. His eyes surveyed the room as if seeking to confirm the suspicion that his actions were being monitored; his voice, however, lowered to a near whisper, was aimed directly into James's left ear. James could feel the breath accompanying Mr Sandler's words against his hair.

'It's a personal hydrolyser. Sprays natural mineral water in a fine, refreshing mist. Evian. See, it's Evian.'

James took the can from his hand. Sandler stood up straight.

'Picked it up on a flight to Hong Kong once. Not this particular can, of course. The airline kept cans of the stuff in the toilets. Cathay Pacific, I think it was. Stops you getting dehydrated. Just a squirt here and there when you need it. Get it from a chemist. Possibly even in supermarkets. Try it. Go on, try it.'

James took the cap off the can and pointed the white plastic nozzle at his face. He held the nozzle down and was instantly rewarded with a fine, refreshing mist of natural mineral water, just as Mr Sandler had promised.

'Thank you, sir.'

'Don't mention it. And of course you know I mean that quite literally. Don't tell anyone around here about it, especially those nosy fucking subeditors over there. We don't want them thinking I'm giving you any special treatment, because I'm not, understand?'

'Yes, sir.'

'I mean it, Bloomington. I can't have you coming in late like this. I'll let it go this time, for your mother's sake if nothing else, but don't let me catch you like this again, OK?'

'Yes, sir.'

Looking past Mr Sandler's absurdly short torso James could see a young woman approaching his desk. Dark-blue jeans covered the swell of her hips. Above the jeans she wore a plain white t-shirt. There was not a bead of sweat on her prominent forehead, although her round cheeks gave off a very agreeable reddish glow. As the distance between the two of them closed, James was struck by the purity and clarity of her eyes, which were as blue as the ocean of his dreams.

She stopped beside Mr Sandler, placed a hand on his shoulder and kissed him lightly on the cheek.

'Hello, Daddy.'

'Imogen? What the fuck are you doing here?'

'I'm here to see you, Daddy. What else would I be doing here?'

'Oh, shit. Are you out of money already?'

'No. Well, yes. But I thought we could have lunch

together. In fact I'll be very disappointed if we can't. And who might this be? He looks familiar . . .'

'What? Oh, Bloomington. James Bloomington. He's one of our junior editors here. We were just discussing the next issue of *Uncommon Cases*, isn't that right, Bloomington? Bloomington, my daughter Imogen.'

James rose to his feet quickly and immediately regretted it. He could feel the blood rushing to his head. He placed his left hand on the back of his chair for support and extended his right hand to Imogen Sandler. He was, he realised, still holding the can of compressed mineral water. Her eyes showed surprise and she withdrew her body from the unexpected gift.

'Evian,' said James, the dryness in his throat and mouth making the word barely audible.

It was then that his nose began to bleed. The rush of blood was strong and sudden and as James ducked his head, reaching for his nose with his left hand and a tissue from his jacket pocket with his right, he knew it was already too late. Blood flowed over the edges of his hand and dropped towards the floor. His eyes followed the first of the drops, rich, heavy and deeply red. He watched it slowly fall and land with a tiny splash on the top of a clean, white running shoe. It was Imogen Sandler's shoe.

As he watched a small, circular stain grow on the clean, white canvas, James imagined the shape of her foot below. Feet, he well knew, were usually the least attractive part of a man or a woman and best kept hidden. His mother's feet, for example, were positively deformed as a result of her days as a dancer, the bones growing to misshapen lumps of hard tissue in an attempt to accommodate the unusual demands placed upon them. His own feet were something of an exception and he generally found them quite pleasing to the eye. There was no overlap to his toes, the nails were strong and well tended, the heels were free of calluses and the arches were clearly formed. Surely the beauty of Imogen's feet would rival his own.

James brought his focus back to the newly formed stain on the shoe. The blood had soaked quickly through the fibres of the canvas, diluting itself as it spread outward. The colour surprised him. At the outer edges of the stain the red gave way to a sickly brown. Though it would gradually fade, it would prove impossible to remove.

Chapter 17

There was no music to greet him as he approached the house on Watterson Avenue at 6.30 pm. Mrs Salvestrin was nowhere to be seen. James assumed she was hidden away in the darkest corner of her bedroom, avoiding all contact with her tenant in an elaborate display of regret and embarrassment over their recent encounter in the bathroom. He suspected that she was incapable of recalling the exact sequence of events (and perhaps even the events themselves), but that she was acutely aware of his nakedness and her own insobriety at the time. In any case, although he had heard her often clumsy movements through the house in the days that followed, James had not seen his landlady since the morning of the incident.

He could feel the crust of dried blood high in his left

nostril. The nose-bleeding was getting to be more than a little inconvenient. Perhaps he should see another doctor about it. However, it was James's experience that most general practitioners were dangerously under-qualified and he simply did not want any more of them prodding about in his nose with implements that may or may not have been properly sterilised. He was sure that most of the GPs he had seen (the total number was now somewhere between five and seven) treated the reported frequency of his nose-bleeds with an unpro-fessional degree of scepticism. Two had simply told him to wash his nose in warm salted water three times a day and wait for the problem to heal itself.

He had been referred to three specialists, one of whom had arranged for a corrective operation to seal a burst blood vessel high in the bridge of his nose. At the final moment, however, James had declined to have the operation performed. There was something about the anaesthetist's eyes that bothered him, some-thing about the deep yellow tinge of the eyeballs themselves that made him sit up straight on the oper-ating table and announce that he had elected to forgo the procedure. He was sorry to have bothered the sur-gical staff assembled but insisted that he be allowed to leave the operating theatre at once. He had walked from the theatre in a green surgical gown, his back and buttocks largely exposed, and called his mother from the public phone in the reception area. She came to fetch her son immediately and, much to James's surprise, kept her silence on the issue of his aborted surgery, a silence she maintained to this day.

James had seen the disgust on Imogen Sandler's face as she pulled her foot away from the overflow of blood from his cupped hand. Her eyes had grown impossibly wide and the flush of her cheeks had spread quickly to her forehead and along the length of her throat. Mr Sandler's reaction had not helped James to maintain his composure. When he had stemmed the flow of blood, he looked up to find Mr Sandler hurrying his daughter out of the building. James cleaned the floor with a crumpled tissue as best he could and returned to his desk. The blood had smeared across the floorboards, against the grain of the wood, as he wiped at it with the sodden tissue.

Clearing his mind of the image of his own uncontained blood, James was surprised to find himself, suddenly it seemed, at the front door to his rented lodgings. He wondered how long he had been standing there. He did not remember ascending the stairs with his final steps. The key was in his hand. When he had opened the door, he took a single step backwards and assessed the silence within. He could not be sure whether or not Mrs Salvestrin was in but thought better of calling out a greeting. Instead, he pulled the door closed quietly behind him and walked down the hall to his rooms.

Locating the remote control on the floor by his bed he turned on the television instinctively, the noise from its speaker announcing to himself and the world that he was home. The curtains to his single window were closed but the early evening sunlight outside was of sufficient strength to force its way through the fabric and fill the bedroom with a soft light, brightened now and then by the flickering of the television screen. James placed his briefcase on top of his unmade bed and began to undress to the agitated chatter from the television behind him.

'Take him then, ya cow! Go on! He's all yours. And tell him never to come near me again. D'ya hear that, Travis? Don't you ever come near me again.'

'Settle down, Jamie. Me and Sharon didn't do anything wrong. It was a dance, right? We were just dancing.'

'Yeah, Jamie. That's all it was, honest. Just a dance, OK?'

'Stay out of it, Shaz. C'mon, Jamie, we just danced, that's all.'

'That was dancing, was it? Outside? Behind the hedge? What sort of an idiot do you think I am, Travis Henderson? I saw you, Travis! I saw you! You don't dance lying down! I know exactly what you were doing – that thing we did under the pier, remember? That's right, Sharon. He did it with me first! Just remember that when you start to itch, ya cow!'

[hysterical sobbing]

'Settle down, Jamie. I knew I shoulda just gone to the footy club . . .'

'What does she mean about the itching, Trav?'

'I told ya, Shaz! Stay out of it!'

'But Travis, it's been itchy for days. Ever since the dance . . .'

In his boxer shorts, James sank onto the bed and

surveyed his room. The air was hot and still; nothing moved except for the images on the television screen. He saw his clothes hanging neatly on their racks, his books stacked neatly on the bookshelf, all contained within four bare walls. He was alone in an empty room. He closed his eyes and thought of Imogen Sandler's pure, white running shoes.

It was inconceivable that Geoffrey Sandler could have fathered such a beauty. Not only was she beautiful but she was well within the range of what could be considered normal height. James had always imagined that Geoffrey Sandler's offspring would possess at least some of their father's physical characteristics. During his less stimulating days at the office James regularly imagined a troupe of energetic circus midgets in Mr Sandler's tow, complete with oversized shoes, bicycle horns, baggy patchwork trousers and red plastic noses. It was for the most part a welcome delusion, although he had become so used to the whimsy of the circus midgets that it was often difficult for him to imagine Mr Sandler without them. James liked to think of the midgets as Mr Sandler's children. Thus he was doubly taken aback to find instead Imogen Sandler.

He could see her face before him, the bottomless depth of her eyes and the fullness of her lips, the slightly asymmetrical nose, the left nostril larger than the right. A barely perceptible flaw that gave context to the beauty around it. He could picture the cords of her neck ending at delicate collarbones that disappeared

171

under the stitched crew neck of her t-shirt. Her breasts rose beneath, the cups of an underwire bra visible as they pressed against the cotton of the t-shirt. Her bare arms were pale, even in the middle of summer, and lightly freckled, the hips wide with promise, hidden, as were her legs, beneath the dark denim of what appeared to be men's jeans. Still, the proportions were excellent.

Even before he began the process of constructing a brief conversation in his head ('My, but it's hot and stuffy today . . .') that would lead to the two of them undressing, conveniently enough behind the closed door of the Jeremiah Sandler Memorial Boardroom, and making quick, passionate love to the hum of the window-mounted air-conditioning unit, James found himself with an erection straining for release from his boxer shorts. He knew Mrs Salvestrin was unlikely to admit herself to his room, a fact he hoped he could rely upon for at least a few more weeks, and permitted himself to reach his right hand underneath the elastic waist of his underwear.

But the touch of his own hand would not satisfy him. Not tonight. He could sense the emptiness of his room pressing in on him, as it sometimes did, and he suddenly felt the need to escape it. He needed to be somewhere else. With someone else. Alison. He would call Alison. Their last evening together had ended pleasantly enough, as he recalled, and his memory could find no objection to either her face or body although, truth be told, he was having some trouble forming an exact picture of either.

Her phone number, written in blue ink on a torn piece of notepaper in small, elaborately looped numerals, was in his briefcase. Alison Gately. He hoped she was at home. James reached for the dirty grey t-shirt that lay beneath the sheet beside his briefcase, pulled it over his head and, paper in hand, walked quickly to the telephone in Mrs Salvestrin's kitchen. He was careful to make his paces as heavy as possible so that Mrs Salvestrin would hear him coming and, if she had ventured from her room, scuttle away. He smiled to think he had this kind of power. But there was no sign of his landlady in either the kitchen or the loungeroom beyond. Reading the digits from the notepaper James dialled the number and waited for an answer. A woman answered in a hesitant voice. He could not be sure that it was Alison.

'Alison Gately?'

'Yes.'

'It's James Bloomington. Hello.'

'Oh. James. Hi.'

'I was wondering if by any chance you are free this evening.'

'Free?'

'Yes. Whether or not you had any plans for the evening. I would like to pay a call on you.'

'You want to go out somewhere?'

'Not necessarily.'

'Oh.'

'Yes, well. If you have plans, perhaps we can leave it for another time.'

'It's OK. I don't have any plans. You can come over if you like.'

'Excellent. I'll be there as soon as I can.'

'OK, I'll see you soon.'

'Yes, you will. One small point, however . . . I'm not sure that I can remember the exact location of your apartment.'

'The exact location?'

'Yes, the address.'

'Oh. It's 54 Calliope Street. Flat nine. Third floor.'

'Of course. I'll be there within the hour, I expect. See you then.'

'OK. Bye.'

'Goodbye.'

James did in fact arrive at 54 Calliope Street within the hour. He knew it would have been polite to have showered, not to mention it being the hygienically correct procedure, but in the interests of making the most efficient use of the time available, he had decided to simply put on his suit again (with the notable addition of a fresh shirt and tie) and make his way to Bondi. He changed trains once at Town Hall Station and caught a taxi from Bondi Junction. The taxi driver, thankfully, was not interested in initiating a conversation of any sort. He kept his eyes fixed firmly on the road (which was commendable), his mouth set in a slight frown and his radio tuned to a deep-voiced announcer prompting callers to share their 'love song dedications'. The driver's origins were not obvious from his appearance – he was heavy-set and displayed a thick tangle of largely grey chest hair – but James would have been surprised if English was his native tongue.

When James got out of the taxi the sun had finally set, leaving a bright half-moon to illuminate the blond-brick apartment block. James remembered the building; he remembered the concrete path on which he was walking and the two flights of stairs he was about to climb.

Alison answered the door. She was wearing a loose-fitting white cotton peasant dress that accentuated the tanned curves of her shoulders. Her hair was loose and she was not wearing any make-up, at least not that he could tell. She was smiling at him, a shy smile, as if they were both in on a joke that no one else could share.

'Hi, James. Come in.'

'Hello.' He did his best to return the smile.

'James, this is my flatmate Rebecca.' She indicated a round-faced, plainly overweight girl of about twenty-five or twenty-six sitting on a lounge watching television. Her right hand was lost in a large foil bag of cheese-flavoured corn chips.

'Hello,' said James. The girl turned her head away from the television and smiled at him. Her teeth were covered with the remains of the masticated corn chips and stained a bright, deeply unnatural yellow. She waved with her free hand, resting the other hand inside the bag on her lap. But she did not say a word in reply.

Alison led James down the narrow hallway to her room. He took off his jacket and placed it over the end of the bed.

'You made pretty good time.' She was still smiling at him.

He placed his mouth over hers and began to kiss her, guiding the dress slowly above her hips and over her head. He could feel her tongue darting from the sides to the roof of his mouth, his teeth mashing against hers. She worked quickly to undo his tie and the buttons of his shirt, releasing the sweat, the dirt, the smell of him. James ran his hands across her shoulders and pulled her close to him, his right arm locked at the small of her back. He used his left hand to work inside the elastic of her underpants, fumbling over her pubic hair towards the moisture within.

Chapter 18

Veronica was in the garden, a rock in each hand, tending to her plants. Ants. There were ants everywhere, crawling over the surfaces of her palm trees and the paved ground below. Because of their tiny size, the ants were proving difficult to crush, and the more she killed, the more appeared. Yes, they were very much like an army. The morning sun was high and fierce, keeping up its daily attack on the people below. It occurred to Veronica that, from the sun, people would indeed look like ants, and a faint smile formed at the corners of her mouth, although if anyone was passing, or somehow looking down on her from the sun, perhaps with a high-powered telescope or other such device, they would not have seen the movement of her lips, covered as they were by the first Safe-T Services Corporation respirator of the day. She allowed the smile to broaden and continued with her work.

She stood upright to wipe the sweat off her brow with a white handkerchief pulled from the top pocket of a lightweight cotton blouse, and saw a man approaching, picking his way carefully along the path to the house. He was carrying a clipboard in his right hand and a large bunch of flowers in the left.

The man was young, perhaps twenty-five, but morbidly obese; a constant stream of sweat dripped from his wet, fleshy face, much of it landing on the front of the oversized khaki work shirt he was wearing. He was gasping for breath and seemed in need of urgent medical attention. Veronica feared that the behemoth would collapse on the spot and imagined the mass of his soft body falling across the path with a solid thud. She could not possibly roll him out of the way on her own; he would just have to lie there until she could get help. But he did not collapse; instead, he somehow managed to take the remaining seven steps required to position himself squarely in front of her.

'Veronica Bloomington?' His whole body inflated to comic proportions as he sucked the air around him into his lungs in a series of slow, purposely modulated breaths. Thin strips of black hair were matted to his forehead and the sides of his face. Rolls of pink flesh covered his knees. Veronica shuddered involuntarily but managed to reply that, yes, she was Veronica Bloomington.

'Hmnpht. Ni hun berboobuna hoominum.'

'Jesus. This isn't an easy house to find, is it? That goddamned path must go for at least a mile . . . I had to park the van way up the hill, up there somewhere. Jesus. Nice view. You wouldn't have a glass of water or something would you, love?'

'Npht, ni hmpht.'

'No need to take that tone of voice about it, I was only asking. Jesus H. Christ, I'm sweating like a god-damned pig. All I asked for was a glass of water. Here, sign this.' He presented Veronica with the clipboard. A ballpoint pen was attached to the metal clip by a tattered length of nylon cord. There was a delivery receipt on the board and a column next to her neatly printed name was marked with an 'X' for her signature. She took the pen and quickly scribbled her initials.

'Full name, please.' She looked up at him menac-ingly but had already begun to complete her first name. When she was finished she thrust the clipboard at the man's chest, creating ripples of flesh underneath his shirt. He caught the clipboard under his right arm and held it against his swollen stomach.

'Jesus! Just take the goddamned flowers.' He held the flowers out for Veronica to take from his hand. A sealed envelope was attached to the cellophane wrapping.

With an elaborate, almost pantomime sigh to indi-cate the discharge of this particular duty (and also that any number of equally perilous tasks were surely in store for him on this unhappy day), the delivery man wiped his right forearm across his brow, clipboard in hand, turned his massive back to Veronica and began his cumbersome climb along the path. Veronica thought the incline might yet prove too much for him; she could not be sure until he reached the street above. As she watched him lumber away she was struck by the height each of his buttocks managed to reach with every step he took, bouncing almost to where she imagined the tip of his shoulder blade might be, buried beneath a thick layer of fat.

Brian was wondering if there was any way for him to be able to tell, to be sure and certain, whether any of the shins that passed him by on any given morning (and he saw a lot of shins from his box) weren't real shins at all, but artificial ones. Made of plastic and not of flesh. Prosthetic. Prosthetic limbs. Prosthetic shins, anyway. It was hard to tell, if a person was wearing long pants. And people did insist on wearing long pants, even in this heat. A person in shorts or even a skirt obviously had nothing to hide, nothing to be ashamed of. Not that anyone should be ashamed of having a plastic shin. No blame to attach there, unless of course you were being a dickhead on a motorbike, say, and had a fall, doing yourself irreparable harm, like fucking up your shin. Then it'd be your own stupid fault. People would ask about your limp, why you never wore shorts even on sunny days, and you'd have to tell them it was because you had a plastic shin – shit, and a plastic foot to go with it. Here, step on my toes: can't feel a fucking thing! How did that happen? Well, I was being a dickhead on a motorbike, just mucking around, pushing my luck and bang! I came off and fucked up my shin. The muscles, the bone, all of it – totally fucked. Even if you told the story with a smile you'd still come off like a prize fuckwit.

A war wound would be much better. Oh, this? I did it in the war, caught some shrapnel behind enemy lines. It stung a little but I managed to get back to base somehow, a couple of the native blokes helped me out – good fellas, those native blokes. Didn't speak a word of English, of course. Just these clicking noises. Click, click, clickety click. Smiled a lot, too. Anyway, by the time I got to the field hospital, the M.A.S.H, the 'Mobile Army Surgical Hospital', it got itself infected. Bloody jungles are like that. Bloody trenches are like that. Bloody mud. Fucking mud. No chance. So the doc had to saw it off, right there below the knee, see? He was a nice bloke, that doc. A bit of a joker, mind you, but you could tell he wasn't gonna let you down. It was in his eyes. Very sensitive eyes. Nurses seemed to like him. They were real nice to me too, if you know what I mean . . .

You could end the story with a wink. A knowing wink and a leer. Then it'd come: Oh, really? You poor thing. And which war was that? That'd put an end to it. Which war? There were no wars, not anymore. Not

181

real ones, anyway. Not like the old days, when you'd talk about 'the war' and everyone'd know which one. Everyone was in it: of course they knew which one. Even Vietnam wasn't a real war. People died, sure, but it was pretty much business as usual. The war? What war? That'd fuck it up. Then you'd be forced to tell them you did it fucking around on a motorbike like a dickhead. A prize fuckwit.

He saw the odd limp here and there, people gimping about, sometimes on crutches. But most of those would be temporary injuries. Sporting injuries, maybe. Falling down stairs drunk. Jumping over fences. I had a little too much to drink. Shit-faced, actually. Well and truly spannered. But how many of them would be prosthetics? Artificial limbs? And how would he be able to tell? Did they always walk in a certain way? A lilt? Favouring the good leg over the bad? The bad over the good? One hip higher than the other? Or would they walk just like everybody else? Perfect balance with a little practice. If you fall over, just stand right on up and try it again! No one here will laugh at you. Be sure to hold the hand rails. But how much practice? And will I ever dance again? That's funny: I never could dance before! Not much rhythm in me, I guess.

He didn't hear her coming. She was just there, standing in front of him, looking down. He refocused his eyes to take in the black leather shoes, strong shins (very fine shins, actually), stockings, the navy skirt. Was it time?

How long had she been standing there already? Should he start the count now? And what about the flowers? She was holding a bunch of flowers, roses mainly, by the look of it. He wasn't sure what the white ones were called. He took a few deep breaths and concentrated on the patch of concrete in front of him. Still she stood there, holding her position above him. He could not measure without counting, and regretted that he had not begun to do so earlier, but already he was sure she had overstayed her time. What was she looking at? What had changed? For the first time since she had begun her visits, Brian felt suddenly, unexpectedly, uneasy.

Behind her desk, Betty Palmer was chewing on the end of a pencil. With no typing to be done and no incoming calls to answer, the receptionist was momentarily distracted. She was looking down her nose and along the length of the pencil's shaft, which served to lend her eyes a strange intensity of focus and, coupled with the saliva that formed at the corners of her mouth and the overall slackness of her jaw, gave her the appearance of a deranged holy woman caught in the midst of some sort of epiphany.

Veronica moved past the front desk with swift, light steps; so light, in fact, that Betty did not notice her go by. Veronica, however, was aware of Betty's inattention and made a mental note to remind her son's boss of the drooling incompetence of his company's receptionist. She was soon standing to the side of James's desk, breathing heavily through her mask. James sat staring at his computer's monitor, the glow of its screen reflected on his pale, damp forehead. He kept his head and body as still as possible, storing his energy against the heat of the day. It was, Veronica noticed, hotter inside the office than it was outside, and the day outside was particularly fierce.

The flowers she was carrying had begun to wilt, surrendering their moisture to the air, and she threw them on her son's desk. He turned his head slowly and looked up at her, lifting his eyes only for the time it took to identify her.

'Hello, Mother.'

'Mnpht. Hni hnee ooh ork hnu.'

'Yes, Mother, it is a wonderful day. Nice of you to stop by.'

'Mnpht! Hni hnee ooh ork hnu!'

'Yes, a truly wonderful day, the sun shining bright and the birds and children singing as one.'

'Hnop hee!'

'Oh, I couldn't agree more. In fact, I was only saying to Mrs Salvestrin – she sends her regards, by the way – this morning over breakfast – '

His words came quickly to a halt as Veronica dug her fingernails into his left shoulder. He could feel their sharpness through his shirt and jacket. She brought him to his feet. Picking up the flowers with her left hand, she thrust him towards the Jeremiah

Sandler Memorial Boardroom with her right, towards the closest secure environment either of them knew.

When Veronica threw open the boardroom door they found Stephen Hunt inside, his back turned to them as he stood directly in front of the air-conditioning unit wearing only his underwear – plain white cotton briefs and a lightweight cotton undershirt. He was holding a leather riding crop in his extended right hand. His tweed suit, a pale-blue shirt and maroon tie were folded neatly on the boardroom table. He turned to face the open door slowly and deliberately. Y-fronts. His underpants were Y-fronts.

'I really must remember to lock that door,' he said. 'A way to beat the summer heat, don't you know.' His smile was not at all weak.

'Please excuse us,' said James. 'I didn't think to knock.'

'Quite all right. Jasper, we have company.' Jasper Jenkins, one of the junior editors of *Saddlery and Stirrups Monthly*, emerged awkwardly from underneath the large oak table in the centre of the room. He too was in his underwear, pale-blue cotton boxer shorts and a white cotton singlet. His clothes were hanging over the back of the leatherette chair to his left. Jasper was tall and exceedingly pale, his fine hair almost colourless against his skin, although his round cheeks were now flushed with colour as he reached silently for his shirt. His body was soft and already swollen with fat around his hips. James noticed the outline of Jasper's breasts under his singlet, the wide nipples pointing to the floor. James and Jasper had started at Sandler and Harris in the same week and had spoken only once since that time. As James remembered it, the conversation (which occurred in the company bathroom) was neither long nor pleasant.

'Hello, Jasper.'

'James.'

'Fancy meeting you here.'

'Yes, quite.'

'Please, take your time. Don't hurry on our account.'

Stephen Hunt had managed to dress himself almost completely by the time Jasper was stumbling, one leg after the other, into his trousers. There was something about Hunt's bearing, the efficiency of his movements, which made both James and Veronica turn their eyes away from him and towards Jasper. Equally, there was something about Jasper's haste, not to mention his bumbling attempts at securing his fly, that invited the onlookers' attention.

'Do hurry along, Jasper,' said Stephen Hunt, arranging his tie into an elegant half-Windsor with a final twist of his hands.

'Coming, sir.'

Veronica was seated opposite Jasper at the table. She was looking straight at the young man and contributing directly to his unease. The mask was obscuring much of her face but the expression of her eyes was such that Jasper was left in no doubt that he would always be remembered by a single word. That word was, possibly, 'buffoon'. Perhaps something less kind. When he had fastened the last button of his shirt he pulled on his jacket and headed towards the door. He had already resolved to attend to his tie only after he had left the room.

Stephen Hunt opened the door for him, stepping aside graciously and ushering him through. Hunt's smile remained fixed and firm as he held his position by the door.

'Thank you both for your patience,' he said, his voice taking on a musical quality. James would later remember him rolling his eyes in mock exasperation, presumably in reference to Jasper's comic role in the events. 'It was a pleasure to see you again, Mrs Bloomington. I trust I'll have the pleasure again soon. Good day.'

When Stephen Hunt closed the door behind him, Veronica removed her mask and placed it with the flowers on the table in front of her.

'That, James,' she began, 'is why I never allowed you to wear white underpants as a child. Nor do I recommend that you wear them now. The story of that man's life was writ large, or not-so-large, as the case may be, on his underpants. Every stain, every trace of his . . . activities. Despite the attentions of what I assume is a first-rate laundry service, the fact remains that it is impossible for white underwear to keep any secrets. And I never wished to know any of your secrets, James, just as I don't wish to know any of them now. Ghastly. And sit down, for God's sake.'

'Yes, Mother. It's a lesson I've taken to heart, let me assure you. But from my brief observation – and I should point out that it is somewhat, well, impolite at the very least, it is impolite or perhaps impolitic to let one's eyes linger for too long on certain areas of another man's body – Mr Hunt's underpants were spotlessly clean.'

'Nonsense, James. Certain stains simply cannot be removed. You of all people should know that.'

'What on earth are you talking about, Mother?'

'Stains, James, stains. You leave them everywhere you go with that nose of yours.'

'Thank you for your understanding, Mother.'

'Not at all. Now tell me what you know about these.'

'They're flowers, Mother. Not particularly healthy flowers by the look of them, although I expect that's the heat. Roses, I think. I'm not sure what the white ones are but I'm sure they were quite lovely at some stage.'

'I know what they are, James. And yes, they were quite lovely. I want to know if you're aware of who sent them to me.'

'Mr Sandler, I assume.'

'So you know about this?'

'Mr Sandler has expressed an intention to show you his regards.'

'You encouraged this?'

'Certainly not. I would not wish you upon any man, Mother. You should know that by now. Mr Sandler is a man of strong convictions, however irrational those convictions might be. It's not for me to encourage him. Nor is it my place to discourage him.'

'Why would such a ridiculous little man — it is that ridiculous little man, is it not? — assume that I would want anything to do with him? He is proposing a period of formal courtship, James, beginning with a dinner engagement between you and I and he and his daughter.'

'Imogen?'

'Yes, imagine. Imagine the nerve . . .'

'No, Imogen. His daughter's name is Imogen.'

'Ridiculous name.'

'Unconventional, perhaps, but hardly ridiculous.'

'It's ridiculous, James. Her mother, at least, should have known better. In any case, I'm here to advise your Mr Sandler that I have no intention of participating in his delusional fantasies.'

'Well, you're a free woman, Mother, you can do as you like. I'm sure it won't affect my career here at Sandler and Harris. That would be very childish on Mr Sandler's part.'

'Your career? It better not affect your career. There are laws against that sort of thing, surely.'

'Of course. And I'm sure he's not the type to hold a grudge. Still, I should tell you that I have a great respect for Mr Sandler, Mother. A new found respect, you might say, and I'm not sure that it would be wise for you to insult him . . .'

'Insult him? What are you suggesting, James?'

'Nothing at all. It's just that it's sometimes foolish to judge a person solely upon a first impression and, well, why not go to dinner, Mother? The four of us, I mean. Why don't we go to dinner and you can take the opportunity to politely explain your position. If I'm there it'll be much easier for you.'

'Easier? Why would it be easier? Easier than what?'

'Than if I wasn't there. I really do think that a dinner engagement isn't such a bad idea, Mother. Providing that Imogen and I are present, of course.'

Veronica remained silent, scrutinising her son's face. His eyes were blinking rapidly and, even in this air-conditioned room, beads of sweat covered his forehead. After a time she reached for her respirator and moved towards the boardroom door, leaving the flowers on the table. She stopped before the door and slipped the respirator over head, leaving it hanging at her chest from her neck. Before she fitted it over her mouth she turned to face James, who remained at the table. She was still examining his face for any signs of weakness.

'Arrange it,' she said. Two words before she adjusted the straps of her mask and walked out the door, leaving James behind her.

Chapter 19

James was having trouble concentrating on the paper before him. He looked again at the title page: 'Push Me, Shove You, Sue Me, Says Who? Letting the Market Decide' by Andrew S. Cummins III. Something to do with trademark infringements and passing off as the inevitable and natural result of unfettered capitalism. As a consequence the author was proposing abolishing both the Common Law cause of action and statutory relief in favour of market forces. James recognised the use of the Hegelian dialectic early on in the piece, which he generally regarded as a sign of intellectual laziness. He had read nothing since to alter his opinion.

Dinner with Imogen. The opportunity was at hand. His mother's presence could present a problem, as could the presence of Imogen's father. Still, this was an opportunity that had to be taken. His mother sensed something was wrong – he could feel it as her eyes bore down on him in the boardroom. She may have guessed that his sudden enthusiasm for Mr Sandler was due to the unexpected involvement of his daughter. James knew his mother. And his mother knew him.

But Mr Sandler's intentions, his clearly stated intentions, were perfectly honourable. Perfectly. The man had to be praised for the strength of his convictions. He wanted to makes James's mother his wife. And why not? She was a handsome woman. As far as James was aware she was not involved with any other men, at least not on a continuing basis. There were always men, and sometimes boys, but none of them had ever mattered. No, Geoffrey Sandler's intentions were honourable. To make her his wife. To make her Veronica Sandler. She would be Imogen's step-mother. Which would make James Geoffrey Sandler's step-son and Imogen's step-brother. His step-sister. Clearly that would never do. Never.

Geoffrey Sandler was standing behind him, looking over his shoulder at the manuscript open on his desk.

'Morning, Bloomington. It is still morning, isn't it? Let me check. No, it isn't – my mistake. Hard at it, I see.'

'Yes, sir.'

'Good submission?'

'It's an analysis of the foundations of intellectual property. As far as I can tell, the author is in favour of a system of ownership that remains in a state of flux. He seems to suggest that intellectual property should belong to the person who can make the most use of it, make the most money from it, at any given time. That's my initial reading, sir.'

'Fascinating, I'm sure. Better than gay whales, right?'

'Sir?'

'*Moby-Dick*. Better than *Moby-Dick*, eh?'

'If you say so, sir.'

'Yes, well I do say so. Sounds like just the sort of thing we're after. Some solid theory. Always good, for the prestige if nothing else, eh?'

'Yes, sir.'

'Yes. I, erm, I hear that your mother was in to visit you today.'

'Yes, sir.'

'Glad to hear it. It was, erm, a pleasant visit, I take it?'

'Yes, sir. Quite.'

'She didn't happen to mention receiving any flowers this morning, did she?'

'Yes, sir, she did.'

'And?'

'And she would like me to act as an intermediary.'

'An intermediary?'

'Yes, sir. She's asked me to arrange a dinner engagement.'

'Excellent!'

'Between yourself and your daughter and my mother and I.'

'The four of us?'

'Yes, sir. It was your suggestion, if you recall.'

'Yes, I suppose it was. I was hoping to avoid it. No offence, Bloomington. It's just that you don't want a woman's son along on your first date, if you know what I mean . . .'

'I'm afraid that I do, sir. Which is why my mother thought it best that I be there.'

'What? Oh, come on. It's not like that, Bloomington. I mean, I just want to talk to the woman alone. To get things off on the right foot. It might be a little stilted with you there. Shit, I can't imagine anywhere not being stilted with you around. Not to mention Imogen, if she's available, that is.'

'Available?'

'Well, I haven't asked her about it yet.'

'Oh. Mother was most specific. She wished for the four of us, and only the four of us, to be there. She wanted to meet your daughter.'

'Yes, well, I'll do what I can. She owes me, anyway. If that girl expects me to keep paying her bills she'll just have to make the time for a couple of father-daughter outings, won't she?'

'Yes, sir. I expect that she will.'

'Dinner for four it is, then. What sort of food does she prefer?'

'Who, sir?'

'Your mother, Bloomington. Who else? Jesus. Stay with me on this.'

'Yes, sir. Italian, she's always been partial to Italian as I recall. Not to mention Italians. Although she's not too fond of Italian women, but I fancy that's a recent bitterness.'

'Italian it is. She's not a vegetarian? Vegan, is that what they call it nowadays? Anything else weird I should know about?'

'I wouldn't know where to begin, sir. However, Mother has always been a woman of healthy and indiscriminate appetites.'

'Right. I'll ask around and come up with a couple of good restaurants. I'll ask Hunt — he's usually good with this sort of thing. What night? Sooner the better, I say.'

'Perhaps you should check on Imogen's availability first, sir.'

'Sure. I'll check with the little cow this afternoon and get back to you. Great. Excellent work, Bloomington. Carry on.'

Geoffrey Sandler clapped his right hand firmly on James's shoulder and gave it a relaxed squeeze. It was a gesture without reserve, unhurried and open, and James was startled. He looked up and saw a face, literally red with excitement, smiling down at him. James had no answer to such a smile and remained silent as Mr Sandler's legs carried him away at an even greater pace than usual.

The evening would bring rain with it. James was sitting at his desk, 'Push Me, Shove You, Sue Me, Says Who?

Letting the Market Decide' open in front of him, and he could feel the heaviness in the air. A brief storm, the night, and the heat would resume. He had not brought an umbrella.

The office was still and almost silent. The working day was coming to a close and those few employees who had not yet abandoned the workplace for their homes were making their preparations for departure, shuffling papers on desks, opening and closing brief-cases and various satchels. These were the only sounds James could hear – the drum of Mr Sandler's footsteps and the intermittent coughs from the office of Mr Whitely-Smalls had ceased. In fact James could not recall hearing a cough all day, which suggested that Mr Whitely-Smalls himself had been absent, if indeed he was ever present.

How had James failed to notice the cough's absence? He lacked focus. Imogen crowded his mind, although he often confused her, parts of her at least, with Alison and, less often, with his mother. That a picture of Imogen's half-open mouth would be followed by an image of the tips of his mother's ears, all within the space of a second, was cause for some concern. James closed his eyes and inhaled deeply, hoping to sink into the blackness and refocus his thoughts on nothing in particular, on nothing itself. Instead he saw himself sitting cross-legged on an unidentified street corner with Byron Jones, in soiled jeans and a heavy woollen pullover, saying nothing but watching an endless parade of feet passing by, the soles of shoes scuffing softly on the pavement.

When he opened his eyes the image was gone and Oliver was standing above him, a wide grin distorting the corners of his face.

'Jimmy! Mate!'

'Hello, Oliver.'

'What's shaking?'

'Shaking?'

'Yeah, what are you doing?'

'Doing? Nothing, nothing. Just resting my eyes. It's been a busy day. I was about to go home.'

'Home? What the hell do you want to do that for? What's there to do at home? Nothing, that's what. You're coming with me instead.'

'With you?'

'With me. Come on, I'll take you out for a drink. Just me, you and anything else we can find with a firm pair of tits.'

'No, thank you, Oliver. I'm really not in the mood.'

'You don't have to be in the mood. My shout, a few quick drinks around the corner and I'll let you on your merry way. Or your miserable way, whichever you prefer. Come on, mate. Don't make me drink alone. You don't want me to look desperate, do you? Like some dicked-about loser? Just for half an hour or so. There's an Irish pub around the corner, you might have heard of it. Paddy O'Murphy's. Big four-leaf clover out the front? Authentic Irish atmosphere. Owned by an

Armenian guy. Phil something or rather. Starts with an "S" and gets progressively more difficult to pronounce. Nice guy. Met him through a client a few weeks back. Thought I'd drop in and check it out . . .'

'Really, Oliver, I'd much rather just go home.'

'Oh, come on. You owe me this one.'

'Owe you?'

'For Alison. For setting you up with Alison. Things seem to be progressing nicely there.'

'How do you know about Alison and I?'

'Hidden camera, mate. Slipped it into your belt buckle when you weren't looking. How do you think? Trudi told me you saw her again. Whatever makes you happy, Jimmy. As long as you're getting an unload, right?'

'Charmingly put, Oliver.'

'Oh, for fuck's sake, come on! A couple of drinks. Relax a little. And as soon as you say go, we're out of there. Help me out. I need you to ride shotgun.'

'Very well. I'll give you half an hour.'

'Excellent! Then what the fuck are we doing here? Let's go, huh? Meet you out front. Leave your case. Hurry it up.'

The rain was beginning to fall as James and Oliver walked from Yeats' Towers and into the street outside. The sun was gone, at least for now, and the clouds had turned the sky to grey. The sidewalk was filled with pedestrian traffic, flowing quickly in both directions.

Like James, Oliver was without an umbrella. The crowd swelled around them as they walked, Oliver guiding James gently by the elbow. Through the rain James could make out the stern faces of those passing by, their padded shoulders pointing the way forward, to shelter, perhaps to home. He could feel his own wet face take on the same resolute expression as a symbol of solidarity. Even those with umbrellas walked quickly against the rainfall, caught up by the pace of those careless enough not to have anticipated the summer shower.

Oliver spoke directly into James's ear without slowing his pace.

'Jesus, Jimmy! Why the hell does it rain every time I'm with you? Huh, Jimmy? Every time. You're a walking fucking rain cloud. Everywhere we go, we get wet. Whenever I walk alone I'm a regular ray of sunshine. Shines right on me, birds riding my shoulders and singing sweetly in my ears. All God's creatures are my friends, Jimmy – all of them. But they see me with you and they run a fucking mile! Except for the women, which is of course why you're here. Almost there. Up on the left. See the sign?'

James raised his eyes, squinting through the raindrops, and saw a large length of neon tubing mounted against a window, twisted into the shape of a four-leaf clover that glowed absurdly green in the dull light. The name, Paddy O'Murphy's, was spelled out in cursive underneath the clover in a white neon strip. People, groups of men mostly, dressed in suits of varying degrees of style and expense, were heading towards the entrance from both directions. James and Oliver joined the huddle around the door, pushing towards the opening, waiting for admission.

A dark-haired girl in a low-cut white blouse, the frilled sleeves pushed off her broad shoulders, greeted them. Both James and Oliver noticed the tan lines from a bikini top that had tied at the back of her neck. A white lace apron, damp at its edges, was tied at her waist above a flowing green skirt. She smiled as if without effort, although not without a hint of impatience.

'Hello, laddies! Welcome to Paddy O'Murphy's,' she chirped, hoping that the high pitch of her voice would make up for her obviously deficient brogue. 'This way, boys, this way!'

She motioned them to follow her and led them inside a large, smoke-filled room; larger than it had appeared through the window outside, at any rate. A smaller girl, also dark haired, passed them on her way to the door to greet the next customers. She wore the same clothes and the same smile as the first girl. The room was noisy and crowded. To ensure they were heard above the din, patrons crowded towards each other and spoke as loudly as they possibly could, which struck James as anything but sensible behaviour. They pushed their way through the centre of the room to a small wooden table that sat against the far wall. There was a wooden chair, the same pale pine as the table, set at each side of the table. Oliver took off his wet jacket and hung it over the back of the chair facing the front window and sat down. James sat opposite him; he did not take off his jacket. The girl picked up two empty beer bottles from the table and wiped it down with her apron. She was still smiling.

'And what can I be gettin' for ya?'

'Please drop that ridiculous accent.'

'Beggin' your pardon, sir?'

'The accent, whatever it is that you think you're doing. Please stop it at once.'

'Easy, Jimmy. Don't mind him, love. You can use whatever accent you like with me. Maybe we'll try a little French later on, maybe some Italian. I'm fluent in all of the major Romance languages, you know. Bring us a couple of beers. Guinness all right with you, James? It'll have to be Guinness, right? Bring us a couple of mugs of Guinness and we'll take a look at the menu.'

'There is no menu. We've got stew or potatoes, skins or wedges.'

'What's the stew?'

'Irish stew.'

'I guessed that, love. Is it beef or what?'

'Beef.'

'Great. Two bowls of stew and some potato skins to share. Sound good to you, Jimmy?'

James was silent.

'Stew and skins it is! Thanks, love. Hurry back, OK? Jesus, James. Lighten the fuck up, would you? Enjoy the atmosphere – it's all part of the atmosphere. She was doing her best, poor thing. Probably never done an Irish accent before tonight. Cute, too, nice set of tits on her. No need to be nasty to a nice set of tits.'

'Really, Oliver, it was ridiculous.'

'So? Who cares if it's ridiculous? All part of the service. Just let the poor girl do her job. What are you so wound up about, anyway?'

'Nothing, nothing at all.'

'Shit, James, it's like the rod up your arse has a rod up its arse or something.'

'Thank you, Oliver. You know how much I've always enjoyed your colourful turn of phrase.'

'Fuck, James. I brought you here to ride shotgun for me and you start by scaring off the first set of tits that comes our way. I mean, I know she's just a waitress, but even just for the practice, Jimmy . . . Besides, if you kick the night off with a bad vibe it can only get worse. Positive thinking, James, positive. Smile and be polite and you never know whose bed you might end up in. Be a miserable old bastard and even I won't take you home. So tell me about Alison.'

'You know perfectly well that I'm not about to tell you a thing about Alison. She's a very pleasant girl.'

'Pleasant? That's all you're going to give me?'

'I'm not going to give you anything, Oliver. It's none of your business.'

'Oh, come on. As a mate, Jimmy. A few details wouldn't kill you. She talks to Trudi anyway, you know.'

'What she chooses to tell Trudi is her business, not mine.'

'Yeah, well, don't worry about it too much. Trudi doesn't know a thing anyway, besides that you've seen her again. Just fishing. Funny, ever since we fucked, Trudi thinks we've got some sort of mystical connection. I mean, it was fucking terrible. I'm not sure I even want to keep going with it. It seemed like a good idea at the time but now . . . Next, please!'

'I need to go to the bathroom.'

'What? I can't hear a fucking thing in this place.'

'The toilet. I need to urinate.'

'Shit, no need to shout. Thanks for sharing that with me. I think it's over that way, the other side to where we came in.'

James stood up and buttoned his jacket and looked across the room for the men's toilets. There was a constant flow of people walking, stumbling, pushing before his eyes, moving in a swirl around him. The smoke added to his confusion. Why people continued to inflict tobacco smoke on themselves and others when it was now perfectly clear to all and sundry that smoking was not only a dirty, disgusting habit but also a virtual guarantee of an unforgiving and usually terminal disease was beyond James. He could understand the impulse towards death, to self-destruction, but why towards a slow, painful and undignified demise? It made no sense at all. And it made making one's way across an unfamiliar room a deeply unpleasant and hazardous task.

He followed a group of men channelled towards the far left corner of the room, where the constricted body movements and grim expressions clearly indicated the presence of a communal bathroom. Through the haze of smoke he could see a swinging door; the constant flow of those entering and exiting, many using their shoulders against it in a display of force and impatience, ensured that it was never at rest.

As James moved slowly forward he looked at the faces around him. There were men in need of a shave, men in need of a haircut, men in need of a better diet. The few women he saw were smiling unnaturally, exaggerating their happiness to fool not only those around them but themselves. He had no wish to look at their faces, distorted as they were with the effort of laughter, and was suddenly quite terrified of catching their eyes with his own. He looked down at the floorboards, slick with spilled foam, and inched his way forward.

To the right of the bathroom door stood a large cast-iron pot, filled with what appeared to be gold coins, around which the hotel's patrons were giving an unusually wide berth. On top of the pot sat a dwarf, a bottle of whiskey in his tiny right hand.

The dwarf was dressed as a leprechaun, a crumpled white blouse tucked into the elasticised waist of a pair of green felt britches, the britches tucked into white woollen stockings and ending in black leather boots fastened on the side with oversized gold buckles. His face was hidden beneath a dark, shabby beard. Ruddy cheeks and a flattened, porous nose rested uneasily beneath a pair of deep-set, bloodshot and brown eyes. The dwarf was slumped quietly against the wall but his eyes gave a deliberate impression of power and not inconsiderable danger. He raised the bottle to his lips and drank, keeping his eyes open and alert to the movements around him all the while.

James stepped away from the bathroom door and stood before the dwarf, looking down at him and at the gold coins.

'They're chocolate, aren't they?' he said. 'Chocolates wrapped in gold.'

The dwarf looked up at him slowly, taking his measure from the ground up. He wiped the whiskey from his lips and across his beard with the back of his left hand.

'Do I know you, mate?' The dwarf's voice was surprisingly deep and slightly gruff, possibly as a result of the whiskey.

'I don't think so.'

'You look familiar. Been in here before?'

'No, never. I'd like a chocolate, please.'

'What?'

'I'd like a chocolate.'

'Go for your life, mate, but I'm fucked if I'm getting up.'

'Would you mind perhaps shifting to one side?'

'As it happens, I would mind.'

'I see. Please excuse me.'

James bent at the waist and reached his hand towards the chocolate coins. To obtain one that had not melted he knew he would have to reach deep beneath the dwarf's buttocks, which he did. He pulled his hand free, stood up and slowly unwrapped the chocolate before examining it briefly and placing it in his mouth. He was immediately disappointed; the chocolate was of poor quality.

'Fuck me,' said the dwarf. 'Does that mean we're engaged?'

'I beg your pardon?'

'Your hands, mate. Mind your fucking hands.'

'I'm sorry, but I did ask you to move.'

'I'm not paid to move, mate. I'm paid to sit here. Right next to the fucking pisser. Very fucking pleasant, that is. Pained expressions everywhere you look and the smell of piss and lager and more fucking piss drifting out of the fucking door all night.'

'Paid? You mean you're not a real leprechaun?'

'Oh, very fucking funny, mate. Very funny. You're lucky I don't smash this fucking bottle over your poncy head and cut you a new smile from ear to ear for that one.'

'You're a very irritable little man. I'm sure you're also paid to be polite to the patrons. You're certainly not paid to threaten them. A smile and a twinkle in the eye, is that too much to ask?'

'A smile? What sort of fucking comedian are you? You expect me to sit here all fucking night dressed up like a fucking extra from *Darby O'Gill and the Little People* and deal with dickheads like you and like it?'

'I was actually quite taken with *Darby O'Gill* as a child. I'm sure many of the patrons here were. Surely it's your responsibility not to disappoint them.'

'Oh, you're really pushing your fucking luck, mate. Don't think I couldn't take you, you fucking oversized faggot.'

'What's your name?'

'My name?'

'Yes, I'd like to report your behaviour to the management.'

'Dopey.'

'What?'

'Name's Dopey.'

'Your name is not Dopey.'

'Sleepy then. Happy. Doc. Grumpy. Yeah, Grumpy. What the fuck do you need my name for? I'm the fucking dwarf! How many other fucking dwarfs do you see here, mate? How many of them are dressed as leprechauns? Don't you think that might narrow it down?'

'Very well, I'll make my complaint directly.'

'Fine by me, it'll hardly be the first. But it's not easy to replace a dwarf willing to demean himself as a leprechaun at short notice, and if you make one fucking crack about that I'll kill you right now. Dickhead. Are you sure I haven't seen you somewhere before?'

'Quite positive. I'm sure I would have remembered you.'

'Why? Because I'm a dwarf? You're sure to have remembered a fucking midget like me, right? I'll take you right now, you miserable fucking wanker.'

'Your stature has nothing to do with it. It's your winning personality. I'm sure you would have made quite an impression had we met before.'

'Are you taking the piss? Are you taking the fucking piss? Don't be fooled by this stupid fucking outfit, mate – I'll do you. I'll do you right fucking now.'

'Thank you for the chocolate.'

'Where the fuck do you think you're going? I haven't done with you yet, mate. I'll get it. I know you from somewhere. I've seen that ugly fucking face of yours before.'

'Perhaps you have, but we've never met.'

'And just what the fuck is that supposed to mean?'

'Again, thank you for the chocolate.'

'Get back here, you prick. I'll kick your fucking arse right here, in front of all these people. All these big friends of yours. How big are you gonna be then, huh? When a dwarf kicks your faggot arse! That's right, walk away. Walk away, you gutless poofter.'

'Jesus, Jimmy. What the hell was that?'

'An irritable leprechaun, if you must know.'

'A leprechaun?'

'A dwarf actually.'

'Jesus, Jimmy. I can't take you anywhere. First you insult the waitress, now the dwarf. What the hell is wrong with you? Why can't you just kick back and relax?'

'I'm going.'

'What? Don't go. The food'll be here any second. At least stay for the stew. Come on, sit down and wait for the stew.'

'I'd really rather not. I'm sorry, Oliver, but I'm going home.'

'Shit. Piss off then. You're not much use to me now anyway, are you? Every woman in the place just saw you in action. They'll all be steering well clear of the guy who picks on dwarfs. And his smiling idiot friend. Fuck it, maybe we can go somewhere else.'

'I'm going home, Oliver.'

'Fuck. Go on then, go. I'll see you later.'

James made his way carefully towards the door through which he had entered. People surrounded him in all directions and it seemed as if the room itself was falling in on him, barring his escape. A girl at the door, a different girl, he thought, different to the one who had led them in but wearing the same outfit, the same frilled blouse, the same skirt, smiled at him.

'Have yourself a fine evening, sir. Be sure and come back to visit us at Paddy's soon.'

A different girl. Or was it the same girl with different hair? A different face? It didn't matter.

When James walked outside he felt the rain falling in thick drops on the back of his neck, running its way underneath his collar and down along his shoulder blades. The rain had grown heavier and the sky had grown darker. Small groups of people, four, five at the most, each huddled around a single raised umbrella, ran across the street as the traffic lights turned red, laughing as their feet trampled through pools of water newly formed on the road's uneven surface.

James pointed himself in the direction of the railway station and set himself against the rain, walking under awnings where he could. By the time he reached the station the water was beginning to soak through his jacket. He squeezed the excess water from his hair and waited for his train. The rain had lowered the temperature, taking much of the heat out of the night air, but inside the station, underneath the city streets, the air was stale and warm.

The train that arrived had air-conditioned carriages and James could feel the cold air against his wet skin as he settled into his seat. He was thankful his journey was short. He closed his eyes and counted the stops.

The rain had not eased when James alighted the train at Waverton. Few of the dozen or so people walking along the platform had umbrellas and they hurried towards the exit. James outpaced them all, clearing the exit first and beginning his walk home at a steady pace. It was difficult to maintain one's dignity uncovered in heavy rain; the best one could hope for was to remain stoic. James affected his most stoic expression and walked, measuring his way by the streetlights ahead.

He could only see the rain falling in the glow surrounding each light but he could feel it on his exposed skin, his face and hands, and hear it as it struck the ground heavily beneath him. He kept walking down the hill as quickly as he could. The post box was up ahead, the telephone booth beyond that. The rain kept falling.

He passed the post box and noticed (with some satisfaction) that the pizza box had gone, presumably removed by a dedicated and efficient postal worker. He could see the neon glow of the telephone booth up ahead. He slowed his pace to inspect the booth for damage. Even from this distance he could see that its walls remained intact. As he got closer to the booth he could also see that the handset was in good working order. Everything was as he last left it. Except there was now an umbrella standing on its tip, resting against the inner left wall.

James pulled back the glass door to the booth. The umbrella was black and it was, as far as he could tell, of excellent construction. The tip appeared to be solid brass, the weatherproof fabric was double stitched and the handle was a polished hard wood, carved with some subtlety in the shape of a duck's head and beak. It was also bone dry. Someone had left it behind earlier in the day, obviously by accident, a rushed caller, perhaps, who had not returned to collect it. And now it was waiting for James. Finders keepers, as the saying went. Losers weepers. He would take the umbrella, of that he had no doubt. It would be foolish of him not to.

He took the umbrella by the handle and slid the plastic mechanism away from his body to open it. It opened in one smooth movement and locked firmly into place. He raised the umbrella above his head and heard the rain fall fiercely onto the stretched fabric, where it came quickly to a stop before sliding over the elegant curves of the dome now formed above him and cascading over its edges.

Chapter 20

Sophia Salvestrin was waiting for him in the hallway. James entered the house wet to the bone, backing in through the door in order to close his new umbrella. He kept the door open with his hip as he shook the excess water off it. He was smiling as he turned around, umbrella in hand, to find Mrs Salvestrin blocking his way. She was wearing the same white bathrobe he had last seen her in. It was tied firmly at her thick waist. Her arms were folded tightly in front of her body, each hand cradling the opposite elbow. She was not wearing any make-up and the lines around her mouth and eyes were plainly visible. Her hair remained uncombed, a mass of tangled black and silver weaved around her face. James was momentarily startled by her appearance.

'Good evening, Mrs Salvestrin.'

'Hello, James.'

'It's good to see you up and about. Have you been unwell?'

'Who is Alison Gately?'

'I beg your pardon?'

'Alison Gately. Who is she, James?' She held out a piece of torn notepaper. 'I found this in the kitchen. Who is she?'

'I'm sorry, Mrs Salvestrin, but I fail to see how that is any of your business.'

'Who is she, James!'

'She's an acquaintance of mine, if you must know. Please lower your voice.'

'Don't lie to me, James. Who is she?'

'I've already told you. She is an acquaintance.'

'Are you fucking her, James? Is she one of your dirty little whores, James? What is she to you?'

'Really, Mrs Salvestrin, I must ask you to get a grip on yourself. These questions are totally inappropriate.'

'Inappropriate? I happen to think they're very appropriate. How can you possibly say that, James? How can you say that to me? What about us?'

'Us?'

'Us. The two of us. The other night. I know I was drunk and I can't remember all of it very clearly but I remember you naked, James. Oh, I remember that. And you carried me to bed. And in the morning I felt . . . violated. But in a good way, James, in a good way. I knew what you'd done, what we'd done, I mean. It was bound to happen, the two of us under the same roof, the tension–'

'Stop right there, Mrs Salvestrin. If you're making accusations against me I demand that you stop at once.'

'Accusations? No, no, James. It's all right. I know what happened, I wanted it to happen . . .'

'This is absurd. Nothing happened, Mrs Salvestrin. Nothing at all.'

'You're lying, James. I could feel it. I'm a woman of the world, James, I know what happens between men and women. Out there, it happens every day. Out there. I've seen it. You know I've seen it, you've seen it too. I've seen it on television, I've seen it on people's faces in the street. Do you understand me, James? I've seen it on their faces. Arrangements, secret meetings, dark corners of dark rooms, dark houses, dark streets–'

'Mrs Salvestrin, you're being totally ridiculous. Nothing happened. Nothing at all. You were drunk in the bathroom and I took you to your room and laid you, that is to say I placed you, on top of your bed and withdrew, er, left the room. I took no advantage of you, Mrs Salvestrin. None at all.'

'You mean, you just left me there?'

'Yes.'

'Alone?'

'Yes. To be perfectly honest, Mrs Salvestrin, I would

never take advantage of a woman of your advanced years, and certainly not in the condition you were in.'

'Advanced years, James?'

'Relatively speaking, of course. I feel no attraction towards you whatsoever and it's foolish of you to assume otherwise. You are my landlady and while I live under your roof I will abide by your rules and endeavour to treat you with the courtesy and respect such a relationship demands, but that is the extent of our relationship. You were drunk and quite unstable so it comes as no surprise to me that your memory of events is somewhat . . . distorted. However, all I took from you that night, at your invitation I might add, was a bowl of risotto. From the refrigerator. And I enjoyed it very much.'

'You did?'

'Yes, very much.'

Mrs Salvestrin was silent, eyes opened wide as she searched his face for signs of weakness or deceit. She could find none. She began to breathe calmly and deeply through her mouth and nose, filling her lungs with air and slowing the beating of her heart. She kept her arms folded tightly around her chest.

'James, please forgive my . . . assumptions. I'm terribly, terribly sorry. You're a good boy, James, a good boy. And, er, I know you would never take advantage of me. I'm sorry I ever doubted you. But the . . . uncertainty these last few days, not knowing what happened, it just . . . filled my imagination with all sorts of strange ideas.'

'Please, Mrs Salvestrin, don't mention it. And I mean that quite literally. I would prefer that we never spoke of this . . . incident again.'

'Yes, but I'm glad we got it out in the open, so to speak.'

'Please, Mrs Salvestrin – that's enough.'

'Yes, I'm sorry. Please, come in. You're wet. You should change.'

'Yes, I should. Please excuse me.'

He moved quickly, flattening his body against the wall to avoid making contact with her hip. When he had slipped past her she moved to the door and closed it. James could hear the tumblers of the door latch falling into place as he walked through the kitchen to his rooms. The water in his hair and through his clothes weighed him down and he suddenly felt the effort of every step. He was hungry but the idea of eating whatever it was he might have in his refrigerator did not appeal to him.

James often wondered why it was that humans should feel the need to constantly eat, whether indeed it was a biologically determined process or a psychological and socially determined need. It often felt to him like a chore. Surely if people could transcend the need for food, it would, at least on one level, free their minds for other, more useful purposes. But what purposes? What then?

He remembered as a child seeing a man on television, possibly the thinnest man he had ever seen, his body composed almost entirely of bones covered in a transparent, fragile layer of flesh. The man's head was disproportionately large, the roundness of his eye sockets and forehead accentuated by the hollowness of his cheeks. His ears were huge, extending from the bottom of his jaw to almost the top of his head, and his black hair was sparse and unbrushed, like the hair of a newborn baby. The man was in an almost empty gymnasium, dressed only in a pair of gym shorts, socks that bulked around his ankles and canvas running shoes. He was smiling for the camera, which panned back from his face to his emaciated body in the centre of the gymnasium. It was impossible to tell the man's age. The film was in black and white.

The television announcer had proceeded to tell the audience that the man was a Breatharian, that he lived on a diet of air and water alone. According to the announcer, Breatharians believed that the air around them provided all the nutrients the human body needed to function. The man on screen was a shining example of the virtues of Breatharianism and James watched him bench-press a stainless-steel bar, his abdomen sinking below his rib cage as he lay flat on the bench, as a demonstration of his strength.

While a diet of air and water would quickly kill a non-believer, a Breatharian would reap the benefits of a food-free life (although, in general, physical exertion was not recommended and in some cases not even possible). Being a Breatharian was an exercise in mental strength and discipline, an attempt at reaching a purity of thought that James found strangely admirable. He had never seen the man or any other Breatharians on television again.

He found the remote control and turned the television on, as much for the soft light it would provide as anything else. He was not interested in watching it or listening to the voices it generated. A quick glance at the screen revealed a group of five people, four men and a woman, sitting around a semi-circular table and talking, about what he did not know – he had muted the sound as soon as the picture formed on the screen.

The light cast by the television flickered through the room, casting his body in shadow against the walls as he removed his wet jacket, shoes and trousers. He looked up to see Mrs Salvestrin watching him from the doorway. She remained silent as he placed his jacket and trousers on hangers and sat down on his bed to remove his wet socks. Her arms were still folded in front of her.

'I'd like to meet her, James. Alison.' Her voice was flat and distant.

'I fail to see why that would be necessary.'

'It's not necessary. I just want you to know that she is always welcome in my house. All of your friends are welcome here, James. This is your home as much as it is mine. You never bring your friends home. They're always welcome, James. I can cook for you, if you give me some notice, and we can eat together. It's always nice to meet new people, young people. We can talk or I can leave you alone, if you'd prefer. These rooms are yours, James, and you can do as you please in them. If you'd like your friends to stay, to stay for the night — I know we've never talked about this before — it's all right. It's all right, James.'

'I'm terribly tired, Mrs Salvestrin.'

'Sophia.'

'I'm terribly tired, Sophia. I'd like to go to bed. Please, close the door on your way out.'

'Dry your hair before you go to sleep. Goodnight, James.'

'Goodnight.'

James removed his tie and shirt. The water had soaked through the shirt's collar and moved down across his breast and towards his stomach. He found a towel and dried his hair and then his shoulders. He lay back on the bed, his head on the pillow, and watched the faces on the television screen as they continued to talk. When one face spoke, the other faces looked on, smiling knowingly, laughing suddenly, always together, occasionally interjecting and laughing some more. The day had been long and tiring and James's one wish was to bring it quickly and finally to a close by falling into a deep and untroubled sleep. He closed his eyes and listened to the sound of the rain striking softly on the roof tiles above him.

Chapter 21

The sun rose early in the morning, bringing with it sufficient heat to evaporate all traces of the previous night's rain. The morning felt especially tropical to James (he had never been to the tropics, of course, but he recalled several movies set in the steamy jungles of the Pacific during the Second World War which evoked the severity of tropical heat splendidly), the sun quickly and ruthlessly reasserting its authority over the people below it. They would bend to its will, some of them quite literally, before the morning was out.

James was already sweating. He could feel the circles beginning to form under the arms of his freshly pressed shirt, and the musty smell from the dampness that ran from underneath his testicles to his anus and along his inner thighs had already come to his attention as he raised himself from his seat in the crowded morning train. There had barely been room to stand but he had somehow managed to find a seat directly to the right of the carriage doors, squeezing his hips into the space that presented itself between an undersized woman passenger hidden behind an opened newspaper (and hence of indeterminate age and appearance) and a graffiti-covered inner wall.

He was waiting for Brian Jones, standing in the shadow of the concrete tower and watching the resigned faces of the people trudging past him in both directions. They walked mostly alone, tilting their eyes slightly towards the ground and away from the sun. Occasionally they walked in pairs, shoulder to shoulder, talking and smiling at each other, hands shielding eyes. He had noticed two couples walking hand in hand; their pace was slower than that of the rest of the morning crowd.

Soon Brian was standing beside him; James had not seen him approach. He was wearing the same pair of scuffed blue running shoes, what looked to be a new pair of jeans, and a red and black checked pullover that James suspected to be acrylic. He was carrying two folded pieces of cardboard under his right arm.

'Here,' he said. 'I had a feeling you'd be showing up so I brought this along. Figured you might want a seat.' He handed James one of the folded cardboard squares. It was printed on both sides in red and green ink, with a picture of a small boy riding a miniature horse below a logo that read 'PONYBOY TOMATOES' in tall, compressed capital letters.

'There ya go. That's right, spread it out and throw it on the ground. Make sure your back's against the wall. It's easier to concentrate that way. Don't know why. Just easier to have people only walk in front of you. If they're walking all around you, not just in front but behind you too, it makes you feel a little uneasy, a little too small. At least it does for me.'

'I'm not staying long.'

'Sure, whatever. But as long as you stay, you should have somewhere to sit. You look like an idiot hovering over me, and it can't be too comfortable on your haunches like that. Besides, you make me nervous otherwise. Where's your briefcase?'

'My briefcase? Oh, I left it at work yesterday evening.'

'Nothing important in it, huh?'

'No, nothing to speak of.'

'It's kind of a prop, huh?'

'A prop?'

'For show.'

'Certainly not. I use it to carry my papers. I often take my work home.'

'And what is it that you do?'

'I'm a junior editor at Sandler and Harris Publishers.'

'And what is it that you do?'

'I work on a monthly periodical, *Uncommon Cases and Commentary on the Common Law*. I edit submissions on a range of legal topics, get them ready for publication. It's a well-respected journal that makes a valuable contribution to legal scholarship and practice.'

'Sounds exciting.'

'Does it?'

'You really do have a problem with sarcasm, don't you? No, it doesn't sound exciting. It sounds goddamn boring as all fuck.'

'But I do find it exciting. Sometimes. The intellectual challenge, the demands of logic, can be quite stimulating.'

'Stimulating, my arse. Stuck in an office reading a bunch of shit no one cares about? Sounds like a waste of time to me, mate. Is that really what you want to do with your life?'

'What do you mean?'

'Just what I said. What do you think I mean? Is that what you really want?'

'It's got nothing to do with what I want or what I don't want. Work is a necessary part of life. Whether you enjoy it or not is irrelevant. It's essential to the social contract, part of the responsibility that comes with being a member of the wider community.'

'Community? Fucking hell, look around you, James. What sort of community do you see? People don't even fucking talk to each other. They're too scared to look at each other. They're scared of me for just sitting here, and all I'm doing is thinking. That's all. But I can see it, not in their eyes — they don't show me their eyes. I can see it in their bodies, the way they step around me and the other guys out here, as if we're not even there. Suits me just fine, I don't want to be disturbed by some fucking do-gooder anyway. But what are they afraid of? What's so bad about me sitting out here? I don't bother anyone, do I?'

'Not that I'm aware of.'

'That's right, no one. All I'm doing is thinking. Taking my time is all. Is that so hard to understand?'

'No, not at all.'

'Ah, fuck it. Who cares anyway. You don't mind people and they won't mind you. You're a young man, there's plenty of time left for you to think things through, start having your own thoughts, not thinking the way other people want you to think. Don't give me that look – I'm not some raving paranoid conspiracy theorist freak. That's Charlie's line, a few blocks up. He's good for a rant or two when you're in the mood. Nah, it's no great conspiracy, at least not that I can see, but if you don't stop every now and then to think about why you think the way you do, to think about thinking, you just end up thinking without thinking. Do you follow me?'

'Surprisingly enough I think I do.'

'Great. So what's on your mind?'

'My mind?'

'Oh, Jesus, we're not going to have to go through this every time, are we? Look, you're here for something or rather, right? As far as I know, it's the sparkling conversation. That's what I'm assuming, anyway. So what's on your mind.'

'Nothing really. Well, something, I suppose, but I'm not entirely sure. I do enjoy listening to you.'

'Listening's fine. You don't want to talk?'

'Not overly.'

'Nothing to say to me at all, huh? Well, I'm not sure how long I can entertain you, you know? I mean, I've got things to do with my day too. I don't get much thinking done with you around. It's too hard to think and talk at the same time, at least properly. I just end up talking about things I've already thought about.'

'Perhaps we could think together.'

'Together? You can't think together. It's just not the way it's done. You have to think alone. It's the only way. How would I know what you were thinking, anyway? We'd have to talk, and that'd be the end of it.'

'I thought we could sit together and think. Independently. We'd be sitting together, not thinking together.'

'No offence, James, but it sounds a bit fruity to me.'

'Fruity?'

'Joke. I'm joking, mate. The smile's usually a dead giveaway. Besides, you can't sit here all day. You've got to go to work, right?'

'Yes, I probably should.'

'And then there's your mother. She'll be along shortly.'

'Yes, I expect she will be. Mother is nothing if not consistent in her habits.'

'No need to tell me, mate. What's going on with her anyway? Something seems to be worrying her?'

'You've spoken with her, haven't you?'

'Nah, settle down. I can just tell. Last time she was here was a little . . . different. Disconcerting. She didn't say anything but I could tell something was up. To tell you the truth she kind of worried me.'

'Worried?'

'Well, more like frightened. She scared me, mate.'

'She's been scaring me all my life.'

'I can see that.'

'What do you mean by that remark?'

'Nothing, mate. Nothing. Just meant that I could see how she might do that. Still, it can't have been easy on a woman like that, what with your dad going away and all.'

'How do you know that?'

'Know what?'

'That my father left us.'

'You told me, mate. You told me that, didn't you?'

'I'm not sure. Did I?'

'Well, how else would I know?'

'Yes, how else? What did I tell you?'

'Don't remember exactly. Just that your father left when you were little.'

'Disappeared. He disappeared.'

'Yeah, that's right. I remember now. He disappeared

and hasn't shown up since, right? That couldn't have been easy on your mother, mate. I mean, a young woman like that with a young baby, all alone.'

'How did you know I was a baby?'

'Everyone was a baby once, mate.'

'At the time. How did you know that I was a baby at the time? When my father left?'

'You told me, mate. You must have told me, right?'

'I . . . I don't recall. I might have told you – it sounds reasonable enough, doesn't it? But I really don't remember. Perhaps it's the heat playing tricks on me. It does that, doesn't it? The heat? Plays tricks with one's memory?'

'Sure it does, James.'

'Yes, well, I, I think it's best if . . . I think I best be off.'

James stood up quickly and began dusting the seat of his pants. What did this man know and what had he told him? He simply couldn't remember.

'You're clean, mate,' said Brian, smiling up at him. 'That's why you need the cardboard. Works a treat.'

'Thank you. Would you like me to fold it?'

'Just leave it there, I'll look after it.'

'Thank you. I'll be late for work.'

'I guess you will. Go on then. I'll see you later.'

James had already begun walking towards the railway station, stretching out the stiffness in his legs and lower back as he emerged from the shadow of the concrete tower. The air around him was heavy and stifling and he felt the full weight of the sun on his crown. Soon it would compress his spine, as it had compressed the spines of those around him, the hollow faces that passed him by.

The heat had made him weary; his head lolled heavily on his neck as he walked. Looking down at his feet he saw that he was moving in slow motion, the pavement blurring into his shoes below him. He reached instinctively for his nose but found no trace of blood, not a single trickle.

Veronica could hear her every breath, resonant and full of life itself, behind the protective screen of the Safe-T Services Corporation (of Boise, Idaho) disposable particulate respirator. She was concentrating on the magnified rhythm of her breathing, blocking out the heat and noise of the day as she walked towards the man on the flattened cardboard box. Even from this distance the top of his head, loose curls covering the protrusion of the skull, was disturbingly familiar. As she moved closer it was the slump of the shoulders, the raised curves of the eyebrows, and the dullness of the eyes themselves (even pointed at the ground, she could make out their distinct lack of vitality) that demanded her attention. It was James, she was certain. Her son. Logically, of course, she was perfectly aware that the man before her was not her son. But on a more funda-mental level, in a way she knew she would never be able to articulate, Veronica was certain this man was a vision of her son.

Her darling son. This is what he was going to look like. She could not divine any resemblance to Cecil — Cecil was far more handsome than this scruff — or to herself. She had always hoped to find a hint of familiarity in James, her own face looking back at her. A feature, perhaps, that she recognised as her own. It had never materialised. It did not materialise now. How was it that a child, the product of its two parents, could resemble neither parent? That it could stand so completely apart?

All babies were essentially featureless, she knew that. James had been especially so, a misshapen lump of dough dusted with flour. Without verifiable proof, distinguishing marks, features of any kind, she could not be sure that the child was really hers. Surely she would feel that connection, that bond, that all mothers are supposed to feel towards their children? Veronica felt nothing of the kind. In fact, it was fair to say that as she lay under the stiff sheets of the hospital bed and the child was first presented to her, she felt precisely nothing. Nothing at all. Cecil was standing beside her, holding her hand tightly in his own. She could not read his lopsided smile, but then she rarely could.

She knew that she would never breastfeed this child, that she would not have its wet, fleshy mouth sucking at her nipple, its tiny pink fingers clutching at her breast, the soft fingernails scratching at her skin. She was aware of recent research, as ceaselessly reported in the daily newspapers and on television news reports, suggesting that children who had been breastfed displayed signs of intellectual and developmental advantage over those who had been fed formula milk, and that this advantage would continue to manifest itself in the child's adult life. The whole idea struck Veronica as absurd and somewhat insidious. Why were women being coerced into abandoning their bodies, their very sense of self, with a thinly veiled threat of a dimwitted, possibly retarded child as a permanent reminder of their selfishness?

Her eyes were still focused on the man sitting cross-legged before her. He knew she was standing over him, looking down. He always knew. Sometimes she would see his eyes climb along her legs and up to her face but his gaze would always quickly return to the patch of concrete directly in front of him. He sat perfectly still, his body barely rising with its intake of breath. Passive, inert, almost lifeless, he would not challenge her right to examine him.

This man was not her son. He was disgusting. Worthless. Useless. He would not bring her closer to James. She had hoped for some sort of insight into her son's life, an understanding not just of who he would be, but of who he was, and she had deceived herself into thinking that this street person could provide it. Of course he could not.

There was little point in coming here, day after day. This man existed, and that was the only important fact she would ever learn from him. She no longer wished to look at him; no, not for another second. She smoothed her skirt along the tops of her thighs and walked quickly away, disappearing into the circle of people that formed around her.

Chapter 22

Something terrible was happening to James. Betty knew it. It was not like him to be late for work, which lately he was making an unwelcome habit of. If he was going to be late, he would certainly follow the required procedure and call the office. At least, he once would have. The James Betty knew and respected a week ago would have called her and let her know he was running late and given her an approximate time of arrival. There was a problem with the trains; he had to stop by the university law school library to research a particularly compelling topic; he was feeling a little nauseous or gaseous and thought it wise to see a doctor: all perfectly valid reasons why he might be late for work.

Of course, until recently James had never been late for work. Not a single day. And he had never forgotten to wish Miss Palmer a good morning. And it was always 'Miss Palmer'. James had never addressed her as 'Mrs Palmer' (as others, including Mr Sandler himself, sometimes did, even when they all knew full well that she was not and had never been married) and certainly never as 'Betty'.

When he did arrive he seemed so . . . unsettled. As if something was bothering him, something terrible. Perhaps it had something to do with his mother, that strange woman in the mask. The mask was odd and a little off-putting. There was nothing friendly about a woman in a mask like that. And why would she want to cover her face? Disfigurement? There were no signs of scarring or marks of any kind elsewhere on her face and neck, none that Betty could see anyway. Besides, she carried herself too straight, too tall, to be disfigured. Perhaps the mask was for some sort of medical complaint, an illness or sickness of some kind. Was she contagious? Terminally ill? Dying? She was dying. That would certainly explain why a sensitive boy like James would be a little unbalanced. His mother, it had to be his mother. She was now an almost regular visitor. More regular than she had been before, when she was not sick. In fact Betty could not recall her ever visiting her son in the office before. Ever. The sickness must have come unexpectedly. Sudden. Sickness these days was always sudden, 'out of the blue', the empty blue sky above them.

No. She was leaping to too many conclusions. She

was assuming the worst. Why was she always assuming the worst? Always. Bad things happened to people all the time, it was true. Random, horrible, evil things. But good things happened too, only less often and always at the end of the bulletin, after they'd done the sport and the weather for the next day, so the host could say good night with a smile. With warmth. Real, human warmth. It all worked out in the end. She just had to remember, good things happened too. She would try not to worry about James, because good things happened too. It would make the morning pass much faster.

She could see James coming up the steps, the sun from the street reflecting off his forehead, slick with sweat. He did not look at all composed; he wasn't carrying his briefcase. He always carried his briefcase with him of a morning. He looked strange without it, confused. It was a confusion Betty was beginning to share. When he saw Betty looking at him, James aimed his eyes to the ground and stepped quickly around her desk, passing by without a word.

'Bloomington!' It was Mr Sandler. His eyes flashed wildly in their sockets as he struggled to contort his face into something resembling a smile.

'Good morning, sir.'

'Oh no, you don't, Bloomington. Not this time. In my office, right now. You and I need a little chat. Now.' He turned and sped away for his corner office; James was expected to follow, and he did.

James had not been inside Mr Sandler's office since the day he was first interviewed for his position at Sandler and Harris. He was not sure that Mr Sandler had been in his office since that day either, such was the man's capacity for constant motion. Mr Sandler's preferred managerial style was to stalk the floor according to his own peculiar pattern, admonishing employees, when it was needed (which was often), as he stood over them. If they raised themselves from their chairs and got to their feet, the illusion would be ruined. At Sandler and Harris every wayward employee recognised the need to stay seated.

Geoffrey Sandler was not comfortable behind a desk (a fact James could confirm from his one previous encounter with his desk-bound publisher), wriggling unhappily in his chair as his extended feet struggled to make contact with the ground below, like a child fidgeting on the lap of an overexuberant department-store Santa Claus at Christmas, longing for relief. James followed him through the office door and watched him cautiously circle the chair behind his desk. James took the seat opposite, across the solid mahogany top, and waited for Mr Sandler to settle himself into the chair.

The office itself appeared unchanged. The furniture (the desk, a large bookshelf against the right wall, a grey metal filing cabinet opposite) favoured function over form. The only decoration was a portrait of Mr Sandler himself, painted (rather haphazardly, in James's opinion) in the style of William Dobell. It was not a flattering portrait and the fact that it hung directly behind and above Mr Sandler's head proved somewhat distracting. James did his best to focus his eyes on the real Mr Sandler's face but could not resist the occasional comparative glance at his painted likeness. Both faces wore an expression of violent disapproval.

'What do you think this is, Bloomington?'

'What do I think what is, sir?'

'This. This office. The job you're supposed to be doing here.'

'I think it's a fine and noble profession, sir.'

'Oh, for fuck's sake – spare me the bullshit.'

'Sir?'

'You're late, Bloomington. Again. You might say, at least the other employees might say, that you're making a fucking habit of it. You just stroll in off the street, dripping with sweat, which I sincerely hope is your own, and expect no one to notice? It's a small office, Bloomington, word gets around and it gets around fast.'

'I'm sorry, sir.'

'Sorry isn't good enough, Bloomington. We've spoken about this before. You're trying to take advantage of me, aren't you, Bloomington? You're trying to take advantage of my relationship with your mother.'

'Pardon me for saying this, sir, but you really don't have a relationship with my mother.'

'Is that a threat? Is that a fucking threat? Are you threatening me? Me, Bloomington?'

'Of course not, sir. Please, sir! I'd feel much more at ease if you'd return to your seat. And please put down that paperweight, attractive as it is. Yes, it really does look very solid, sir. I can see why you admire it so. That most certainly was not a threat. I was merely pointing out that you have yet to establish a proper relationship with my mother. I can hardly be accused of trying to take advantage of a relationship that does not yet exist. Given our best efforts, however, I'm sure the relationship will blossom.'

'Blossom?'

'Yes, sir.'

'Yes, well, I still don't like it, Bloomington. And it's not just your late arrivals that are bothering me. I can appreciate that there may well be valid excuses for lateness, even habitual lateness – no, don't bother giving me any, I'm sure that's not necessary. But Whitely-Smalls tells me that your work hasn't been up to standard lately.'

'Tells you, sir?'

'Well, of course he doesn't actually tell me – I haven't spoken to the man in years, not since he came back from Cairo. No one has. He slipped me a note under the door.'

'Cairo, sir?'

'Yes, Cairo. El Qahira. It's the capital of Egypt, the largest city in Africa and the Middle East. But that's beside the point. The point is, he tells me your work is getting sloppy. That's not like you, Bloomington.

Whitely-Smalls has a high opinion of you, thinks you're a fine junior editor. But your progress of late has been anything but satisfactory. Well? Don't just sit there. What have you got to say for yourself?'

'About dinner, sir.'

'Yes?'

'Has Imogen confirmed her availability? Mother is most anxious that we set a date.'

'Is she?'

'She most certainly is, providing that the four of us will be able to attend, of course.'

'Of course, of course.'

'A horse is a horse, of course, of course.'

'What?'

'And no one can talk to a horse, of course.'

'Who's talking to a horse? What the fuck are you babbling about, Bloomington?'

'Dinner. We were talking about dinner. And Imogen's availability.'

'She'll be there. I've had a word to Imogen and she'll be delighted to attend. How does Thursday sound?'

'It sounds fine to me, sir. I'll have to check with Mother before I can give you final confirmation, but I'm sure she'll be able to make it.'

'You're sure?'

'Quite sure. Have you picked the restaurant?'

'Yes, a new little place on Norton Street, just outside the city. It's called Mama Luigi's. Strange name, I know, but what can you expect from wogs? Hunt tells me it's obscenely expensive and that the waiters are all arrogant, impertinent little cunts in tight black t-shirts. Not that I really give a shit what they wear, but it's a good sign, right? The ruder the staff, the better the food. Besides, it's all part of the atmosphere. That's what Hunt says, anyway.'

'Sounds delightful. I'm sure Mother will be thrilled.'

'You're sure?'

'Quite sure.'

'That's great news. Fine work, Bloomington, fine work.'

'Thank you, sir.'

'But we're still going to have to do something about your arrival times. I can't have you coming in late all the time, if only for the sake of the other employees. Office harmony, you know how it is.'

'Yes, sir. I'll do my best to arrive on time and I'll endeavour to improve the quality of my work.'

'That's all I wanted to hear from you, son. Back to work with you.'

'Yes, sir.'

James got to his feet and slid the chair he had been sitting on under the desk. He could feel that he was being scrutinised, which added to his sense of discomfort. As he opened the door to return to his own desk he looked over his shoulder to see both of Mr Sandler's faces smiling back at him with barely contained joy.

. . .

'Wake up, Jimmy!'

'Oh, excuse me, sir. I was . . . I was just checking a point of evidence.'

'Jimmy, it's me.'

'Oliver?'

'Who were you expecting? Jesus, Jimmy, were you asleep?'

'I was . . . I was just resting my eyes, Oliver. What time is it?'

'It's 5.45. Thereabouts, anyway. Looks like this place is winding down. So what have you got planned for your evening?'

'My evening? Nothing. To be honest, I haven't given it much thought. I should probably take some work home. I haven't really been keeping up of late.'

'Having trouble keeping it up, Jimmy? I think I can help.'

'Please, Oliver, I'm not in the mood.'

'No, seriously, James, I've got just the thing – me, you, Alison and Trudi hitting the town for a double date.'

'I'm sorry, Oliver, but it's not possible.'

'It better be possible, mate. I've already organised everything.'

'What?'

'They're meeting us at the pub.'

'Which pub?'

'Paddy O'Murphy's.'

'I'm sorry, Oliver. I don't care what arrangements you've made, it's out of the question.'

'Oh, come on, James. It's a good pub. I like it in there. The stew was really good. Fucking great, in fact. And they won't remember you in there, they really won't, if that's what you're worried about. Probably different staff every night, and it's not like they'd have put up a "Wanted: Wanker" poster just for you. Besides, it'd be more like "Unwanted: Wanker", wouldn't it?'

'Very amusing.'

'You'd look great on a poster, Jimmy. Stick-on bandito moustache, a bit of a poncho happening, ten-gallon hat. I won't even mention the spurs, for fear of turning you on. And besides, when was the last time you saw Alison? She wants to see you.'

'Whether she wants to see me or not is entirely immaterial, Oliver. I have work to do.'

'Oh, come on, James. I'm really getting sick of pleading with you to have some fun. A few drinks, that's all. Maybe dinner afterwards, if you're in the mood. It's not going to kill you. You'll have plenty of time to work tomorrow.'

'Perhaps just one drink. But I want it understood that I'm free to leave at any time.'

'Fuck, James – no one's trying to hold you captive. Piss off whenever you like. I'll come back down in fifteen minutes or so and we'll do it, OK? And try to wake yourself up a bit. You look a little dozy. Want to come up and use my bathroom?'

'No, thank you. Just give me a minute and I'll be fine.'

'Right. See you in a while.'

James watched Oliver bound away from his desk and towards the elevators. There was an energy to his movements, a sense of excitement about him, which James could never share. In fact, in all the years James had known Oliver, he had yet to determine whether the excitement was genuine or not, or an element of a facade, perhaps, that sheltered a more delicate soul. This was the hypothesis advanced by a certain malleable girl from their university days (why she had felt compelled to share her theory with James was still beyond him). James, however, was inclined to suspect that if Oliver did indeed have a soul (which was possible), it would be anything but delicate. Unfortunate as it may have been, it was likely that Oliver was all that he seemed to be and nothing more. In James's experience, people often met but rarely exceeded his expectations of them. So far Oliver had failed to prove an exception.

He looked about the office. The few employees present when he and Oliver began their conversation had now departed. It was still light outside; the sun showed no sign of weakness or lethargy and continued to scorch the earth below it. It would continue to do so for at least another hour before it faded into the night sky.

James tidied his desk and shut down his computer. He would gather his papers and retrieve his briefcase from underneath his desk and wait for Oliver in the foyer. As he stood, he heard what he thought to be a shuffling noise, paper shuffling, from behind the closed door of the central office of Mr Whitely-Smalls. He stopped in front of the door and listened, closing his eyes and holding his breath in an effort to identify even the softest sound. Nothing. He knocked at the door, three sharp raps with the knuckles of his right hand.

'Mr Whitely-Smalls? Sir? It's James Bloomington.'

Nothing.

'I wanted to apologise for the poor quality of my work recently. You see, I spoke to Mr Sandler today.'

Nothing. Still James stood by the door, his ear pressed against it. He spoke slowly and carefully, projecting his voice through the wooden fibres of the door.

'I've always wanted to visit Cairo. It must be very beautiful.'

A loud, violent cough, quickly smothered by a hand-kerchief, erupted from behind the door. James kept still, listening, waiting. But he would hear nothing more. Abandoning the door, he walked to the foyer and waited for Oliver.

'You might want to try smiling a little, Jimmy. Might help you to relax.'

This was not new advice from Oliver, and James saw no new reason to respond. They were walking with and against the afternoon crowd, to Paddy O'Murphy's. The sun was shining straight into their eyes. Oliver took a pair of black-framed sunglasses from a black leather case he removed from his top jacket pocket. The suit was new, a dark-grey summer weight, flannel by the look of it. The cut was excellent, accentuating Oliver's shoulders and drawing attention away from his waist. This was obviously not an off-the-rack suit and James was impressed (although he stifled any urge he may have felt to compliment Oliver and they continued to walk in silence). Oliver held his head high and straight; eyes shielded, he dared to square his jaw and look directly into the sun above. James kept his eyes aimed at the tops of his shoes, squinting as the sunlight reflected off their polished surfaces with every step.

'Head up, Jimmy. We're here.'

A dark-haired girl in a white blouse and green skirt stood inside the door. She was not wearing an apron. It was the same girl. Or was it? James could not remember her face in any detail (did she wear her hair up or down?), and the fact that Oliver greeted her with a familiar smile meant nothing: Oliver treated everyone he met to the same broad grin. To the best of James's knowledge he kept no special smile in reserve for those he actually knew. The girl responded with a faint smile of her own but James could not be sure if it was a smile of recognition or merely a smile of professional courtesy. The latter seemed more likely as the girl proceeded to lead them to a table in the far right corner of the room and take them through the menu (which had not changed since their last visit) with a marked lack of interest. She did not attempt to affect an Irish accent at any stage. Oliver explained they were expecting company and would prefer to wait until that company arrived before placing any order. (Of course, if for any reason their guests failed to arrive, she was more than welcome to come back and join them, and could expect to find a warm and comfortable seat in his lap.)

It was still early and there was no rain outside to drive people through the door, so the room had yet to fill. Waitresses moved listlessly from table to table; patrons were spaced irregularly across the room, standing or seated loosely around tables in small, conspiratorial groups. James let his left hand fall beside his chair; he had stood his briefcase upright beside the chair, as was his habit, and he was feeling the contours of its plastic handle, running his fingers and palm across its familiar, smooth surface. Seated opposite, Oliver smiled his smile and looked around the room, craning his neck to ensure that he covered its entirety.

'Girls aren't here yet.'

'No.'

'Guess they're closing up the shop.'

'Probably.'

'Anything you want to tell me about Alison before they get here?'

'Such as?'

'You know.'

'I'm not sure that I do.'

'No, I'm not sure that you do, either. She's got a tidy body on her, that's for sure.'

'Whatever you say, Oliver.'

'Whatever I say? Jesus, that's not like you, James. It's never whatever I say. We both know how danger-ous that could be. C'mon, at least put up a fight. I was expecting some indignation. A little of that a-gentleman-never-tells shit.'

'Sorry to disappoint you.'

'You are a constant disappointment to me, James. One big disappointment after another. But at least you're consistent. And no matter what you will and won't tell me, I know for a fact you're fucking Alison, and that knowledge fills me with joy. Genuine joy, James. I'm thrilled for you, mate, really I am. You should listen to me more often.'

'Yes, I probably should.'

'You know, if you really want to thank me, you'll take a few snapshots of her next time you, uh, get the opportunity.'

'Snapshots?'

'With a camera, Jimmy. Hell, a video camera's your best bet. You can set it up so she won't notice a thing. Throw it under a towel or something, just make sure you leave the lens sticking out. And the sensor. Move-ment. The camera reacts to movement and turns itself on and you're away . . .'

'Whatever you say, Oliver.'

'And once we've got her on video, we'll use the tape for blackmail, OK? String her up and take turns, what do you say to that?'

'Yes, Oliver. Sounds lovely.'

'Are you even listening to me? Hey, how many fingers am I holding up?'

'Pardon?'

'Never mind. Listen, why don't you head over to the bar and get us a couple of drinks? Guinness for me. Grab one for yourself too – here, take a tenner. That should cover it. Go on, move it. Bar's that way . . .'

James took the ten dollar note from the table and followed the direction of Oliver's outstretched hand. He could see the bar and the steward standing behind it. The steward was wearing a black vest over a white shirt, both of which seemed too small to contain the body within. An absurdly large green bow tie was clipped around the thick muscles of his neck, its edges falling limply across his broad chest. He was wiping a glass tumbler inside and out with the end of a thin strip of towel that lay across the top of the bar. He looked up as James approached, continuing to wipe the tumbler with a slow, circular motion.

'Top of the morning to you, sir. And what can I be getting you on this fine summer's day?' He spoke in a flat, low voice, with no trace of an Irish accent. Although he was relieved not to hear another ridiculously overemphasised and inappropriate brogue, James was nevertheless offended by the steward's lack of effort. The man's job demanded a certain level of enthusiasm, real or otherwise. He was evidently bored, as well he might be, given the nature of his work. But while he remained behind that bar, he had a role to fill.

'If you'd care to consult the rather gaudy timepiece behind you, which I presume is some sort of cheap, imitation Harrison, or perhaps your wrist-watch, you would find that it is now the early evening. It is not the morning.'

'Top of the early evening to you, then. And what can I be getting you as this fine summer's day comes to a close?'

'I'd like two pints of Guinness, please. And I'd prefer a more generous level of service.'

'Generous level of service?'

'Yes, generous. A smile would be a nice place to start, perhaps followed by a leer and a wink. A bit of playfulness with the customer. Something a little hearty, a little more . . . well, a little more Irish, frankly. This is supposed to be an Irish pub, is it not?'

'That's what the sign says.'

'I think you'll find that the sign does not actually say anything of the kind, but the four-leaf clover certainly does imply it. As such, I think a customer is entitled to expect a certain level of banter with the staff.'

'Which would you prefer? The banter or the beer?'

'I'd prefer both. I assume the price of the beer will be inflated regardless. It only seems fair to expect a generous level of service to make up for such inflation.

Or would you prefer that I had this conversation with your manager?'

'I know who you are.' The steward's cracked lips stretched across his teeth to form a broad smile; the man was obviously pleased with himself, as if he had just uncovered whatever secret James had been trying to conceal. James was momentarily stunned.

'I beg your pardon?'

'You. Tommy told me about you.' The smile had yet to fade.

'Tommy?'

'The leprechaun who used to work here. Sat right over there, on the pot of gold. You remember the leprechaun, right? Little guy, green suit, bushy beard. You wanted to complain to the manager about him too, right?'

'Perhaps I did. That leprechaun was a very disagreeable little man.'

'He's not a real leprechaun, you know. He's a dwarf.'

'Yes, of course I know he's a dwarf.'

'Skeletal dysplasia, that's what it is with Tommy. He warned me about you. Warned everyone about you. Said we should all watch out for the uptight smartarse with the shitty perm.' His smile had grown even wider, threatening to extend beyond the square edges of his jaw. He was smirking now: the grin had become an unrestrained smirk.

'Now I really must insist on seeing the manager.'

'Settle down, mate. I figured you'd get a laugh out

of it, that's all. I can tell from here it's not a perm. You've gotta laugh, right? No one ever really listened to Tommy. Any trouble he got in, he always made for himself. Short tempered, if you'll pardon the expression. But loveable all the same.'

'I didn't find him the least bit loveable.'

'You weren't the only one, mate. We had to let him go just yesterday.'

'Let him go? Where?'

'We had to fire him, mate. He glassed another customer, third one this month, and that was it.'

'Glassed?'

'You know, you smash a bottle and use the broken glass. He glassed the bugger all right. Just missed a major artery. Wasn't pretty, blood everywhere. Now, what can I get you again?'

'Two pints of Guinness.'

'Two pints of the black stuff coming right up.'

James could feel the nausea rising from the pit of his stomach as he watched the dark, thick liquid flow from the tap until the soft, white foam appeared, spilling over the rounded rims of the tilted beer glasses. The foam gathered where the soft flesh of his palms met each glass as he took them from the bar and walked back to his seat, suddenly unsteady on his feet.

'Back so soon, Jimmy? I just saw the girls come in and head straight for the toilet. Typical, huh?'

James placed the glasses and Oliver's change on

the table and returned to his seat. His forehead was covered with sweat; still the beads continued to form.

'Shit, Jimmy. It's not that hot in here, mate. What's wrong with you?'

'Wrong? Nothing. Actually, I don't think I'm feeling particularly well.'

'Cheer up, mate. Smile for the girls.'

Alison was walking across the room with Trudi, the two of them smiling and laughing softly, apparently at a shared joke. She held herself tall and straight, hair falling across her forehead. She smiled at James, took a chair and placed it directly next to his, seating herself close and letting her arm fall gently across his. Her hand came to rest on the inside of his thigh. She turned her face away from him and continued her conversation with Trudi, who was now seated next to Oliver.

'Oh, I never thought she'd leave, Trude, never!'

'I know – she must have tried on everything we had in stock, in four or five sizes, too! And she looked like a dog in all of it.'

'Oh, I know. She was just too heavy. I mean, even if she lost a few kilos it'd be hopeless. She might squeeze into a few things, but they're just not cut for a woman of that build. Especially the new range.'

'I know. She was in the wrong store, poor dear, but you can't tell them, can you? You just have to stand there and smile.'

'There was this woman in the store, James, and we just couldn't get her to leave, right, Trude?'

'I thought we were going to be stuck with the fat cow all night!' Oliver joined Trudi and Alison in their laughter, faces stretching and distorting with the effort.

'Never mind, girls!' he said. 'You're out on the town with us now. And you won't have to watch us try on any clothes, right, James? Except for your underwear, Trudi, I'll be trying them on again later. They were a little on the snug side, but you can't beat silk for that undeniably feminine feeling. Right, Jimmy?'

James could feel Alison's fingers squeezing the flesh of his thigh as she laughed along with Trudi and Oliver. The heat from her palm was unbearable, burning through the fabric of his trousers, and he could feel the sweat flowing freely from his temples and along both sides of his jaw. The room itself was closing in on him; fragments of conversations, hideous laughter, reverberated through his head. He wiped his forehead with the palm of his hand and turned to see Alison looking straight at him, lips drawn from her teeth in a canine snarl. Her eyes were two perfect spheres in their sockets, her skin too tight for her skull. And still she continued to laugh.

James stood quickly, hitting his knees against the underside of the table as he steadied himself on the thin wooden arms of his chair. He began to speak almost immediately, even before he could straighten his body to its full height.

'I'm sorry,' he said, his voice clear and unrushed. 'I'm not feeling terribly well. Please excuse me.'

His thigh knocked heavily against the table, rattling the glasses but not knocking them over, as he stood and then stooped to pick up his briefcase. He freed himself from Alison's grasp and evaded Oliver's outstretched hand. He could hear them calling his name, voices high and shrill, but he did not stop to look back as he made his way for the door, moving as quickly as his bloodless legs would allow.

The sun had all but disappeared when James stepped into the street; only a faint orange glow lingered above the towering office blocks that surrounded him. The street was cast in continuous shadow. It was still light but much of the heat of the day was gone, carried away by a gentle southerly breeze sweeping across the city. James could feel his entire body coated with a thick, sickly film of sweat, large areas of his flesh sticking to the insides of his shirt and trousers. He was aware of a sudden chill creeping down his spine, the sweat on his face and neck evaporating quickly into the air as he walked towards the railway station.

As he walked, his blood resumed something of its regular flow throughout his body but it also gathered at his extremities at an alarming rate, swelling his hands and feet. His steps felt unusually leaden; his shoes were suddenly too tight for his feet, and he could feel the hardened strips of leather tight around his ankles. The shoes, standard black Oxfords, were not new, but after five months of almost daily wear they retained a degree of hostility towards his feet, particularly towards his left heel, that continued to amaze him. A new blister would form before he was home.

He moved through the ticket turnstile at the station and up the stairs to his platform, where he was relieved to find an empty aluminium bench. The platform was only sparsely populated with post-rush-hour commuters, most of whom hid themselves from view behind broadsheet newspapers. The bench would be uncomfortable but he was grateful for the opportunity to rest his feet. As he sat, he heard the static crack from a loudspeaker above his head. An announcement would follow; James knew from bitter experience that it was likely to be unintelligible, thanks to both the poor quality of the public address system and the announcer's heavily accented English (probably Mediterranean).

To James's surprise, the announcer's message was delivered in clear, if somewhat nasal, unaccented English.

'Attention, passengers on platform three. Due to a signal failure at Central, trains are running late and out of order. City Rail apologises for any inconvenience.'

James was not particularly inconvenienced. As long as he could sit in peace, he did not mind waiting. The platform was largely silent (except for the general murmur of discontent that immediately followed the announcement but soon subsided) and the underground air was cool and reassuring. But the tranquillity would not last: he looked up to see a young woman smiling as she approached the bench with the obvious intention of taking a seat. There were empty benches further along the platform but, rather than walk any further, she had decided she would share James's bench. This was the price he paid for sitting at the bench nearest the stairs. He shifted his buttocks along to the left edge of the bench, ceding authority to the right side.

She was probably in her mid-twenties, her long, silver-blonde hair circled into a bun that sat at the base of her neck. She was dressed conservatively, a loose-fitting white blouse falling over a floral-patterned skirt. Her features were almost masculine, although her flawless, pale complexion ensured that had she indeed been a man, she would have been an exceedingly pretty one. The general effect of her face was further softened by a pair of large, pale-blue eyes that moved slowly from side to side as she followed the text of the paperback she had opened as she sat down. Despite the heat of the day and her general solidity, she looked fresh and clean, and James was pleased to discover that her scent was equally pleasant. He began to resent his own musky odour. He was about to look away when he was struck by the title of her book: *Learned Optimism.*

'*Learned Optimism?*'

She looked up from the book, greeting his question with a welcoming and patient smile.

'Learn-ed,' she said. 'It's pronounced "learn-ed".'

'I believe you're mistaken. Given the context, I'm sure it's simply, *Learned Optimism*. What a ridiculous title for a book.'

'Why do you think it's ridiculous?' Her voice was gentle but insistent.

'Surely optimism is something that can't be learned or taught. It's part of a person's very nature: either you're an optimist or you're a pessimist. It's one of the fundamentals of a person's being, part of their unchangeable make-up.'

'Oh, no. The book makes it very clear in chapter one that you can change who you are, if only you want to change. All you have to do is want it. Anyone can be an optimist if they just learn to apply the principles of positive thinking. Identifying the right time to be an optimist is the first step, knowing that you're faced with a choice: to be a pessimist or an optimist. To see the glass as half empty or half full.'

'Oh, dear.'

'No, really. It works!'

'But there are certain things, certain parts of personality that are unchangeable. A person's essence, if you will, remains constant, despite any indoctrination to the contrary. Even if a pessimist learns to apply the principles of optimism, that person remains essentially, at their essence, a pessimist. You may be a pessimist trying to be an optimist, but you're still a pessimist. The whole notion is absurd.'

'I think I see what you mean. You're a very smart man, Mr . . .?'

'Bloomington. James Bloomington.'

'You're a very smart man, Mr Bloomington.'

'Please, call me James.'

'Thank you, James. It's a thrill for me to talk to another educated person and I really do see what you mean. Some things about themselves people can't change.'

'Exactly.'

'Like their skin colour.'

'I was thinking more of their internal characteristics, but I suppose skin colour is an example.'

'Oh, it's the perfect example. No matter what he does, a black is always black. And white people, like you and me, are always white.'

'I beg your pardon?'

'Don't you see? A nigger will always be a nigger and people like you and me will always be members of the white race.' She was still smiling sweetly, looking intently into his eyes.

'What on earth are you talking about?'

'The great Aryan brotherhood, silly! And the sisterhood. I'm a sister from ADFAB – Aryan Daughters For A Better Tomorrow. We drop the "T" to make it sound better. It's much nicer that way, don't you think?'

'You're a Nazi? A self-improving Nazi?'

'Oh, please don't use the nasty "N" word. It's not

like that anymore. We've got nothing against niggers, or even the Jews. We're not too crazy about Asians, of course, but nobody is these days. It's the Zionists who are the biggest threat, the real enemy of the white race, and the Zionist Conspiracy controls World Government, but everybody knows that. Not all Jews are Zionists – that's just plain discrimination. They did kill Jesus, Our Lord and Saviour, but that's historical fact. And there are plenty of Zionists who aren't even Jewish, even some white people are Zionists. But they're just doing like you said: fighting against their very nature. They all need to come back to the fold. Would you like to come back to the fold?' She reached across her body, revealing an ample bosom, and grasped James's hands in hers. He pulled his hands away quickly, lurching further across to the left so that only one buttock, his right, remained in contact with the bench.

'Please, stop right now.'

'Oh, James, what's wrong? You should come to a meeting. Someone smart and handsome like you would fit right in. You can't come to ADFAB, of course – that's just for the sisters. But you should go and meet with the Aryan Sons. Aryan Sons Surviving For Action Today. We don't use the acronym, it's just "Aryan Sons" for short. But the Sons hold regular socials with the Daughters. We get all dressed up! They look so dashing in their black boots! And you'd look dashing too, James! Although you're really quite dark, aren't you? Dark hair. That curl. Dark eyes. You're not French, are you?'

'No, I am not French!'

'It's all right if you are. We've got lots of French brothers. We're all white underneath! James? Where are you going, James? Don't run away. I thought we could sit together on the train! Come back! I wanted to give you a flyer for the next meeting!'

He heard her voice trail into the distance as he hurried along the platform, sheltering behind an automatic snackfood dispenser as soon as he judged himself far enough away from her gaze. He stood with his back pressed against the machine until the train pulled up alongside the platform, waiting until the last possible moment before throwing himself through the doors of the front carriage.

It was a pair of new shoes. Waiting for him in the telephone booth. He should have known, as soon as his feet began to hurt, that they would be there.

The girl from ADFAB had not followed him into the carriage. Nevertheless, James spent the entirety of his journey home looking over his shoulder. Even as he got off the train and began his walk to Mrs Salvestrin's, he continued to watch out for her, hoping the moonlight would fall upon her silvery hair and provide him with advance warning of any approach. Despite the general lethargy he felt in his limbs and the discomfort of his heel, he knew he could run, at least for a long enough period to find a suitable hiding place.

Thus preoccupied, he almost walked past the telephone booth without slowing to check it for damage. A sudden, unexpected flicker of its neon light snapped him back to attention and he stopped in his tracks and turned his eyes to inspect the booth. The walls were free from graffiti, exterior and interior; the dialling mechanism, coin slot and handset were all in good working order. And at the base of the booth, on the square slab of concrete, was a pair of black Oxfords. He knew immediately that they would be his size, 10 EE.

They were not new; there were signs of wear on the heels and the leather of the outer soles, and slight scuff marks on the toe of the right shoe. Inside the booth James held the shoes up to the light. There was a small, circular mark on the upper of the right shoe that he wiped off with his thumb. It looked like dried red ink. Perhaps it was blood. The shoes themselves were of excellent design and quality, hand-stitched by the look of it, and made entirely without synthetic materials. There were no labels on the inner sole, no other identifying marks aside from the size, '10EE', stamped on the bottom of each tongue.

There was nothing left for him to do but take the shoes and go home.

Chapter 23

He dreamed that night not in colour but in black and white, the many shades of grey lending a softness to the scene that did not belong.

He was standing on the wide wooden balcony of a dilapidated building, a boarding house or motel of some kind. The walls were painted white, a layer of thick enamel that would crumble at his touch. The blackness of the night surrounded him, the steps from the balcony disappearing into nothingness. A light, perhaps from a single globe, shone above him, casting his shadow long and thin across the balcony. The boards creaked with his every step, as if each might be his last, but the light continued to follow him as he moved to the edge of the balcony and looked out into the void.

He was dressed for summer in a dark-grey sports shirt, open at the neck, and light-grey trousers. The night itself felt cool and calm and he was comfortable in his clothes, the fibres brushing softly against his skin. Looking down at his feet he saw that he was wearing his new black Oxfords, freshly polished and buffed to a vibrant sheen. When he stood still the night stood still with him: there was no sound except for that of his own breathing, no movement save for the rise and fall of his chest.

Someone was standing behind him. He heard the sound of a match being struck and turned to see the heavy-jowled face of a man illuminated briefly by a flicker of flame. He was lighting a cigarette, cupping it to his mouth and inhaling in slow, greedy puffs. He shook his right arm to extinguish the match and stepped forward, three slow, deliberate paces, moving into the soft sphere of James's light.

The man wore a dark-grey suit, single-breasted and crumpled, a white shirt and a thin black tie. A grey fedora was pulled low across his forehead. His eyes, dark as the night, stared at James from beneath the brim of the hat. The circles under them suggested sleepless nights, the stiff sheets of cheap hotels, bedside ashtrays piled high with half-smoked cigarettes, endless meditations on the task at hand. He continued to smoke, wrapping his chapped lips around the filter of the cigarette and drawing the smoke deep into his lungs, expelling it slowly through his nostrils.

Something, someone, had disappeared. Vanished. That much was clear. The man was a private detective. He questioned James without ever speaking.

Q:

'James, James Bloomington. Would you like a room?'

Q:

'Oh, no. We don't get many folks passing through here. Not since the freeway went up, anyways.'

Q:

'Oh, no. I'm pretty sure I'd remember. We can take a look at the register if you like. Are you sure you wouldn't like a room?'

Q:

'Just me. And Mother. That's Mother's room up there on the hill.'

Q:

'I grew up here. It's all I've ever known. Don't care to know much else.'

Q:

'Not really. After all, a boy's best friend is his mother.'

Q:

'No, never. I mean, there were kids at school. Not many, but a few. Kids that I liked. It was hard on Mother though, and very few of them ever came back.'

Q:

'Oh, she didn't mean it like that, no sir. But with just

the two of us around, there wasn't much room for anyone else.'

Q:

'I wouldn't know about that, sir. But it's just like they say, a son is a poor substitute for a lover.'

Q:

'Who? Who did you say?'

Q:

'I . . . I've already told you. I don't know anyone by that name. No, don't go! Wait, please! I need to ask you something.'

But the man was already gone, enveloped by the darkness. All that was left behind was the cigarette smoke, which dissolved slowly into the night air.

James awoke to the morning heat. His forehead was beaded with sweat; a faint taste of blood clung to the back of his throat. He would visit Byron Jones this morning and he would wear his new shoes.

'Nice shoes.'

'Thank you. I mean, thank you. For the shoes. They're very comfortable.'

'They look it.'

'Yes, the fit is almost perfect. It's often a difficult width. Thank you again.'

'What for?'

'The shoes. These shoes. You left them for me, didn't you?'

'Those shoes? Never seen them before in my life. You picked those shoes up off the street? Around here? Nice.'

'No, they were left for me. They were meant for me to take.'

'Where were they left?'

'In a phone booth.'

'A phone booth?'

'Yes, in a phone booth.'

'Who by?'

'I don't know. I assumed it was you but I'm obviously mistaken.'

'Obviously. Are you feeling all right, mate? You look a little . . . damp. No colour either. Maybe you should sit down?'

'Yes, I think I should. It's this heat. The sun, it never stops.'

James fell quickly and ungracefully to his haunches, the weight of his buttocks suspended over the heels of his Oxfords, his left arm pressed against the concrete tower for support. Byron looked at him and slowly shook his head.

'Summer, mate. It's always the same. Every summer since I was kid, it's always been like this. But heat is just a state of mind. Think cool thoughts and pretty soon you'll start to feel cool. People have a lot more control over their bodies than they realise.'

'Nonsense. A person's body heat is a purely physical

reaction. Granted there are internal and external causes, but they're always physical, not mental.'

'Then why am I sitting out here in a woollen jumper?'

'Because you're sedentary. You don't move a muscle. And it's actually rather cool here, as you well know, given the shade and the concrete.'

'And my mind, mate. And my mind.'

'It has nothing to do with your mind.'

'It's got everything to do with my mind. It's all in my mind, mate, this whole thing.'

'What are you talking about?'

'This, all this. It only exists in my mind. You, me, everything. Even the sun.'

'I doubt that your mind's powers are strong enough to control the sun.'

'Why not? You think I haven't learned anything, sitting out here? What is it you think I do out here all day?'

'I know what you do. You think.'

'That's right, I think. I expand my mind and it's getting bigger and bigger all the time. It's getting fucking huge. You think I can't create this, you, with my mind? Of course I can. Why should you be any more real than that guy over there? Why should you be more real than him, than her, that little guy over there?'

'Stop it.'

'Why? You scared? How big is your mind, mate? Is it big enough to create me? Big enough to create you? Big enough for any of this?'

'Who are you?'

'You know who I am.'

'Who are you? I need to know.'

'You know who I am, James.'

'I know you're Byron Jones.'

'Brian. It's Brian.'

'All right, Brian Jones. How do you know me, Brian Jones? What do you know about me?'

'Jesus, keep your voice down.'

'What are you here for? Why are you here?'

'Look, calm down. We've been over this before, James. To think. I'm out here to think. I'm just sitting out here minding my own business. Why should it have anything to do with you? What makes you think I've got anything to do with you? I never asked you to come and talk to me, did I? I never asked your mother to come out here and fucking stare at me, did I? Strange fucking woman. Although she's stopped now.'

'What do you mean, stopped?'

'Stopped. She doesn't come anymore. At least she hasn't for the last couple of days. She might come back again, I guess, but I doubt it.'

'How do you know?'

'I can just tell, mate. I could feel it when she left. It just felt like she'd had enough, like she wasn't coming back.'

'Perhaps I shouldn't come back either.'

'Mate, do what you like. Just don't expect any answers from me. I haven't got the answers you want.'

'No, I don't expect that you do.'

'You probably don't even know the right questions. You've got to know the question before you can expect an answer.'

'I thought you were the question.'

'Me? I've got enough questions of my own, mate.'

'You can't sit out here forever, you know. Sooner or later something will happen. Someone will want something from you and you'll feel obliged to give it to them. Your wife – she'll want you to go back to work someday.'

'Maureen? I reckon you're right. She's already moaning about me sitting around at home all day doing fuck all. She wouldn't be too happy if she knew I was out here. She'd say I was embarrassing her, and she'd be right. I seem to embarrass everyone else by sitting out here, why not Maureen too? Shit, she'd die if she saw me. But she never has much cause to come into the city so the odds are in my favour.'

'Do you love her?'

'Love? I don't know about that, mate. I'm not sure I ever loved her, not sure that it matters either. Love would just confuse us both. See, what most people don't understand is that love and happiness aren't the same thing. They're not even necessarily connected. I guess they can be, but it doesn't seem to happen that way, at least it never did for me. Love is a violent thing, a reaction, it burns like an allergy. Makes you do stupid things, say stupid things all the time. There's nothing even about it, nothing steady. And steadiness is what you need in a marriage. Stability. That's what happiness is all about, two people who know what to expect from each other.'

'I'm not sure I like the sound of that. What about romance?'

'It's overrated, mate.'

'Will you stop coming out here when she asks you to?'

'Yeah, of course.'

'But where will you think?'

'I reckon I'll be done with thinking by then. I'll just enjoy it while I can.'

'Do you mind if I stay here with you for a while? I'll be quiet.'

'Sure. Here, take this.'

Brian shifted his weight and pulled a second flattened cardboard square from beneath the one he was sitting on. He handed it to James. It was the 'PONYBOY TOMATOES' box.

James set his briefcase on the ground and placed the box to the left of Brian's. He sat with his back against the wall, legs crossed underneath him, eyes set straight ahead. The wall pushed against his curved spine, cold and hard, immovable. Soon he was hunched forward, shoulders over his thighs, settled comfortably into position. Time began to accelerate as his breathing began to slow. He watched the legs of the people passing before him blur into a continuous whole, a giant centipede rushing headlong into a sunburned concrete city.

Chapter 24

James was not at work. It was three o'clock and he still had not arrived at the office; nor had he telephoned to provide an explanation for his absence. It was not like him. A woman, presumably the drooling idiot at the front desk, had phoned Veronica to inform her of these facts and to ask if she might know where he was. Why was she expected to know her son's movements? He was, after all, a grown man and this was no longer his home. He had made a home of his own with that Italian woman, hadn't he? Why didn't she try and contact her? Surely she had the number? Oh, there was no answer there, she was told. Oh, no answer? What a pity. Perhaps Mrs Salvestro or whatever her name was had felt the presence of an imbecile at the other end of the line and, blessed with a premonition of the utter stupidity of the incoming caller, had decided not to pick up the receiver. If only Veronica had been similarly blessed she could have avoided the entire conversation she now found herself subjected to. Oh, she was only following company procedure, was she? In future she could kindly shove her company procedure, indeed, the entire company itself, if the mood took her, right up her useless, wrinkled old arse. Good afternoon? Good afternoon, indeed.

Veronica had been trying to sleep. She took an afternoon nap whenever she was able, escaping into the depths of her dreams. But the telephone had begun to ring and she had felt compelled to answer its call. Given her mood, she was somewhat disappointed it had not been her usual gentleman caller; she would have welcomed his silent attentions. She was listless and had been so all day, unable to find any pleasure in any of her innumerable routines, whether inside the house or out.

In her garden she had chased a large army of ants with a pesticide spray, killing many of them in their frantic spread for safety. The sun had sat high above her head, watching in silent approval as the ants abandoned themselves to the cloud of death that pursued them, no matter which direction they took. Breathing freely behind the STSC-720 N95, Veronica sprayed the pesticide liberally, stooping close to the ground to follow every chaotic movement, every second of the insect drama she had created. Despite her stooping, her speed and balance were excellent. But she could find no satisfaction in the extermination of the ants; even the demonstration of the strength and flexibility of her own body (usually a guaranteed crowd-pleaser) failed to rouse her from the moribund state she found herself in.

It was that damned man in the lane. She had become accustomed to building her day around a morning visit to the city, where she would view the man who looked like her son – so much like him, in fact, that she had granted the wretch an importance he did not deserve. It turned out that he was just another worthless beggar in the city; no more, no less. She no longer felt any need to look at him (or any other street person she could think of, for that matter) but it would take some time before she could completely let go of the ritual of her daily visit and all that surrounded it.

Without this visit there was no need for Veronica to travel to the city, no need for her to dress and prepare for the journey, no need for her to leave the house at all. She was alone in its big, empty spaces. Only the air-conditioning kept the rooms from going stale. No movement, no people, save for the shapes projected into the loungeroom from the television screen.

She could not remember turning the television on; perhaps she had done so earlier in the day. The sound was muted.

A poorly dressed studio audience was seated before a raised stage. The stage was not large; indeed, the studio itself was uncomfortably small and the people in the audience often appeared to be sitting on top of each other, hollering and whooping and swinging their arms at the elbow in a circular fashion. In the centre of the stage sat a large, apparently teenaged girl. Her hair, which fell across her broad face, was dyed a deep purple-black; her very white, puffy body was covered in an oversized black t-shirt. She wore a silver ring through her septum and a scowl on her face. Her t-shirt bore a slogan in red, lower-case letters across the chest: 'nobody understands my pain'. She was holding the hand of an older, even fatter woman, obviously her mother, who sat to her left. A short distance to the right of the women sat a middle-aged man in a blue and white checked shirt and dirty blue jeans. The shirt was not tucked into the jeans. The camera focused on the man's sun-scarred, leathery face. Fresh shaving cuts marked his left cheek and the cleft of his chin. He shook his head continuously as the girl spoke, clutching at his forehead with the fingers of both hands. His bloodshot eyes and blank stare spoke clearly to the audience: 'Do you believe this crap? Why me? I'm a hard-working man. What have I done to deserve this?' There was an empty chair to the man's right, and two more empty chairs to the left of the two women. The camera focused again on the women. A caption across the bottom of the screen read: 'I'm a Lesbian and so is my DAUGHTER!'

The small-screen spectacle reminded Veronica of a

miniature-scale Roman amphitheatre, her vision shaped by countless Hollywood movies of the 1950s: a desperate, impatient crowd surrounding the frightened gladiators, smiling, laughing and baying for the blood they could smell in the air. The humiliation of others would provide a counterpoint and veracity to their own trivial lives. There was an ugly, repulsive sensuality to it, which gave it an unstoppable momentum. Veronica did not need to hear these people speak (her nightmares were overpopulated as it was) and she did not need to watch the inevitable conclusion. She found the television's remote control and quickly shut the picture off.

She looked through the glass doors and over the balcony to the sea and the sky. Nothing but blue, cold and dazzling in the afternoon sun. She knew better than to trust her eyes. The sun was relentless, heating the air and destroying the skin of any living creature foolish enough to test its strength. Sunburn, sunstroke, skin cancer, melanoma. The damage could be immediate or triggered at an unspecified future date. A cancer, for example, might not surface for twenty or thirty years. The sun had all the time in the world; the sun was time itself.

Byron had gone, taken his cardboard and left; James did not know when. He had not moved for hours. His buttocks were beginning to ache, his legs stiff and lifeless underneath him. He stretched his hands towards the sky and willed himself to return to his surroundings, rotating his head in a clockwise direction and opening and closing his eyes rapidly against the afternoon light. He looked at his watch: it was seventeen minutes past four.

A scattered collection of gold and silver coins surrounded him, money thrown at him and Byron from passers-by. Byron had, judging by the spread of the coins, attracted a larger number of contributions than he. He had not noticed Byron leaving. Perhaps he had gone home at lunchtime; perhaps even earlier.

Now it was time for James to leave. Balancing himself on his outstretched palms, he rose unsteadily to his feet. He could feel people's eyes on him as he stood up and brushed at the seat of his pants and the backs of his thighs. He did not immediately regain his sense of equilibrium. He leaned his shoulder gently against the wall, loitering (and he was loitering, there was no other word for it) in the shadow of the concrete tower while he waited for his balance to return, which it quickly did.

It was too early for him to go home and too late for him to go to work. He would visit his mother instead. The sun was high above him and he knew instinctively that the heat would begin in earnest as soon as he left the safety the shade had provided him. He folded his cardboard square and rested it against the tower wall. Byron would find it there tomorrow morning; there was a chance, of course, that he would not.

James would need to take a bus to reach his mother's house but first he would need to take the train north to

Wynyard. He took a deep breath and stepped into the heat and glare of the afternoon.

The bus dropped James at the top of the path to his mother's house. His trip had not been unpleasant; in fact he had barely been aware of the people around him (there must have been many at this time of day) and he could not clearly remember having made the transition from the train to the bus. But here he was, making his way carefully along the crooked concrete path towards the house at its end.

The path took him past three other houses, each older but not grander than his mother's. He would smile and wave at the old couple (and they always appeared as a couple; James had never seen either of them without the other) in the house immediately next to his mother's, if they happened to be on their balcony (and they always happened to be on their balcony) and they first smiled and waved at him (and they always did). He had never known their names and they had, as far as he knew, never known his, but that had never stopped them from being polite, and their smiles always struck him as genuine. Perhaps one day he would introduce himself to them.

The smell of fertiliser rose from the front garden of his mother's house, the thick, sweet odour of blood and bone, ground into a white powder and spread across the dark earth. James could feel the fertiliser forcing its way up his nostrils and down into the pit of his stomach. He could see the half-empty plastic sack, slit open at the top right corner, resting against the terracotta tiles of the front step to the house. His mother had been in the garden.

The steps ascended in a gentle curve to a thick, transparent glass door covered by a black iron gate. James mounted the steps as quickly as he could and pressed the button of the intercom.

He waited for about thirty seconds, holding his right hand over his mouth and nose, before the intercom crackled to life.

'Hmpht ho?'

It was his mother's voice. She was wearing a mask inside the house.

'Mother, it's James.'

'Hname?'

'Yes, Mother, it's me. Come and let me in.'

The intercom fell silent and James could hear the muffled sounds of his mother's movements as she made her way down the stairs, quickly and efficiently but without undue haste. She came to the door wearing a respirator and dark-green rubber gloves up to her elbows. The gloves appeared to be wet; she was holding her elbows to her sides and her hands straight up in the air in an effort to prevent the water from dripping off her fingers.

Her gloved hands fumbled with the lock of the glass door. James tried the iron gate and found it was already open. When his mother finally hit the latch of the door he grasped the handle from the outside and opened it. His mother took a step back and allowed him to come inside.

'Hello, Mother.'

James stretched past his mother's stiffly held forearms and kissed her lightly on the side of her mask. Veronica was moving her head rapidly up and down and from side to side, indicating to him that he should take her mask off.

'Hmnel he nako hne nas.'

'I'm sorry, Mother, but I can't hear you.'

'Hne nas!'

'Sorry, Mother? You'll have to speak up. It's the mask.'

'Hne nas!'

She pressed her mask to his chest and pushed her head up, wriggling her face free from the STSC-720 N95, which now hung by its elastic straps around her neck. She took a step back from her son, her face red with effort and her eyes red with anger.

'Thank you for your help, James!'

'Don't mention it.'

James looked at his mother blankly.

'I've been cleaning the toilet.'

'Oh, I see.'

'There's ammonia on my gloves. Help me take them off.'

'And get the ammonia on my skin? No, thank you.'

'Very well.'

Veronica turned her back on James and walked up the stairs towards the kitchen. James followed at a distance, his eyes measuring the spaces he passed through for signs of change. He had not been to his mother's house since he had moved to Mrs Salvestrin's. Everything appeared to be perfectly in its place: the six chairs around the dining table, the finely finished ceramic vase (imported from China by his father many years ago) on the display stand at the top of the stairs, the magazines arranged on the glass coffee table in the loungeroom. This was the dust-free, static environment in which his mother insisted she live her life. She emerged from the kitchen with the gloves removed.

'You weren't at work today.'

'No, I wasn't. How did you know?'

'That idiot woman from your office rang here, of all places, looking for you.'

'I'm sorry about that.'

'Why should you be sorry? You're not sleeping with her too? Another old woman, James? I'm beginning to find it somewhat disturbing. You really should see a professional about this. Oh, James, you're sleeping with her, aren't you?'

'No, Mother.'

'Where have you been? I suppose you're aware that your suit needs to be dry-cleaned. Urgently. And where did you get those shoes?'

'The shoes? They're new. Do you like them? I suppose the suit could use a clean. I did intend to go to work this morning, Mother, but something came up.'

'What came up?'

'Something.'

'I see. Something you don't want to tell me. What are you doing here anyway?'

'I felt like I wanted to be here.'

'You felt like it? Why? You've never felt like it before, certainly not since you moved in with that old Italian whore.'

'Mrs Salvestrin is my landlady, Mother.'

'I'm sure she is. It's just a question of how you pay the rent.'

'Yes, Mother. I'm sure you don't need me to go into the details of our transactions, do you?'

'I'd rather you didn't. Now, to what do I owe the pleasure of this visit? The truth, James.'

'I wanted to see you, Mother.'

'Please, James.'

'To talk about our dinner arrangements for tomorrow.'

'And we couldn't talk about them over the telephone?'

'Yes, I suppose we could have. But as I said, I felt like I wanted to be here. You should be flattered – a son's outpouring of emotion for his enfeebled old mother. I'm concerned about your welfare. How can I be sure you haven't turned into one of those old women with cupboards full of cat food, or taken up with a troupe of Russian acrobats, unless I come out here to see for myself?'

'Stop it, James. This dinner is that important to you?'

'Yes, Mother. It is.'

The telephone began to ring; it was attached to the side of the loungeroom's display cabinet and James was closest to it.

'Don't answer that!'

'What are you talking about, Mother? I'm right here.'

James lifted the receiver and held it to his ear.

'Hello? Hello? Who is this? Hello? Look, it's obvious you're there. Who is this? Hello? Hung up. You'd think a person would at least have the decency to admit they'd dialled a wrong number and apologise. He just said nothing.'

'He? What makes you think it was a man?'

'I could hear his breathing. Very nasal. And quite irregular. The man should probably see a doctor.'

'Yes, well, where were we?'

'We were talking about dinner. Tomorrow night, seven-thirty, at a place called Mama Luigi's in Leichhardt.'

'Leichhardt? I suppose I'm meant to think that's terribly chic.'

'Mr Hunt says the food is excellent.'

'Who?'

'Mr Hunt. You met him in the boardroom. In the white underwear.'

'That old fairy? He's given the dinner recommendation?'

'I'm sure it will be fine. And I hardly think you should be leaping to conclusions about the man's sexual orientation. He's a very respected editor.'

'James, we caught him with that plump boy, remember?'

'We didn't exactly catch anyone doing anything, Mother.'

'Oh, James, you're so naive. No wonder old women find you such an easy target. I expect they ask you to watch *The Graduate*.'

'Hardly ever, Mother. Please don't be late for dinner.'

'You know you don't need to remind me to be punctual, James. But I'm yet to understand your motives. Why are you so intent on me giving myself to this man?'

'I'm intent on no such thing, Mother.'

'You know his intentions, James, if not your own. He intends to marry me. Me, James, not you. Is that what you want? You want this man to be your new father? A step-father – is that what you want?'

'Really, Mother. I'm not sure I ever had an old father. What use would I have for a new one?'

'Don't speak that way about your father, James.'

'What way?'

'Don't try and deny you had a father, James. He was a wonderful man, a wonderful father. Without him we wouldn't be where we are today.'

'And where are we exactly?'

'Secure, James. Happy and secure.'

'I'd really rather not talk about this, Mother. Not again.'

'Very well. Is it your career, James? Although to call it a career is probably somewhat ambitious, even for a mother who loves her son. Is that why I'm doing this? Is that why I'm to give myself to this man at dinner? A noble sacrifice for the good of your career?'

'Let's get this clear, Mother. You are not giving yourself to anyone. We're there for dinner. A pleasant evening. Pleasant above all else. Just the four of us, smiling and laughing all night.'

'The four of us? Of course. The daughter. It's the daughter, isn't it? You want his daughter. That's it, that's why we're doing this.'

'Really, Mother. I want no such thing. I barely know his daughter. In fact I've only ever laid eyes on her once. She looks pleasant enough. I just thought it would be easier if we were there.'

'Stop it, James. You always were a fool. And not a particularly good liar. Very well, at least the reason for this farce is clear to me now. I'll try not to disappoint you. Now, if you don't mind, I'd like to finish cleaning my toilet.'

'I thought you might like to have dinner together.'

'Tonight? Whatever for? Won't we be having dinner together tomorrow?'

'Yes, but . . .'

'That will be more than enough excitement for me for one week, I should think.'

'Very well. I'll let myself out then, shall I?'

'Lock the door behind you.'

'I'll see you at the restaurant?'

'Of course.'

'Goodbye, Mother.'

'Goodbye.'

James made his way slowly down the stairs. He had never thought of this house as his home; his mother's presence infected every room, morning and night. It was as if she lurked around every corner and behind every door and could be expected to spring out of every cupboard at any moment, silent, stern and beautiful.

He was afraid to masturbate in this house and had never done so, relieving himself instead, quickly and efficiently, in school and university toiletblocks. It was an enterprise always accompanied by a certain element of risk, hence the need for speed and silence. He knew she would have known (his underwear, his sheets, something would betray him) and that she would have felt nothing but disgust for his inability to control himself. He could not have lived in her house under such circumstances.

But now he did not want to leave; he wanted to stay. His mother was upstairs, waiting to hear the sound of the door closing behind him. He went to the door, opened it and closed it, remaining inside.

She would be stretching the gloves carefully over her

narrow fingers, refilling the bucket and making her way to her toilet. He stood perfectly still until he heard her footsteps above his head.

She was on her knees on the hard tiled floor, scrubbing relentlessly.

James walked slowly and silently to his empty bedroom and sat on the edge of the unused bed; he had left nothing behind in this room. His mother had insisted on it. Four white walls and a flat white ceiling. The thick curtains were drawn against the light and the air was dry and stale. James looked up at the ceiling, carefully removed his penis from the zip of his trousers and began to masturbate. His mother was above him.

He finished quickly, cleaning his fingers, palm and penis with a tissue from his inside jacket pocket. He placed the tissue under the bed, as far back as he could reach while still sitting down. His heart was beating strongly, matching the efforts of his lungs.

James rose from the bed and moved to the front door. He closed the door behind him with a barely audible click and slipped silently into the warm summer evening. Sweat was running from his temples as he hurried along the path, waving a second time to his mother's neighbours as he went by.

Chapter 25

He chose to walk to Mrs Salvestrin's from his mother's house, a choice he regretted almost immediately. Still, once a choice had been made, James was not one to deviate from it, and he willed himself to keep a steady pace along the wide concrete footpaths that would carry him home.

He walked west into the sun, which had begun its slow descent towards the horizon where it would finally disappear, marking the end of another day. It had lost none of its heat and continued to cast a stark, even light over the scorched earth below it.

James kept his eyes to the ground, trying to avoid stepping in the lengthening shadows cast by those people walking in front of him. As a child, something had told him, warned him, not to step in shadows; that a person's shadow was a separate, living entity, alive but not breathing. The person might walk away, but the shadow, the aggrieved shadow, could always come back for you, invisible in the dark. It was not a fear that lasted long and James had stepped in many shadows since, without suffering any ill consequences. It was often unavoidable, especially in the crowded streets of the city. Still, the habit remained and he saw no reason to break it in his adult years.

The streets were filled with traffic, a steady stream of cars, motorcycles, buses, trucks and other assorted vehicles, commercial and otherwise, crawling towards various destinations along a common path. James was outpacing much of the traffic travelling in his direction; even when a section of it would pass him, he would catch up and overtake it as it slowed to a halt at the next set of signal lights.

He had built up a rhythm to his movements that allowed him to ignore the heat and exhaust fumes that surrounded him. He concentrated solely on the mechanics of walking, his legs driven by an intricate series of cogs and pulleys, and as he walked he was surprised to find himself relaxed and remarkably content. He was (and this was a source of some concern) almost happy. Happiness, in himself and others, had always made him nervous; he needed to know its source before he could attempt to trust it. He had spent the day doing nothing, absolutely nothing, sitting on a crushed cardboard box in a dirty lane as people walked by, oblivious to his presence, and the sun had maintained its cyclical vigil overhead. Time passed and he achieved nothing. He had neglected his responsibilities, his contractual duties. Why should this make him happy? The peace he had found could not be real if it was based on neglect and abnegation. Which left only Imogen.

He would see Imogen tomorrow.

The footpath had narrowed considerably, the lines of cars now broken by long intervals. He was almost there. He passed the railway station and began the final, familiar route home. He had been walking for over an hour and the flow of his sweat was constant. His feet, however, were perfectly comfortable, the heels unblistered. Toes, ankles, instep: the shoes had protected them all, the leather already stretched to accommodate every irregularity.

The telephone booth was ahead; he could see it clearly in the evening light. The sky was a pale, faded blue. The streetlights above him flickered to life, the fluorescent tubes emitting a steady hum as he passed beneath and walked towards the booth.

It was clean. And empty. Nothing. Not a single coin in the return tray. Even from a distance, this distance, he knew.

James stood inside the narrow booth, letting the glass door swing to a close behind him, and examined every corner. The top phone book on the tray was folded back in place, the dog-eared pages open at the name 'REID'. A number was circled in fresh red ink under the entry 'REHABILITATION SERVICES'. The handset sat limply in place. He lifted it to his ear and checked the dial tone; satisfied, he placed the handset back in its cradle, bringing the booth back to silence. He opened the door and slowly circled the booth, checking the walls and the blades of grass that surrounded it on all sides. Again there was nothing.

But there may yet be something. All that was required of him was patience. He would find a hidden vantage point and watch, wait for something to happen. Off the footpath, behind a low, white fence – a strip of wood suspended no higher than his knees – was a hedge, not five metres away from the booth. This would be his vantage point. James glanced quickly over each shoulder before he raised his left leg and stepped into the hedge, separating its branches with his hands and plunging within. He shielded his face with his raised forearms and succeeded in pushing his way through the web of branches and foliage. There was no longer any question that his suit would be in need of dry-cleaning.

He turned to face the telephone booth, brushing fine, broken branches from his arms and shoulders. The hedge was thick and sturdy, its shape obviously maintained by the regular, strenuous attentions of a professional gardener (if not a professional, at least an enthusiastic amateur). He could not clearly make out the shape of the telephone booth through the hedge unless he separated its branches with his hands and thrust his face into the rapidly contracting hole through which he had emerged. With his head, neck and shoulders halfway into the hedge, his view was excellent. He was, however, aware that this position left his rear (quite literally) somewhat vulnerable. Still, he held the branches off his face as best he could and set his eyes on the telephone booth.

The colour slowly drained from the sky and the light began to fade as the sun retreated to gather its strength for the day that would follow the night. James continued to keep watch but no one, save for the occasional passer-by — office workers, like himself, making their way home — strayed into his field of view. And none of them showed the slightest interest in the telephone booth that stood before them.

He was beginning to tire of the discomfort when he noticed a girl approaching the booth. She looked to be around fifteen years of age, possibly younger, and wore cut-off denim jeans low on her hips, the elastic of her cotton underpants showing at her waist, and a tight-fitting t-shirt. She was barefoot and couldn't be far from home. She carried the correct change for a local call in her hand and walked confidently into the fluorescent glare of the booth. James watched as she deposited the coins and dialled the number. Soon she was giggling with excitement, leaning her shoulder against the glass of the booth and running her free hand repeatedly through her shoulder-length hair. Her hair was wet and obviously freshly washed. It was equally obvious that she was speaking to her boyfriend. Either her parents had not permitted her to use the telephone at home or she wanted the privacy that only a public telephone booth could provide.

James continued to watch the girl. He could not clearly see her face but he saw that the skin on her arms and legs was smooth and tanned, her broad shoulders matched by her thick waist and hips. She was strong and healthy, and whatever surplus weight she was carrying was evenly distributed over the curves of her body – a blessing she might not carry into adulthood. She laughed: an occasional high-pitched, nervous shriek carried through the glass and the dense hedge to James's ears. He smiled at her in return, sharing in the exultation of the moment.

It was then that something struck him, sharp and hard, across his lower back.

'Hey! What the fuck are you doing to my hedge?' It was a man's voice, sharp, and equally hard as the instrument that struck him a second time.

'Motherfucker! Get the fuck out of there!'

The muscles of his back hardened reflexively to meet the third blow, but James knew there was only one way out: through the hedge. He stretched his arms wide, pulled the branches aside and kicked forward, scrambling his way clear. As he burst out of the hedge he caught his right shin on a plank of wood and tumbled to the ground. The momentum of his flight had been momentarily halted. He had forgotten about the fence.

He could hear the man attempting to follow him through, screaming further obscenities as the branches blocked his passage. James sprang to his feet and saw the girl in the booth looking at him over her shoulder. Her eyes were wide and her lips moved at great speed. She was describing the events she was witnessing to the boy she had called: a man coming out of a hedge, tripping over a fence and running off down the street.

James kept running. Whoever was chasing him had obviously thought better of it part way through the hedge. There was no one behind him as he bounded up the steps to Mrs Salvestrin's front door. After briefly fumbling with his keys, he was inside. He locked the door behind him.

Alison met him in the hallway. The sound of 'That's Amore' drifted in from the loungeroom.

'James!'

'Alison? What on earth are you doing here?'

'Waiting for you. I've been waiting for at least two hours. Why are you out of breath? And what have you done to your clothes? It looks like you've been through a jungle. And your face is bleeding, James. What have you done to your face? It's all red.'

He reached his hand up to his right cheek and brought it away to see a thin smear of blood.

'This? It's just a scratch. At least it's not my nose.'

He began to laugh softly, to himself. His lips showed a broad smile.

She pulled a handkerchief from her skirt pocket and began to wipe away the blood and sweat from his face.

'What are you smiling at? Happy to see me?'

'Not particularly, no. Certainly surprised. What are you doing here?'

'Mrs Salvestrin called me and asked me to come over for dinner. She said you were expecting me, that you'd be home by 6.30, no later, but to come a little earlier so we could meet. You didn't know about this?'

'No, not a thing.'

'She's been feeling my legs, James.'

'What are you talking about?'

'My calves. She's been feeling my calves.'

'Is that so?'

'Yes, it is. I got such a shock when she reached down. She said they're nice and firm. She could see why a young man like you would take after a pair of calves like these. And my teeth. She's been looking at my teeth.'

'Your teeth?'

'She made me open my mouth, James, and she looked at my teeth. Like a dentist. She didn't seem all that impressed by the teeth. I think it was the fillings.'

'Fillings?'

'I've got two fillings in my back molars. Right side. Then we stood in the kitchen and talked, I guess, while she made the pasta sauce.'

294

'Carbonara?'

'I think it's a bolognaise. She talked about her husband and how unambitious and weak he always was. And we talked about you and how long I'd known you and where we'd met and all that, and I told her there wasn't really much to tell and she said young people never appreciated anything, it was only when you got older that you learned how precious love was, and then she started to cry. She said it was the onions, but she finished chopping the onions way before that and she was fine. And then she said excuse me and walked off into the loungeroom and she's been playing that song, over and over again, and I've been waiting for you in the kitchen, trying to make sure the sauce didn't all dry up.'

'Did it?'

'Did what?'

'Did the sauce dry up?'

'Not completely, no.'

'Good. I'm hungry. Starved, really.' He continued to smile.

'James, what have you been doing? Why are you so late?'

'I went to visit my mother. I was helping her in the garden.'

'Some garden. You look like shit.'

'Do I? I'm feeling rather fine, actually.'

'Here, let me brush some of that off.'

'Thank you. Now, about that dinner.'

'You should talk to Mrs Salvestrin. Let her know you're home.'

'I'll do that.'

He walked into the loungeroom. A standing lamp in the far right corner provided the only light. The lampshade was made from a stiff orange fabric and the room was cast in its colour. James found his landlady sitting in a faded brown leather lounge chair next to the record player. 'That's Amore' continued to play but the track was coming to its end. Mrs Salvestrin's eyes were closed but it was difficult to tell if she was asleep. She was wearing a white apron over a blue gingham house dress. The apron invited all those who read it to 'Kiss the Cook!'. Beside this printed invitation was a cartoon pair of oversized, over-amorous lips. There was an empty bottle of red wine and a half-full glass on the side table to her left.

James moved to the record player and lifted the needle from the spinning vinyl.

'I was listening to that.'

'So I hear. Good evening, Mrs Salvestrin.'

'Hello, James.'

'You've been drinking.'

'Only a little, darling. Only a little.'

'Thank you for preparing dinner.'

'My pleasure. I just wish you were home a little earlier. Alison is a lovely girl, James.'

'Is she?'

'She has lovely calves.'

'I really hadn't noticed.'

'You should notice these things, James. Women like men who notice the little things. What have you done to your suit, James? It looks ruined.'

'It'll be fine. It's a secret. I've been doing secret things all day.'

She had never seen him smile as broadly as he smiled now.

'How exciting! Will you tell me about them?'

'Of course not. Then they wouldn't be secret, would they?'

'I suppose not. I'm sorry I didn't tell you I'd invited Alison over for dinner. I wanted to meet her.'

'It's quite all right. As it happens I'm in the mood for company.'

'Really? I thought you'd be angry.'

'Not in the slightest. Will you join us for dinner?'

'No, I don't think so. You go ahead and eat. Leave everything. I'll clean it up in the morning. I think I'll go to bed.'

'It's still quite early.'

'I'm tired, James. Tired and old. You wait till you get to my age, you'll see what it's like then.'

'Good night, Sophia.'

'Good night, James.' She reached for the glass of wine and turned her head away from him, smiling as he walked back into the kitchen.

Alison had prepared two bowls of pasta for them;

she had already begun eating from hers, standing over the kitchen bench.

'The pasta's a little cold and sticky but the sauce is really good. Can't beat real Italian cooking.'

'No, I don't suppose you can.' He picked up his bowl and began to eat.

'James, if you don't want me here, I can just go.'

'What makes you think I don't want you here?'

'After the other night in the pub, I just thought . . .'

'I wasn't feeling well. That's all. Tonight, on the other hand, I'm feeling quite splendid and I'll be only too happy to share my joy with you. Now hurry up and eat.'

When they finished eating James led Alison through his kitchen and into his room; he did not turn on the light. He began to kiss her before they reached the bed. His face had stopped bleeding but he knew that the skin would be red and irritated. The pasta had been good; he had not eaten all day and he could feel the oil from the sauce coating his throat as the pasta settled in his stomach, thick and heavy.

His clothes were soiled with sweat and dirt and he was glad to be rid of them as he lay naked on his bed with a girl whose name he knew but whose face he could barely remember when he closed his eyes. It was Imogen's face he pictured as he slid Alison's underpants from her ankles and buried his face between her thighs.

It was then he realised that he had lost his briefcase somewhere during the day; he had not come home with it. He had no idea where he had left it: perhaps in the lane, perhaps on a train or bus, perhaps at his mother's, perhaps in a hedge. He began to laugh, a laugh that started deep within his stomach and moved up his chest and throat, gaining momentum as it left his open mouth. Dizzy from the heat, the smell of Alison, the smell of his own body, he fell back on the bed as the laughter continued to escape him. It was only when Alison covered his mouth with her own that it stopped.

Chapter 26

James is waiting for Byron in the laneway. It is Thursday morning. He is wearing his double-breasted navy suit with a clean white shirt and maroon tie. A diagonal line runs from the top of his right cheek to the corner of his mouth, a thin, reddish-brown crust of dried blood almost parallel to his jaw. In profile, the mark delineates the skull from the jawbone, giving a clear impression of the skeleton beneath his skin. His face and neck are marked by other scratches, barely perceptible in themselves except for where the skin has taken on a slight irritation. Shaving this morning brought its own special discomfort, further irritating his skin and leaving his entire face noticeably flushed.

A layer of grey clouds has formed high in the atmosphere, threatening a rain storm that will never appear, at least not today. The sun will see to that, rising above the mass of cloud and burning a series of holes through it that will gradually expand in diameter until the holes themselves have become the sky, an endless blue expanse of heat and light. But now the sky is overcast, the air warm and wet, and James is content to conserve his energy for the day ahead, leaning against the concrete tower as he waits for Byron to appear.

He had expected Byron to be there when he arrived, serene and smiling on his cardboard square. It was now forty-two minutes past ten and there was still no sign of him.

James woke late after a dreamless night, his body still weary from the exertions of the previous day. Alison was gone when he woke up. She left no note. He could not remember if she had stayed the night: once he had spent himself he fell almost immediately into a sleep as heavy as death itself, oblivious to everything except his need to rest. It was almost 9.30 before he showered (ridding himself of a thick film of dirt and salt, his own and Alison's), dressed, and left the house for the railway station. He had not stopped for breakfast and he had not seen Mrs Salvestrin.

He watches the faces of the people approaching from the direction of the railway station; most keep their eyes pointed firmly at the ground in front of them, despite the fact that the sun's glare has been diffused by cloud cover. He looks directly into their faces, challenging them to lift their eyes and meet his own.

Some do, if only for a few seconds, and are rewarded with a smile; most do not, preferring instead to quicken their pace and shift direction sideways until they have successfully negotiated a path around him.

He sees Byron approaching, crossing the street with obvious (James thinks exaggerated) difficulty, lurching slowly towards him. Byron's movements are slow and almost comically uncertain. His body is hunched forward from the hips; his head balanced precariously on the left side of his neck. Each step sends a visible shiver of pain along his left side. His right arm is wrapped around the front of his body to cradle his ribs. James watches every step he takes with a mounting horror. Eventually Byron teeters to a stop, swaying from side to side on unsteady feet.

James barely recognises his face. The left side is heavily bruised and swollen, as if it has been inflated, like some sort of grotesque purple and yellow balloon. There is a deep cut underneath the right eye, five stitches visible under thin, white strips of sticking plaster. The eye socket is a raised blue-black circle, the eye itself struggling to see past the swollen flesh that surrounds it. The right ear is covered by a square, flesh-coloured sticking plaster, the hair surrounding the area shaved in haphazard strokes to ensure the adhesion.

'What happened to you?' It is Byron who speaks first, through distorted, swollen lips. His voice is still and familiar. James doesn't answer.

'That's a nasty scratch you've got there, mate.' Byron

is attempting to point to James's right cheek, raising his left arm no higher than his chest.

'This? I was helping Mother in the garden. It's nothing. Not cosmetically pleasing, granted, but no real harm done. Really, it's nothing. And what . . . what happened to you?'

'Same.'

'What?'

'Gardening accident.' He attempted to smile but only succeeded in dribbling a thin white stream of spittle down his chin. He wiped the spittle away with the sleeve of his right forearm.

'Are you all right?'

'Do I look all right?'

'No. Tell me what happened. Please.'

'I was mugged.'

'One mugger did . . . did this? What did he take? Your change?'

'Didn't take anything. And it was a bunch of guys, as far as I remember.'

'A group of men beat you? For nothing?'

'I don't know if it was for nothing. I assume they had a reason. At least I hope they had a reason, otherwise it'd all seem pretty pointless, wouldn't it?'

'And no one helped you?'

'What do you think, James? Does it look like anyone helped me? Someone must've called the police when they were done with me, but otherwise I guess they stood around and watched. Or didn't watch. Some of them may have joined in the fun. Whatever. Police took me to hospital. They patched me up and let me go. Few broken ribs, couple of cuts, otherwise I'm solid.'

'When did this happen?'

'Yesterday. I went home in the afternoon but Maureen got called in to the hospital to do a late shift so I figured I'd come back and get a few more hours in, till it got dark. You were gone by the time I came back, must've been around five or so, I suppose. So I sit down, make myself comfortable and slip straight into it. I'm thinking about when I was a kid, must have been six or so, and Dad took us to the beach. I think it was east somewhere, maybe Bronte. I don't know where Mum was; it was just me, Dad and June. We all got burnt to a crisp by the end of it.

'We were off playing in the water, in the shallows, right near the sand. The waves were breaking pretty far out and the whitewater came shooting in, all froth and foam. We were throwing wet sand from the bottom, grabbing big handfuls and chucking it at each other before it melted away. And I got June smack in the middle of the face, a big clump of mud right in her eye. She was pissed off something rotten. And she ran at me, screaming. Dad was off somewhere getting a beer or something, so he didn't see anything. She was bigger than me, just a couple of years older, but at that age a couple of years makes all the difference. She grabbed me by the neck, one hand on the back of the neck, one on my shoulder, and dunked me, pushed me under the water and held me there. The water was so shallow my face went right into the sand. I could feel it, feel the grains of sand grinding into my face, into my teeth and gums, and she kept pushing me down, further and further into the sand. I was struggling, kicking and thrashing around, but I couldn't get her off me and she wouldn't budge. She was strong. Real strong, the bitch. And she held me there, pushing her knee into my back, and I knew she wasn't going to let me up. She just wasn't going to. And I didn't much care. Once the struggle was out of the way, the instinct, I didn't much care. I could feel the whitewater washing over my back and hear the water in my ears, people splashing around and laughing, and everything went black. And she would have killed me. She would have fucking killed me, except a bluebottle washed in on the next wave and wrapped itself around her forearm. Stung the fucking shit out of her and she let me up.

'When I came up I could see her running up the beach, screaming and crying, holding her arm out. She ran right into Dad and he tried to settle her down. Ripped the bluebottle off and rubbed wet sand into her arm. But she wouldn't stop crying. Cried all the way home. And she would have killed me and I would have been happy to go. Funny, eh? And I only just remembered it all yesterday. Plain as the day.

'So I'm sitting here, right there – there, look! You can see the blood. Fucking hell, that's my blood. And I open my eyes and I'm smiling, thinking back to the beach, and there's a whole bunch of guys standing around me. Big guys, mostly. Blond hair. Black boots. White shirts. Good-looking boys, I guess. And they're talking to me, all at once, leaning over and snarling at me, shouting at me, faces right up close, right next to mine, spitting stuff out about me being the waste product of Zionist rule and how they had to clean shit like me off the streets. Then they started hitting me.'

'ASSFAT!'

'What? Whose ass?'

'The Aryan Sons Surviving For Action Today. It was the Aryan Sons!'

'I guess they were all somebody's sons. And I think they had a midget with them. Angry little fuck. Almost bit my ear off, yelling and screaming about how I was an oversized piece of shit, and how big did I think I was now? Although I might have imagined the whole midget thing. I rolled up as best I could but I'd already taken a few whacks to the head. Everything was a little bit hazy from that point on, so it's hard to say what was real and what wasn't. Sure seemed like a midget to me, though.'

'Are you sure it was a midget? Not a dwarf?'

'What's the difference?'

'It's one of proportion.'

'What do you mean?'

'How big were his arms and legs?'

'They were tiny. He was a midget, for fuck's sake.'

'But were they proportionate to the rest of his body or disproportionably small?'

'How the fuck do I know? I didn't exactly pull out a tape measure.'

'Listen to me. A dwarf is usually someone suffering from a condition known as skeletal dysplasia, the most common form of which is achondroplasia. It results in disproportionably short arms and legs, relative to the trunk length. The head is also large. A midget, on the other hand, is a proportionate dwarf − the arms, legs, trunk and head are the same size in relation to each other as would be expected with an average-sized person.'

'What the fuck does it matter whether I got stomped by a dwarf or a midget? Besides, I told you I might have imagined that part.'

'It matters. If only for the sake of correctness.'

'Correctness? Fuck me, James!'

'I'm sorry. I didn't mean to upset you. How, er, how did you explain this to your wife?'

'Maureen? Lucky I didn't end up at her hospital. I told her I got belted up outside the pub by a bunch of young thugs. Beat me up, robbed me. I'll get the royal treatment for at least a week, all the sympathy in the world. She's a good woman, my Maureen.'

'And what are you doing here? Shouldn't you be in bed?'

'Yeah, I probably should. But I figured you'd be here and I didn't want to disappoint you. Besides, I wanted to say goodbye.'

'Goodbye?'

'I've had enough, James. It's not safe out here any-more. Not for me, anyway. And I'll need some time to recover. Hurts like fucking hell. Besides, I figure I've done enough thinking. It's time for me to start looking for work. Too much thinking is no good for you. I reckon I'll just cut down on the thinking time. Buy a banana chair or something and stick it in the backyard. Maybe string up a hammock. Lie about and have a think on the weekends where no one feels inclined to kick seven shades of shit out of me.'

'You mean you won't be here anymore?'

'That's exactly what I mean.'

'Can I visit you at home sometimes, perhaps?'

'Why would you want to do that?'

'I don't know. I think I'd enjoy it. I'd like to meet your wife and see your home.'

'No offence, James, but I don't think it's a good idea. You don't need me anyway. You want to come out here and think, just come and do it. I'll give the patch to you. Draw up a title deed and everything, if you like. And if you need someone to talk to, surely you can come up with someone better than me? How about your friend, Oliver.'

'How do you know about Oliver?'

'You've mentioned him before.'

'No, I haven't.'

'Yeah, you must have. Otherwise, how would I know?'

'I don't know.'

'Look, whatever. You've got to have other people to talk to besides me.'

'But I want to know what happens to you.'

'Why?'

'I . . . I don't know why.'

'I'll be fine, mate. Just fine. And so will you. Oh, Jesus! Fucking ribs hurt like all hell. James, I've got to go. I've got to go, mate. See you around, OK?'

'Goodbye, Byron.'

'Brian. It's still Brian.'

'Goodbye, Brian.'

Brian lets his bruised right hand fall away from his ribs and raises it towards James.

James can feel the warmth of the other man's blood flowing through his fingertips, strong and alive. He holds the hand in his, afraid to let it go. It is Brian who finally pulls his hand away.

James stands perfectly still, keeping his eyes on Brian as he crosses the street and shuffles off towards the railway station. His appearance is sufficiently grotesque that oncoming pedestrians grant him a wide berth, fearing that the faintest contact with such misfortune will bring misfortune on themselves. There but for the grace of God? Not likely, but it's better to be safe than sorry.

Brian's progress is slow but steady and James sees the distance between them growing at a constant rate. Because Brian's back is hunched as he walks, because he is buckled over, James loses sight of him from moment to moment as pedestrians weave in and out around him, hurrying to pass him, hurrying to forget the battered, bloody face that smiles up at them. James sees the top of his head, the greying curls of hair, disappear behind the shoulder of a middle-aged woman whose face betrays no sign of recognition, no acknowledgment of the human pain and frailty that has just passed her by. So close, so far.

High above, the sun is beginning to break through the clouds.

And then he is gone.

Oliver was descending the steps of Yeats' Towers as James approached them from the street. It was one of the rare occasions that James could recall Oliver not greeting him with a smile. He attempted to compensate for this with a broad smile of his own.

'Hello, Oliver.'

'Hi.'

'Where are you off to?'

'Sandwich. I'm going to get a sandwich. How about you? Just showing up for work? Lucky for some.'

'I've been doing some research.'

'Oh. Is that where you picked up that scratch?'

'I did it in the garden at my mother's house.'

'Oh.'

'How about you? Been busy?'

'I'm always busy, James. So many arms and legs, so little time. You know how it is.'

'I'm not sure that I do. Oliver, I'm sorry for walking out on you at the Irish pub.'

'Forget it. It's not like I'm not used to you being a prick. I didn't even have to explain it to the girls much, told them that you're always pulling shit like that and that I've learned to expect it. Alison didn't seem too put out by it. Probably thinks it's all part of your dark and mysterious persona. Mr Enigma and all that. We had a good time. Like I said, the food there is great.'

'Again, please accept my apologies. I felt suddenly quite unwell and thought it best if I left.'

'I said forget it, didn't I? You don't have to apologise to me. You don't mean it, anyway. You don't even like me, right? You think I don't know that? Don't shake your head at me. It's true. You don't give a shit about how I might be feeling. Never have, never will. Sit there in whatever fucking world it is you inhabit, sucking up your rarefied air and leaving whatever's left over for dickheads like me. I don't know why you bother with me, really. Everything I do repulses you, right? Every effort I make. I have to drag you along everywhere we go, force you to try and have some fun. Well, I'm fucking sick of it, James. You think I'm that desperate for your acknowledgment, that desperate for your affection, that I'll put up with whatever you care to dish out?'

'No, of course not, Oliver. I apologise if I've been out of sorts of late, I've had a lot of things to deal with.'

'Of late? Fuck that, Jimmy, it's always been the same. Always. You've always been a prick and you're not going to change. I know what you think of me and you can fuck right off.'

'Please, Oliver . . .'

'No. Fuck you, James. You think you're the only friend I've got, huh?'

'No, of course not.'

'That's right. I've got plenty of friends, and I don't need some trumped-up prick like you hanging around thinking he's better than me. You think I'm so fucking eager to please that I'll bend right over while you fuck me and say thanks? Is that it?'

'Please, Oliver. I'll try to explain everything to you later. Please don't be upset.'

'Upset? I'm not upset. Calm, reasonable and rational, that's me. Bearing that in mind, I'd like to say fuck you, James. Fuck you very much.'

'I'm sorry, Oliver. I have to go. I'll talk to you later.'

'Fuck off.'

James bounded up the steps and through the doors to Sandler and Harris in an attempt to convey a sense of urgency. He wasn't late. It was not past midday. He simply had important business to attend to, and that was that. He was grateful that the sun had made its final breakthrough as he walked to the office from the railway station. Its heat caused his red face to break out in a sweat that added to the overall impression he was seeking to make: dynamic, rushed, a young man in a hurry with places to go and people to see, a young man who should not be disturbed. It was a trick he was borrowing from his mother, although he evidently still had much to learn. Betty Palmer stopped him with a single word as he attempted to streak past her desk.

'James!'

'Good morning, Betty.'

'Your face.'

'Yes, Betty. It is my face.' He fixed her with his most enigmatic smile, which unsettled her almost as much as the fact that he was referring to her by her first name.

'What happened to it?'

'You mean this? Just a scratch. Gardening accident. I was helping Mother in the garden yesterday.'

'But I rang your mother yesterday afternoon and she said you weren't there.'

'Late afternoon. Probably after you called.' He continued to smile at her as directly as he could.

'Is that why you didn't come to work yesterday? Because you were helping your mother? I'm afraid that's not really an adequate excuse.'

'Oh. No, that wouldn't be adequate at all. I simply didn't feel well enough to come to work. In the morning, that is. I felt better in the late afternoon. And my landlady's telephone wasn't functioning correctly so I couldn't call to let you know. Of course, I could have walked up to the public telephone booth, but I could hardly have been expected to have done so in my state, could I?'

'No, I wouldn't have expected that. And the telephone was out of order? That would explain why I got no answer there.'

'Yes, that would explain it.'

'I'll need a doctor's certificate, James.'

'Of course. First thing tomorrow.'

'And are you feeling better now, James?'

'Yes, thank you, Betty. Never better, in fact. Never better.'

Geoffrey Sandler was sitting at James's desk, his legs dangling from the seat of James's chair, suspended in the air. Only the extended toe of his left shoe was touching the ground; his right shoe was swinging above it in wild, counter-clockwise circles. He was attempting to hold his hands still, fingers crossed and resting in his lap, which only served to make his agitation all the more apparent. He saw James charging towards him and sprang out of the chair to meet him, taking his hand and shaking it rapidly.

'Bloomington!'

'Good morning, sir. I mean, good afternoon, sir.'

'Morning, afternoon – whatever it is, it's good. That's a nasty scratch you've got there, by the way. Today is the day, Bloomington. Today is the day!' He placed his tiny right hand on the small of James's back and began guiding him towards the Jeremiah Sandler

Memorial Boardroom, talking as he walked with his customary haste.

'Which day, sir?'

'Thursday, Bloomington! Thursday!'

'Of course, sir.'

'What do you mean by that? Don't tell me something's wrong, Bloomington. Don't tell me that we're going to have a problem tonight.'

They were now in the boardroom, standing just inside the closed door at the head of the circular table.

'No, sir. None that I'm anticipating. Mother will be there at 7.30 sharp, as I trust we will be.'

'Excellent!'

'And Imogen, sir?'

'Imogen? Oh, her. She'll be there. Can't vouch for her punctuality, but she'll be there all right.'

'Mother will be pleased to hear it.'

'Whatever makes her happy, Bloomington. Whatever makes her happy. I've got the flowers arranged for the restaurant and some chocolates for afterwards. Belgian or French or something. Hunt picked them out for me, said they were the best money could buy.'

'Yes, sir. I'm sure they are.'

'They better be, right? Now, Bloomington, any last-minute instructions for me? Topics of conversation, places of interest? Your father. Can I talk about your father or should I avoid the subject entirely?'

'Why would you want to talk about my father?'

'Well, you can learn a lot about a woman from the

company she keeps. Or kept, in this case. And it'll help me see if I can measure up to a dead man's legacy. Always tricky, dealing with dead guys.'

'What makes you think my father is dead?'

'He is dead, isn't he?'

'Legally, yes.'

'Legally? That's all that counts. Your mother is free to marry again, right? Tell me I'm right.'

'Yes, sir. She is free to marry whomever she chooses.'

'Excellent. Excellent, Bloomington. I've got a good feeling about tonight. Something good is going to happen.'

'Yes, sir. If you say so.'

'I say so. So, I can talk about your father, right?'

'Perhaps it would be best not to bring it up too suddenly, sir.'

'You're probably right. Save it for dessert, huh?'

'At the very least, sir.'

'If things look like they're going well, I might get you to take Imogen home, if that's all right with you. I'll slip you the money for a cab.'

'Very thoughtful of you, sir.'

'Not at all. I've got you to thank for setting this up for me, Bloomington. And I won't forget that. You've got a great career ahead of you here at Sandler and Harris. I'll make sure of it.'

'Thank you, sir.'

'In fact, as of next week, you'll be in charge of *Uncommon Cases.*'

'In charge, sir?'

'Acting Editor. Only temporary, of course, while Whitely-Smalls takes a little holiday. He's off to Cairo again. Left me a note. A matter of some urgency, apparently. In fact I think he's already gone, although you never can tell with Whitely-Smalls.'

'Will he be gone for long, sir?'

'Didn't say. I assume he's coming back. I'm sure he'll let me know when he does. In the meantime, you're in charge. I know you won't let me down.'

'Yes, sir.'

'Well, I expect you've got quite a lot of work to do. Check your desk. Whitely-Smalls left a pile of material for you. You're going to be a busy boy for a while. Right! I'll see you at the restaurant tonight. I'd give you a lift but I'm getting a haircut before dinner. Here, take some money for a cab.'

'Thank you, sir.'

'Pleasure. Now hop to it.'

James walked back to his desk. Mr Whitely-Smalls had indeed left him a large stack of papers: a mix of unread, uncorrected and corrected manuscripts, an incomplete pagination for the coming issue, the food-stained takeaway menu for a nearby Indian restaurant, a list of contributors' contact details, and a torn, yellowed classified advertisement that offered 'Cheap,

Discreet Asian Massage, After Hrs, All Areas'. He had not left any further instructions.

James looked at the title of the first manuscript on the pile, 'In Defence of Duelling: The Alternative to Alternative Dispute Resolution'. It was marked by Mr Whitely-Smalls' hand as 'possible' and was as good a place as any for James to start. He tidied his desk, placed the open manuscript before him and readjusted his chair. Once he began to read, the hours would quickly pass, which was all he hoped for.

He was not surprised to find that the author, one Brian K. Chiselbottom, began by establishing his terminology:

The gentlemanly art of duelling draws its name from the medieval Latin 'duellum', meaning 'a combat between two'. A duel, as I would like to define it, is a formal fight to settle a quarrel or avenge an insult, fought between two persons (the duellists) in the presence of witnesses, called seconds, according to rigid laws and rules (the 'code duello', the established code of duellists, which lays down the rules of engagement and the various roles of the seconds, such as inspecting weapons and calling for medical aid). A duel is usually fought with guns (duelling pistols), swords or other weapons. It is not necessary that the duel be fought to the death.

Chapter 27

James arrived at the restaurant a full half-hour early. He was told by a waiter with impossibly proportioned biceps bulging from a tight black t-shirt that he would have to come back later (that is, in half an hour). He could not wait at the Sandler table until the booking took effect at 7.30. Right now, Mama Luigi needed the table. James would have to wait outside. Sorry for the inconvenience, but what could he do? Mama was in demand.

He waited outside on the footpath, resting his back against the restaurant's wide front window and watching people pass him by in small, jovial groups. Almost every building on the block, and for blocks in either direction, was an Italian restaurant or cafe, and all of them were doing good business. It was still early, and many of the restaurants would have tables available for casual diners, but Mama Luigi's already appeared to be operating above its modest capacity. James was only inside for a moment but he was struck by the vitality of what he had seen. The dining area was not large and the edges of the small square tables were pushed close together in an effort to squeeze in the maximum amount of patrons.

He turned to look through the window at the scene inside. There were, he guessed, between forty-five and fifty-five people crowded along the wooden benches and around the various tables. A steady stream of waiters, each identically muscled and dressed, appeared from behind the swinging kitchen doors to the right, carrying steaming plates of food on their large, flattened palms. He noticed one of the waiters grasp the buttock of another with his empty hand as he passed by, causing the second waiter to drop the stack of plates he was carrying. A narrow staircase at the rear left corner appeared to lead to another dining area; waiters and patrons ascended and descended the stairs in single file, flattening themselves against the side walls when it was necessary to let others pass.

He had been looking through the window for only a few minutes when he felt a large, open hand descend on his right shoulder. The hand spun him around clockwise and he found himself face to face with the waiter who had initially turned him away. The waiter's blond hair was slicked back from his tanned face and stuck to his scalp with thick wads of hair gel. His face was flat and hard but he was attempting a shy, almost embarrassed smile.

'Excuse me, sir. Would you mind moving away from the window?'

'I beg your pardon?'

'Move away from the window, please. You're disturbing the customers.'

'How am I disturbing them?'

'They're just trying to have a peaceful meal, sir. And you're out here staring at them and blocking the view. Mama Luigi's is not a fishbowl, sir. You wouldn't like it if someone was staring at you as you were trying to eat, would you?'

'No, I wouldn't. I'm sorry. I have a reservation here for 7.30, remember? I was waiting for my companions . . .'

'Would you mind waiting further along, sir? Past the window at the corner, perhaps? We'll be able to seat you soon. I'll let you know when the table is free.'

James began to apologise again but the waiter was already heading back inside the restaurant, adjusting the strings of the white apron he wore over his black trousers. James moved past Mama Luigi's front window and stood with his back against the brown-brick facade, waiting to be allowed inside.

He knew he would need to compose himself quickly if he was to counteract the initial poor impression he had surely made on Imogen, not to mention the waiter. The navy suit was not his favourite but it couldn't be helped. The real problem was that he had been reading submissions solidly for five hours and he suspected that his whole face, including his eyes, was now the one colour, a deep crimson, flushed with blood. The briefest glimpse of his own reflection in the restaurant's front window had confirmed his suspicion. A red face was not a good starting point. On a positive note, the early cloud had kept the sun at bay and he had spent much of the day (and the entire afternoon) immobile at his desk, thus holding his overactive sweat glands somewhat in check. Besides, the restaurant was dimly lit and filled with its own odours, so he was confident he would be able to sit beside her without undue fear of discovery.

His strategy would necessarily be to side with Imogen against his mother and her father. He hoped Mr Sandler's behaviour would appear as ridiculous as possible. They would join together in their mockery of the old people and their vain attempt to find companionship to help them through their advanced years. Fools. Love was for the young, the strong. James knew it; Imogen would know it too. And their eyes would meet, sharing that knowledge and all it implied. Their lips would follow. Of course, it might not happen exactly like this. He would need to be prepared for any eventuality.

Geoffrey Sandler was the first of the party to arrive. His hair had been freshly cut into an inappropriately youthful fashion, short and layered at the back and sides but a little too long on the top. He was wearing casual tan trousers, a lemon shirt, open at the neck, and a navy sports coat. He walked towards James and grasped him firmly by the elbows. James could not be sure, but Mr Sandler appeared to be at least two inches taller than he had been earlier that afternoon at the office.

'Evening, Bloomington! What are you waiting out here for?'

'I'm waiting for our table to become available, sir. Shouldn't be long now.'

'And they expect you to wait out here on the street? Worse, they expect me to wait out here on the street? We'll see about that.'

'Really, sir, it's only for a few more minutes . . .'

But he was too late. Mr Sandler was already through the door. He was speaking to another waiter, tall and sharp-featured, whose long, dark hair was pulled back into a ponytail.

'Sandler. Table for four. We have a reservation.'

'Yes, sir, you do, but not until 7.30. You're early.'

'I'm five minutes early.'

'It's closer to ten, sir.'

'Five, ten − I don't give a fuck, sunshine. I'm here for my table and I expect to be seated at it right now.'

'Yes, sir. I'll just check with the maitre d.'

'You do that. Wanker.'

Two minutes later and they were seated at a small table on the left-hand side of the room. The waiter had quickly cleared a couple who had obviously finished their meal some time ago and were content to occupy a space that was no longer rightfully theirs. They both seemed happy enough to go, as if they had known it was only a matter of time before they were discovered. James sat on the bench that ran against the wall, the tops of his knees hitting the underside of the table, the table edge pushing deep into his contracted stomach. Geoffrey Sandler sat opposite him on a high-backed wooden chair. A thick red candle flickered on the table between them.

'Jesus, it's fucking noisy in here.'

'Pardon, sir?'

'I said it's fucking noisy in here.'

'Yes, very.'

'I hope your mother likes it.'

'So do I, sir.'

'I gather she's a fussy woman, Bloomington? Very particular about certain things.'

'Yes, sir, that's quite right. I'm glad to see that you've chosen a restaurant with a no-smoking policy.'

'Have I? That's a stroke of luck. I had no idea. All down to Hunt. I don't know why, Bloomington, but I've got to have your mother. She's a very, very handsome woman, I think I've told you that before, and there's something about her that's penetrated my very soul. Plus, she's got a real sweet caboose. And that's about as poetic as I'm ever likely to get. I hope you don't mind me speaking that way about your mother, but after all, you're a grown man, aren't you? You understand the needs of other men. You do understand what it is to be a man, don't you?'

'I'm working on it, sir.'

'Sorry? You'll have to speak up.'

'I said I'm working on it, sir.'

'Working on what?'

'Never mind, sir.'

'Let's see if we can get the attention of one of these dick-head waiters. Get them to clean off the table. Wouldn't mind a drink, either.'

While Sandler looked around for a waiter, James looked through the front window to see his mother passing on her way to the entrance of the restaurant. She was wearing one of her respirators and a sleeveless purple sheath of a dress, her body straight and powerful, arms swinging defiantly. He had often been struck by his mother's movements; it sometimes seemed she had the ability to slow down time itself, passing through it at her own pace, separating herself from the colourless world that spun around her. She was beautiful, it was true. He watched her appear at the doorway and make her way inside.

James sat up, as straight as the table in his stomach allowed, to catch his mother's attention. Even in the dimly lit room she spotted him almost immediately. She took a single step in her son's direction when she was stopped by an outstretched arm. It was another waiter, slightly shorter than the others, with black, shiny hair and parchment-coloured skin. The waiter kept his arm raised, like a military guard at the checkpoint of an occupied city. He motioned with his other hand for Veronica to take off her mask. His voice was pitched high, almost hysterical, although he was trying his best to keep it to a whisper. As a result, his words came out in a hiss.

'The mask!' he said. 'It has to come off!'

Veronica stood her ground, glaring at the boy who had halted her progress.

'What do you want with that thing on your face in here? It's clean in here, madam. The air is fine. You'll scare the other customers off, wearing that contraption. They'll think we've added some kind of poison to the menu. I'm sorry, madam, but either you remove the mask or you'll have to get out. Off or out!'

Veronica pulled the respirator slowly and deliberately from her face by its exhalation valve, up and over her head, where she held it in her right hand. Watching her from the table, James could see the muscles of her neck tighten with anger.

'This is not a mask. This is an STSC-720 N95 disposable particulate respirator. I do not wear it for show; I wear it for the simple and scientifically verified reason that the air outside is hopelessly unclean. I have no idea about the quality of your air, but I did fully intend to remove the respirator as soon as I reached my table. It may surprise you to learn that I have come here for dinner. It would be difficult for me to enjoy my meal and keep the respirator on. It also makes conversation rather difficult.'

'Yes, ma'am.'

'And I am neither your madam or your ma'am.'

'Yes, sir.'

'Wrong again.'

'I'm sorry, Miss . . . ?'

'Mrs. Mrs Veronica Bloomington.'

'I'm sorry, Mrs Bloomington.'

'And so you should be. You're really quite theatrical, aren't you? Perhaps you should audition for *Les Miserables* next time a production comes to town. I'm sure they'd find a place for you in the chorus. Please ensure that you do not come within five feet of me for the remainder of my evening here. If you do, I'll be forced to inform both the maître d'hôtel and the owner of your rudeness.'

'Yes, Mrs Bloomington.'

Veronica reached the table and stood before her son.

'Hello, Mother.'

'Hello, James. Please don't get up.'

'I can't get up, Mother. I'm really quite cramped.'

'So I see. And your face?'

'It's just a scratch.'

'Yes, I can see that too.'

Geoffrey Sandler had sprung to his feet and pulled out a chair for Veronica, directly to the right of his own. He stood with his hands on the back of the chair, smiling up at her. She was wearing open-toed sandals with only a modest heel, but still she hovered above him.

'Good evening.' The voice was strained with effort. 'Lovely to see you again, Mrs Bloomington.'

'Good evening, Mr Sandler. Please call me Veronica.'

'Thank you, Veronica. Please call me Geoffrey.' He slid the chair under her as she took her seat. Before he sat down, he looked quickly over his shoulder and clapped his hands sharply to draw the attention of the nearest waiter. He was finding it difficult to tell one waiter from another. He placed his hand on the waiter's shoulder and drew him down to whisper directly into his ear. The waiter acknowledged him with a nod and cleared the empty plates from the table before hurrying away to the kitchen.

Just as Sandler was settling into his chair, smiling so widely that his lips threatened to tear at their edges, the waiter returned with a large wicker basket of flowers that he placed on the table without a word. The base of the basket was as large as the table top and the flowers rose so high from it that James could no longer see Mr Sandler or his mother from his seat opposite them. The flowers extended wildly in all directions, a mass of soft colours and scents, so that James doubted Mr Sandler and his mother could see each other either. He heard Mr Sandler's voice from somewhere on the other side of the table. He was shouting to be heard above the crowd, as well as to provide an indication of his direction.

'These are for you, Veronica.'

His mother's voice answered, clear and controlled.

'Thank you, Geoffrey. But perhaps we should have them removed from the table.'

Her voice was joined by a new voice.

'Daddy? Daddy, are you in there?'

It was Imogen. Somewhere behind the flowers was Imogen. His nasal passages irritated by the various pollens surrounding him, James sneezed loudly, three times in succession.

'James! Do try to control yourself. His nose always was very delicate, you know.'

'Imogen, I'm down here. Grab one of those fucking waiters and have them take these flowers away, would you?'

Imogen did just that. The next thing James knew, the flowers were lifted from the table and carried away by a pair of large, tanned arms. They belonged to the blond waiter with the slicked-back hair. And there was Imogen, in a plain grey t-shirt and dark-blue jeans, her face a dazzling smile, the whiteness of her teeth start- ling, the colour in her cheeks just as he remembered it.

'Thanks, Heinrich.'

'Heinrich? Who the fuck is Heinrich?'

'That was Heinrich, Daddy. He's one of the waiters. I think he's quite sweet.'

'How do you know his name?'

'He told me his name. He introduced himself as I came in.'

'Fantastic. You manage to pick up the waiter before you even sit down. Your mother would be very proud.'

'Stop it, Daddy. Aren't you going to introduce me to our guests?'

'Of course. Veronica Bloomington, my daughter Imogen.'

'My, what a lovely name. Pleasure to meet you.'

'And you remember her son, James. One of our star young editors at Sandler and Harris. You met him at the office once, remember?'

'Yes, I remember.'

'Lovely to see you again.'

'How's your nose?'

'Fine, thank you.'

'His nose has always been very delicate. Very fragile, even as a child. He'd often come home from school with a bleeding nose.'

'Thank you, Mother. That's enough.'

Geoffrey Sandler stood from his seat to allow Imogen to squeeze through the tables and slide onto the bench beside James.

'Sorry I'm late.'

'Please, Imogen. Let's not start that again. Do we have enough menus? I'll order some wine. If that's all right with you, of course, Veronica?'

'Fine, as long as there's at least one good red. And speaking of red, James, what have you done to your face?'

'I told you it's just a scratch, Mother.'

'It's not just a scratch, darling. Your entire face is red.'

'It's pretty red, all right. Look at him, Daddy. That's exactly the colour your face gets when you're angry.

That's just how you look most of the time. Not pretty, is it?'

'What happened, James?'

'Please, Mother. Let's just look at the menu.'

'He probably caught his face on a branch, trying to climb a tree to some poor girl's window so he could watch her as she undressed. Is that what happened, darling? You can tell Mummy. I'm sure he's just too embarrassed to tell everyone in front of his mother. He never was much of a tree climber, really. Never had a head for heights, or lows for that matter.'

Veronica laughed suddenly and loudly, as if she had never laughed before in her life, and Imogen and Geoffrey Sandler laughed with her, looking at each other occasionally to confirm they were enjoying the moment equally, sharing the laughter as father and daughter. The laughter would not subside. James attempted to break it by calling over a waiter. It was not Heinrich. He ordered gnocchi in a gorgonzola sauce and the first chicken dish he saw from the mains list, holding the menu up to the waiter and pointing at his selection with a finger quivering with rage and humiliation.

He could feel his face positively glowing red, the blood surging at his temples, and he found the atmosphere suddenly hot and oppressive. Dinner had begun − off to a wonderful start, in fact − and he had already been excluded. It was his mother who would charm both Geoffrey and Imogen Sandler, not him, and he sank back against the wall as they made their selections from the menu, still laughing among themselves. It was over, before it had even begun.

James fell silent and remained silent while the food arrived, shutting himself off from the conversations of his dinner companions and the conversations of those around them. He drank the wine, the sweet, syrupy liquid sliding down his throat and into his empty stomach, and answered all questions directed at him with a simple yes or no, but otherwise retreated within himself, into silence. He saw the pictures but could not hear a sound. Inside, Mama Luigi's continued its bustling business; outside, through the window, he could see darkness beginning to set over the rooftops that stretched off into the distance, row after uniform row.

He looked to his left to see that Heinrich had somehow managed to squeeze himself between their table and the next; he was on his knees or his haunches, his heavy arms crossed on the table, the square chin atop his arms, looking up, smiling and talking to Imogen. Across the table James could see his mother and Mr Sandler eating, drinking wine, laughing, talking, smiling, the wetness of their teeth and tongues flashing in the candlelight.

Halfway through his chicken he decided it was time to speak. He spoke loudly and clearly and addressed himself directly to Heinrich, who turned his face to listen.

'You know, I was reading a fascinating article today, a submission at work, on the gentlemanly art of duelling.

That comes from the Latin "duello", Heinrich, meaning "a combat between two". You know the sort of thing. It's a staple plot device of nineteenth-century Russian literature, for example – pistols at twenty paces and all that. I'm sure we're all familiar with the romantic ideal. The author – and this is the interesting bit, I'm sure you'll agree, Mr Sandler – was arguing quite seriously and eloquently for the reintroduction – or really the introduction, seeing as how duelling has traditionally been of dubious legality – of the duel into the legal system. Officially sanctioned duels could take some of the burden off the judicial system, but sanctioned only in cases where both parties agreed to participate, of course. The parallels to accepted adversarial legal processes are already quite startling. Two opponents facing each other according to clear sets of rules and a laboriously defined code of conduct, etcetera, etcetera. The beauty of the duel, as opposed to the two-party counsel system that has developed under Common Law, is that the parties start on genuinely equal terms and are assured of a just outcome. At least that's the theory. In practice, things can always turn out differently. But it's really quite a fascinating idea, and it certainly flies in the face of the so-called "win-win" mentality that much of the current Alternative Dispute Resolution theory is seeking to establish as the orthodoxy.'

He was breathless when he finished, sweat running freely from his forehead and onto the table top. Heinrich had raised himself to his feet and walked away,

333

smiling blankly at James, shortly after the second sentence. The rest of the table, and even a few interested spectators from neighbouring tables, looked at him in silence. Veronica spoke first.

'That's really very lovely, darling.'

'Yes, Bloomington. First rate. First rate.'

Imogen did not say a word.

James took the napkin from his lap and wiped his forehead and returned to his dinner, knife and fork in hand, his eyes focused on the strips of flesh and the stringy muscle fibres of the chicken. Thick drops of sweat were falling from his forehead and chin and onto his plate, mixing into the rich cream and tomato sauce. He could taste nothing except for the blood deep at the back of his throat.

Imogen placed her hand on top of her father's and addressed the table.

'Well, good night everyone. Heinrich gets off in a few minutes and we're going to go out for a drink. It was lovely meeting you, Veronica. I had a really nice time, Daddy. Thank you so much for dinner.'

She stopped to kiss her father on top of the head as she walked past. He placed a crumpled fifty dollar note into her palm and kissed her on her glowing cheek in return.

'Goodbye, James.'

'Goodbye.'

James got up from the table and excused himself, thanking Mr Sandler for dinner and saying goodbye to his mother. His movements were slow and heavy, somehow disconnected from his mind, as if he was looking in and watching himself through the front window from the footpath outside. His legs were carrying him to the door, right before left, left before right, right before left. He walked past Imogen, who was waiting near the kitchen doors, on his way out. His nose began to bleed as soon as he stepped into the warm night air.

Chapter 28

James Bloomington had arrived early. According to Betty's watch he had entered the Sandler and Harris office at 8.42 am. He wished Miss Palmer (he distinctly said 'Miss Palmer') a good morning as soon as he arrived. He looked quite dashing in his pale-blue shirt, navy tie and navy suit, although a little tired around the eyes. He could definitely use a good meal and a good night's sleep, that much was obvious. His face, however, had returned to its normal complexion. The mark, the deep scratch on his cheek, was still visible, but less noticeable for the fact that it was no longer surrounded by a sea of inflamed skin. He went straight to his desk and sat before a large pile of papers, shuffling through it until he found a suitable place to begin the day's work. He had neglected to bring a doctor's certificate to explain his absence earlier in the week but Betty was willing to forgive him for this; she would complete and authorise his leave payment before lunch.

Stephen Hunt was the next to arrive, some twenty minutes later. Jasper Jenkins followed him through the door. Neither of them wished Betty a good morning. She watched the two men walk into the office, Jasper a measured three paces behind Mr Hunt's every step. When Mr Hunt stopped in front of James's desk, Jasper kept on walking past them to the right. She could see that Mr Hunt was attempting to engage James in conversation, resting his thigh against the corner of the desk and repeatedly stroking his moustache, the right elbow of his tweed jacket rising again and again as his hand reached for his face. He held his back stiff; the jacket fell in perfectly straight lines from its wide, heavily padded shoulders, serving to disguise the bony frame underneath. He stood above James for only a few minutes, obviously receiving some small satisfaction from their exchange, a sour smile playing over his lips as he walked away, still stroking his moustache.

Betty returned her eyes to her work, raising them occasionally to watch the small square of the street she could see from her chair. The city had begun its day under the vengeful eye of the sun, which had risen that morning with a peculiar venom, sending a warning to all who felt its early outburst that the day, today, would be a particularly unpleasant one. Betty had felt it as she made her way to the office from the railway station, and she could see that others, those who walked through her little square of the world outside, were feeling it now. The heat would level them by the end of the day.

And now she lost herself to a slow-motion image that had formed suddenly, without invitation, in her mind: herself and her sister Angela, neither more than eight years old, in white cotton underpants, their pale, puffy bodies shining in the sun, running through the water sprinkler in their frontyard, over and over, looking down at the wet green grass as they ran, careful to avoid the patches of bindies that waited to puncture the soft pink flesh of their feet should they take a false step. The colours were so vivid.

'Morning, Betty!'

It was Mr Sandler's voice, booming in her ear, that brought her back to her desk.

'Oh! Good morning, sir.'

'And what a wonderful morning it is.'

He had stopped at her desk. He had never stopped at her desk. He was leaning on her desk, smiling. Was he talking to her?

'Yes, sir, it's lovely. But it might get a little too hot later in the day. I was . . . I was listening to the radio this morning at breakfast and the weather forecast is for a hot one. A real stinker, I think he said, sir.'

'Is that so? And how was your breakfast?'

'It was lovely, sir. I've got a lovely jar of genuine

English marmalade that I'll be very sorry to see the end of. It's really lovely on toast in the morning.'

'I'm sure it is, Betty. I'm sure it is. Why don't you take a little break at lunch and go out and grab yourself another jar? Mustn't deprive ourselves of the things that give us pleasure, eh?'

'Thank you, sir. That's a lovely idea. Just lovely. I'll be sure to do just that.'

And he was gone, almost as quickly as he had appeared. She heard his quick little steps carry him into the office where he too stopped before James's desk. His voice carried clearly to the reception area, strong and full of life.

'Morning, Bloomington! Come and see me in my office as soon as you're done with that page, would you? Great work you're doing there, by the way, son. Great work!'

James was in Mr Sandler's office. Mr Sandler sat behind his desk, beaming up at him. Mr Sandler's portrait hung from the wall, beaming down at them both.

'You wanted to see me, sir?'

'Sit down, son. Sit down.'

'Thank you, sir.'

'Last night was wonderful, Bloomington! I can't thank you enough.'

'I expect you should be thanking my mother, sir.'

'I did that this morning, son. And I hope I'll be doing it a lot more from now on.'

'I see, sir. Is that all you wanted me to know?'

'No, no, of course not. I just wanted to reassure you that my intentions towards your mother are still perfectly honourable. She's a wonderful woman, Bloomington! Wonderful! And so flexible!'

'Yes, sir. I'd really rather we didn't have this conversation.'

'I also wanted to assure you that your place here at Sandler and Harris is secure just as long as you're performing at your peak, Bloomington. You'll get no favours from me, none at all, despite my relationship with your mother. I know you'd prefer it that way, anyway. And so would your mother. No favours, no special treatment. You'll be just another employee to me, even if you should happen to become my son.'

'Yes, sir. Thank you, sir.'

'Work hard, Bloomington, and success will come your way. Be a part of the Sandler and Harris team and the team will love you back. My father founded this company with the sweat of his own brow and I've built it up to where it is today with the same philosophy. I want you to carry on that tradition. I know you've got the sweat we need. Hard work! That's all there is to it. Hard work!'

He was still shouting after James as James left the office and walked back slowly to his own desk, gripping its edges for support as he sat down. As soon as he was seated the telephone rang, loud and shrill in his ears. It was his mother. Of course it was his mother.

'Good morning, Mother.'

'Hello, James. James, I wanted to talk to you about last night.'

'Mr Sandler has already talked to me about last night, Mother. I'm glad you had a good time.'

'Yes, well, you did want me to have a good time, didn't you? That was the whole idea, was it not? For me to be nice to your boss?'

'I really didn't expect you to be that nice, Mother.'

'Yes, well, neither did I, James. He really is a rather sweet, insecure little man, James, almost like a boy himself. Not at all what I expected, really. Did you know he wore lifts in his shoes, just to impress me?'

'That's lovely, Mother.'

'I want you to know that I intend to see Mr Sandler again, James, at least in the short term. No pun intended. I hope that you approve.'

'Really, Mother? Would it make any difference if I didn't approve?'

'None at all. But it would be nice. And what did you do to your face, James?'

'Nothing, Mother. My face is fine. It's perfectly fine.'

'If you say so, dear. And I'm sorry it didn't work out with Imogen for you. She's quite lovely, isn't she? But really, James, Heinrich was a very strapping young fellow and you weren't exactly at your most charming. Hardly said a word all night and when you did, you came out with some nonsense, challenging Heinrich to a duel.'

'I wasn't challenging Heinrich to a duel, Mother.'

'I should think not, James. He'd probably kill you.'

'Yes, Mother. I'm sure he would. He's probably a master of the Heinrich manoeuvre.'

'I should think you should ask your Imogen about that. You didn't look well either, James. Frankly, I was glad to see you go home.'

'Thank you, Mother. But I'm not at home now, I'm at work and I really can't afford to spend all morning on the telephone. I've got a lot of work to get through today.'

'Fine. I just wanted to make sure you were all right.'

'I'm busy, Mother. Goodbye.' James placed the handset firmly onto the receiver before his mother had a chance to answer.

The office walls were closing in on him. He was sure the ceiling was pulsing, matching the pulsing at his temples. It was unbearably hot inside and out but James felt a deep chill within and pulled his jacket around him for warmth. The day was unfolding in a way that he had absolutely no control over and he had no alternative but to abandon himself to it, watching himself from above, waiting to see what would happen next, waiting for the next collision.

It was Alison, talking to Betty Palmer at the reception desk. Betty rose from her chair with a broad smile, raised her arm straight and pointed her extended finger at James. Alison followed the direction of the finger towards James. He watched her approaching him from all directions, above and behind her, all around her, all at once; watched the sway of the narrow hips under her skirt, the loose muscles of her long legs tightening with every step, the fine layer of sweat that covered her bare arms and upper lip. He heard the sounds of the low heels as they met the polished wooden floorboards, heard the scratch of stiff fabric as her upper arms brushed against the linen of her blouse, and the friction high on the inside of her thighs as the dimpled flesh met and rubbed together as she walked.

She was standing above him, smiling, and then she was sitting on the edge of his desk, her legs stretched to the floor. She was talking to him and he was talking back. He was smiling too. Her words echoed in his head, high inside his skull.

'Sorry to bother you at work. Oliver gave me directions. I'm on a break and I needed to talk to you. I know we talked about this and we talked about not forming any emotional bonds and all of that but I just wasn't prepared for this kind of . . . distance, James. This coldness. Sometimes I feel a warmth from you, the other night at your house I felt it. I mean, I know we're just having fun and everything and it's really too early to start thinking about anything else but I just can't help forming an attachment. And I'd like to feel some sort of attachment from you but I just don't. And it's wrong, James. It's just wrong!'

He answered her, watching her face, every ripple of her mouth, every movement of her eyebrows, counting

343

each and every freckle across the broad bridge of her nose. He was telling her he was sorry, that he didn't know what was wrong with him, that he did very much like spending time with her and would like to continue to do so, but that as far as he understood, it was primarily a sexual and emotional need he was trying to fulfil and that he thought it best not to place her under any illusions as to his intentions; that he understood if she no longer wished to see him, and if that was the case, he would no longer bother her.

And then he was laughing, bent over in his chair, a laughter that rose from the very pit of his stomach, that he could not stop. It was not of his will; the laughter would have to run its own course. He watched the tears begin to form and well in her eyes from every possible angle, he watched the edges of her crooked front teeth bite into her bottom lip, and he watched her turn and half walk, half run past the reception desk and out into the street.

He continued to laugh, cradling his head in his folded arms on his desk, closing his eyes to black. When the laughter had finally subsided he watched himself stand up, straighten his jacket and smooth the curls of his hair with his palms. He watched as he told Betty Palmer that he would not be back for the day, smiling at the look of disbelief on her face, and walked down the steps of Yeats' Towers and into the merciless glare of the midday sun.

. . .

He went to the lane but Byron Jones was not there. He knew that Byron would never be there again but his legs had carried him there regardless, through the crowded, burning streets, to stand in the shadow of the concrete tower that rose into the blue and orange haze of the sky. All that remained of Byron was his blood, staining the footpath in dark patches that would remain, not forever but for some time to come, until the sun, wind and dirt would combine to carry the stains away.

Sweat was now flowing freely across his body and he could feel that his face would soon glow red again. The walk had drained him and there was nothing left for him to see or do but to stand perfectly still, which he did, leaning against the tower wall and gradually sliding his back down until he was sitting cross-legged, without a scrap of cardboard to protect his trousers. He sat where Byron would have sat; the blood stains on either side provided the perfect indication of the position he had habitually occupied.

James already knew he would sit here until the sun went down, that he would watch the fiery ball set over the city and bring an end to another day. It was a cycle that would never end, a cycle that he would have to live within until the day the sun finally rose no more upon him. So he sat in place and waited, watching the shadow of the tower grow longer and sharper as the world continued to spin on its axis in the perpetual, frantic motion that carried all – that carried children who would grow into old and feeble men and women – into and out of his life, day after day, hour after hour.

It was dark and almost cool. A thin sliver of the moon revealed itself occasionally from behind thick passing clouds, lighting his way to the telephone booth. He knew it would have something for him tonight, this night, and he was afraid of what he might find. He walked towards the glass door with slow, careful steps, trying to anticipate what would be waiting for him inside, afraid of his own desires.

The fluorescent tube of light that usually glowed so steadily within the booth was flickering in a repeated pattern, three or four quick sparks as it struggled for life, followed by a sustained, bright burst of pure white energy that would die abruptly after only a few seconds; then the pattern would begin again. The flickering light made it difficult to examine the booth from outside; he could not concentrate his eyes on any given area for any length of time. He would have to go inside.

The tube continued to blink, buzzing with effort, as he eased open the door. The light may have been tampered with; most likely the tube had grown faulty and would need to be replaced. As he stepped into the booth his foot struck something hard and hollow. He looked down and saw a Samsonite briefcase, lying flat on the concrete square, appearing and disappearing with the light. As he bent down to pick it up, he knew that it was his briefcase and that it would not be empty.

He placed the briefcase flat on top of the phone books that lay on the narrow metal tray to the side of the telephone. The briefcase was just below his chest; he raised his hands to the latches on either side, clicking them back in unison, and slowly opened it. Inside was a magazine. On its stiff, glossy cover he could see the red lips and white teeth of a woman biting into the head of a man's penis; her full eyes looked directly into his, as if she was asking him a question; and then she was gone.

He held the magazine up and flicked through its pages, each page flashing in and out with the light. He saw women, girls, all thin, none pretty, and men, dark, hairy, faceless, in various (and often acrobatic) sexual positions involving a number of different combinations, the most common being one man with two or more women. He saw white edges to each page, filled with short paragraphs of text in what looked like English, German, Spanish and Italian. Their eyes were empty and only occasionally showed any sign of life, let alone pleasure. Drug addicts. They were all drug addicts, weren't they? He didn't care. There was something about a woman held captive to her addictions, something about a woman so willing to have these ... *things* done to her that gave him an immediate erection and filled him with longing and an inarticulate anguish. But he could not stop flicking through the pages.

Towards the end of the magazine he saw an image of a man lying underneath a glass coffee table, masturbating as a woman, her back to the camera, squatted above him and defecated on the table. He was struck with the sudden realisation that there could be no other reason for anyone to own a glass table. What else were they for, if not for this? His mother had kept a glass coffee table for as long as James could remember.

He put the magazine in the briefcase, closed it, and left the telephone booth behind him.

Chapter 29

James woke before sunrise. Outside, the world was in darkness; it would not remain so for long. The night was over but he would not leave his room until the sun had risen, until he could see its rays shining through the gaps of his curtains. The sharp pain in his stomach was from hunger and he knew it would go away if he could ignore it for a sufficient length of time. Besides, there was nothing in his refrigerator. He got up from the bed and turned on the light.

The bare bulb illuminated his room with a harsh, fierce glow, reflecting off the pale, white skin of his naked body. Despite the sparsity of the furnishings, the room still managed to appear to be in a state of disarray. He had thrown the jacket of his suit and his shirt over the television set, where they lay slumped across the dusty screen. The pants lay on the floor, his shoes not far away. He could not see his tie; his belt was still looped through the trousers. The open briefcase lay on the floor near the foot of the bed. The magazine, folded open at a particularly unsavoury page, lay on the floor within arm's reach of the bed. If he was to continue living with Mrs Salvestrin, he would need to hide the magazine or destroy it, one or the other.

The scratch on his face would not leave a lasting scar. James ran his fingertips along its length, tracing the crusted blood from his cheek down to his mouth. Soon he would peel it away, picking at its corners until it lifted.

There were no clean boxer shorts in his drawer so he was forced to pull on the pair he had worn for the last two days; he found them lying on top of his trousers. He did, however, find a clean grey t-shirt and a pair of light cotton pants to cover his naked body, and a wide-brimmed, white canvas cricketer's hat to protect his face from the sun. He pulled the sneakers and socks from beneath his bed and sank his buttocks to the floor to finish dressing.

The first rays of sunlight had begun to filter through the curtains, falling harmlessly as shapeless patches on the floor beside him. The sun had risen in the space of a few minutes, beginning its weary arc through the sky.

It was time to go.

James walked through his kitchen and along the darkened hallway, careful not to make any sound that would disturb Mrs Salvestrin. He hoped she was asleep, safe in the dreams and lovers of her youth.

He opened the door to the morning, squinting into the rising light. A man and a woman, no more than twenty-eight years old each, were jogging along the street, talking excitedly as they ran. He had always admired people who could run and talk at the same time with no apparent shortage of breath; he waved at them and they waved back, smiling at him as they moved quickly past the house. He took three deep, exaggerated breaths, pushing the air forcefully from his lungs through his nose, pulled the hat low across his brow and stepped off the patio onto the grass below, landing with a soft thud.

He was walking towards the telephone booth. He could see the morning sunlight reflecting off its glass panels as he approached it. The booth's light had turned itself off, a timer switch engaging for the daylight hours. James circled the exterior and gave it a cursory inspection. Nothing had changed since the previous night. He hoped someone would replace the faulty light before nightfall. Perhaps he would call the service line from the booth and alert them.

He did not intend to hide. He would sit right here on the grass, in front of the telephone booth, out in the open, taking whatever shade was provided to him and keeping his hat tilted against the sun. This is where he was meant to be. He did not know what or who to expect but he knew he was not alone and that in itself was enough.

He watched as the first of the early morning commuters walked by, making their way up the shallow gradient of the hill towards the railway station and the trains that would carry them to the city, to the desks and ergonomic chairs that greeted their arrival every morning of their working lives. The men wore light-weight suits, the women loose, floral-print dresses. Their footsteps were slow and laboured, their eyes heavy with sleep. In winter they would walk the same route at the same time, in the dark, and their frosted breath would rise into the air with every step as confirmation of their exertions. As children they would pretend they were steam trains, huffing and puffing and hooting the whistle until their throats and mouths were dry. The moisture gone, they would be forced to slow down, stoking the fire with more coal until they could begin again. The phenomenon of evaporation remained but the wonder did not.

But it was summer. The sun was shining high in the sky and it would be a beautiful day. James could feel the sun's rays soaking through his clothes and into his skin; he could feel the stiff blades of grass, the morning dew all but gone, pushing against his outstretched palms and fingers, and he could smell the rich, warm earth below the surface. It was reason enough to smile, and he did just that.

The day could be short or long. Time could stretch

the day into night, the night into another day. James did not know. He sat on the grass watching, waiting for whatever would come.